Twinchantment

Twinchantment

Elise Allen

Disney • Hyperion
Los Angeles New York

For information address Disney • Hyperion, 125 West End Avenue, New York, New York 10023.

First Edition, April 2019

1 3 5 7 9 10 8 6 4 2

FAC-020093-19053

Printed in the United States of America

This book is set in Century Schoolbook Pro/Monotype

Designed by Jamie Alloy

Library of Congress Cataloging-in-Publication Data

Names: Allen, Elise, author.
Title: Twinchantment / by Elise Allen.
Description: First edition. • Los Angeles : Disney Hyperion, 2019. •
Summary:
When magic and other potentially magical beings, such as twins, are outlawed in Kaloon, royal twin sisters Flissa and Sara pretend to be one princess until dark magic puts their mother's life in danger.
Identifiers: LCCN 2018031538 • ISBN 9781368008624 (hardcover)
Subjects: • CYAC: Sisters—Fiction. • Twins—Fiction. • Princesses—Fiction.
• Magic—Fiction. • Blessing and cursing—Fiction.
Classification: LCC PZ7.A42558 Tw 2019 • DDC [Fic]—dc23
LC record available at https://lccn.loc.gov/2018031538

Reinforced binding

Visit www.DisneyBooks.com

THIS LABEL APPLIES TO TEXT STOCK

To Maddie, who continues to astound me
each and every day.
I'm so proud to be your mom.

The Kingdom of Kaloon Magic Eradication Act

In acknowledgment of the grievous harm visited upon King Lamar by practitioners of the Dark Art of Magic, the following rules shall now and forever forward be enforced in the Kingdom of Kaloon:

1. Only designated Keepers of the Light may practice magic, and only as part of their duty to protect Kaloon.

2. There shall be no other practice of magic within the Kingdom's limits. To ensure this, those with magical abilities must vacate the kingdom immediately.

3. Should a person develop magical abilities, they must report directly to the Keepers of the Light, register their skills, then prepare for mandatory relocation outside the kingdom.

4. All magical amulets, charms, and other talismans are strictly prohibited.

5. Children born with physical evidence of a propensity for magic may not be raised in the kingdom, and instead shall be surrendered to the Keepers of the Light for re-homing. Such physical evidence includes:

   a. Polydactyly—extra fingers or toes
   b. A caul over the face at birth
   c. Left-handedness (should it persist after active retraining)
   d. Twinhood

These rules are absolute. Any defiance will be answered with swift and certain punishment, ranging from life imprisonment, to exile, to execution.

So it is written and sealed from this day forward.

Prologue

Magic had brought the dark times to the kingdom of Kaloon. And only magic—tightly controlled magic—could sweep them away again.

Every Kaloonian knew the story. The nobles of the castle, the merchants of the village, and the farmers of the vast countryside had all taught it to their children. Anyone could describe how the Dark Mage Maldevon hid his true nature for years. He pretended his magic was simple and harmless. He won everyone's trust performing tricks at local festivals and making mystical poultices to heal wounds and ailments. Even the great King Lamar had admired Maldevon—had even invited him to live in the castle.

It was a fatal mistake.

At exactly midnight on the day of King Lamar's son's Ascension Day—the day Prince Alistair turned twelve and would officially take his place in the royal line—Maldevon and his followers swept through the castle, unleashing spells and curses that extinguished the lives of everyone in their path. By the time King Lamar understood what was happening, many in the palace had already fallen. The king immediately summoned his army, but their strength and weapons were nothing in the face of Maldevon's hateful magic. With a flick of a finger or a muttered syllable, the mage could steal the air from their lungs or thicken the blood in their veins.

Despite the danger, King Lamar wanted to fight Maldevon himself, but his personal guard wouldn't let him. Though the king raged and fought against them, his guard overpowered him and brought him into a secret chamber of the castle for his own protection.

It should have been a pointless ploy. Hidden nooks and tunnels were no match for Maldevon. His very senses were magical. He had the power to find anyone he wanted and destroy them with barely a thought.

And he would have succeeded, had it not been for a single man. A mage who only used his power for good.

As Grosselor would later tell it, he was reading in bed when he heard the commotion. Not with his ears. He was miles away. Back then, he had already lived a very long life and found simple happiness on a sprawling farm on the outskirts of Kaloon, surrounded by others like himself. He was a mage, but unlike Maldevon, he didn't want attention or accolades. He only wanted to spend time with his friends and family, other mages with the same philosophy. They could create anything they needed, so they lived together in harmony and left the rest of Kaloon alone.

Yet on this night, anguish seared like lightning through Grosselor's head. He heard terrified screams and felt each life ripped away as if it were part of his own soul. He knew instantly what was happening, and although he'd never dreamed of approaching the castle, he knew what he had to do.

Humble Grosselor would always decline to talk about what happened next. Stories passed down through the years simply said that Grosselor and his allies appeared at the palace out of nowhere. What they did is a mystery, but by the time they were done, Maldevon and all his followers were in Grosselor's custody, and King Lamar was safe.

His family, however, wasn't so lucky. Most of them had perished. His wife, his siblings, his children. Even Prince Alistair, who'd just turned twelve that day.

Only one member of King Lamar's family survived: the second of his six children, Prince Regland. Just one year younger than his older brother, Prince Regland was now the one who'd have an Ascension Ceremony at age twelve, but King Lamar swore no dark mages would get in the way this time. He enacted the Magic Eradication Act, forever banning all magic from Kaloon, except that which would be used to protect it. He insisted Grosselor take charge of securing the kingdom at all costs. At His Majesty's decree, Grosselor formed the Keepers of the Light.

From the beginning, this group of magical men and women dedicated themselves to eradicating all dark magic from the land. Hand in hand with the royal family, Grosselor and his Keepers kept Kaloon safe for generations. Dressed in their yellow cloaks and doublets, they were like glimpses of the sun, and gave Kaloonians the same warm feeling of comfort.

Kaloonians born in the years after the Magic Eradication

Act couldn't even imagine a world where magic was allowed to run rampant, nor would they want to. The very idea was terrifying. Grosselor himself was the only person old enough to remember that time clearly, and his stories made it sound terrible. Of course, Grosselor didn't look his age, nor did any of the older Keepers. Their timeless youth and vitality were the only outward signs of their powerful magic. They didn't boast about this or showcase it, though. None of the Keepers spoke about magic. They saw the power as a duty to bear, one to protect the kingdom they loved.

Like when they saved the life of King Lamar's great-great-grandson's firstborn child, Princess Flissara.

It happened at a party in Queen Latonya and King Edwin's high-ceilinged throne room. The space was so stuffed with celebratory banners and bunting, it was a wonder there was any room for people; yet its stone walls seemed to echo with the voices of the whole kingdom. Men, women, and children crammed together, sweating in their finest hand-stitched brocade dresses and tunics. They ignored the oppressively thick air and stood on tiptoe, the ones in the back stretching and straining to see the king and his very pregnant queen on their rich purple thrones.

With the exception of the Keepers in their ever-present yellow, purple was the color of the day. It was Queen Latonya's favorite, and everyone wanted to please her. She and King Edwin were the most beloved royal couple ever to rule Kaloon—the only royal couple who had married for love. King Edwin had met his bride while shopping in the village. Her family owned a cheese shop. One look at her mane of dark curls, laughing brown eyes, and sparkling smile and he was smitten. Latonya had loved him just as much but wasn't sure she could trust the fancies of a king. He wooed her tirelessly for an entire year. When she finally said she'd marry him, the whole kingdom celebrated for weeks.

Now, nearly nine months later, she glowed with joy as she rested one hand on her giant belly and addressed her people.

"Friends, family, fellow Kaloonians. I am so honored you've all joined King Edwin and me today to share our happiness as—"

What happened next moved too quickly for anyone to intervene. Gilward, the court jester and a lanky noodle of a man, somehow muscled to the front of the crowd. In a single motion, he ripped his hands from his pockets, thrust his arms out like talons, and screamed arcane words at the top of his lungs.

Bright light filled the throne room, so intense it hurt, and everyone shut their eyes and turned away. When they opened them again, the light was gone, but Queen Latonya stood on the dais staring down at her swollen belly in horror as a thick green mist swirled around it. The king leaped to his feet and drew his sword. "What did you do?" he roared down to Gilward. *"What did you do?!"*

In an instant, Grosselor magically appeared at Gilward's side. His whole body sparkled with his unique magical signature, and those same sparkles glistened on Gilward as he slammed to his knees, his forehead banging on the floor and his arms jerking painfully behind his back. He rose as if yanked by the elbows, until he hung a foot off the floor . . . and then he changed. As those around him watched in a mix of awe and horror, Gilward shrank within his purple unitard. His skin crumpled closer to his bones, suddenly crepe-thin and wrinkled. Eyes wide with terror, he turned desperately to Grosselor. "What are you doing to me?" he croaked in a suddenly ancient voice.

"Nothing," Grosselor said impassively. "Whatever's happening to you, it isn't me."

And it wasn't. Every witness said Grosselor's magical signature, those sparkles, glistened only around Gilward's elbows, from which the jester dangled as if on a hook. They were nowhere else on his swiftly deteriorating body.

Just then, Mitzi, a young woman from the kitchen staff, shrieked from across the room, "The mist!" She thrust her arm out to point at Queen Latonya. "It's going *into* her body!"

King Edwin gasped and ran to his wife as she looked down at her belly and screamed. Mitzi was right. The thick mist that had been swirling around her was now seeping through her gown and into her womb. The queen tried to claw it away, crying out in panic, but it wouldn't stop. It sank into her, until every wisp was gone.

Then Latonya jolted upright as a bolt of white-hot pain shot through her body. She yowled in agony.

No one saw anything else after that. The royal nurse, Katya, heaved her enormous body onto the dais and ushered Queen Latonya away, King Edwin by her side the whole time. Grosselor blinked onto the dais to join them, leaving Gilward to be ushered out of the room in the grip of a craggy-faced Keeper named Rouen. Within moments, everyone involved with the incident was gone, leaving only a handful of Keepers to stay with the crowd and keep them calm and quiet, as everyone anxiously waited to hear what had happened.

When Grosselor reappeared on the dais an hour later, his smile glowed almost as brightly as his yellow doublet.

"May the Light keep us all," he said. "The queen is fine . . . and so is her new baby girl. Long live Princess Flissara!"

(Almost) Twelve Years Later

Chapter 1
Sara

BONG! BONG! BONG!

Again and again the bell in the castle's highest turret bonged, and with each repetition, the knot in Sara's stomach tightened.

She was late. Supremely late. Un-princessly late, and there was absolutely no way she could make it across the fields, past the stables, through the gardens, and up the endless steps to the throne room's balcony before the tenth bong of the bell.

No way at all. Unless she ran faster than she'd ever run in her life. She took a deep breath, then sprinted, top speed—

—for about a second. Then she tripped over the hem of her skirt and belly flopped onto the grass.

"Ugh!" she groaned. "This is the *worst*!"

She dragged herself to her feet and peered down at her favorite rose-red dress.

Grass stains all down the front. Of course.

"Worser than worst!"

For a second, Sara considered blowing off the Weekly

Address entirely, but that would be an even huger disaster. Every time she went to one of Kaloon's county festivals and spent time among her people, they always told her how much they loved the Weekly Address. They said they eagerly awaited that reliable break in their workweek, which made them feel connected to the royal family, even when there was nothing to report. If Sara didn't show up, Kaloonians would worry. And they'd talk. And no matter how much Kaloon loved her, some people would *definitely* spread stories about where Princess Flissara had been instead—and Dad would hate that.

Of course, the truth was, they'd talk anyway once she flew in with a stained dress and nightmare hair that burst from its braids like straw from an overstuffed mattress.

Still, better to be there than not. Sara gripped her skirt in her fists and ran with her eyes pinned to the ground so she wouldn't miss any stray roots or holes. She was a princess by birth, but as her mother never failed to point out, Sara was also Queen of Uncoordination.

She cursed herself for letting time get away. She hadn't meant to. She'd spent the morning with a sketch pad in the rose garden specifically so she'd be close at hand while she waited for the Weekly Address. But then she'd heard high-pitched giggles and looked up to see two little kids playing hoodlehoop. Hoodlehoop! How fun was that? The small boy and girl each had a hoodlehook and used it to roll the hoop back and forth between them, and they just looked so free and happy that Sara wanted to capture it on paper . . . but then the kids ran off, rolling the hoodlehoop as they went, and the only way Sara could finish her drawing was to chase after them!

Normally she'd have needed a cleverly crafted plan to slip away from all the servants and Rouen, the family's officially assigned Keeper, but when Sara looked around, she realized that for this one blissful moment, she was *alone*.

Was someone slacking on the job? Was something exciting going on somewhere else in the castle that had everyone's attention?

Sara didn't know, and she didn't care. She tucked her sketch pad and charcoals into her satchel, slung the bag over her shoulder, and ran after the kids. Keeping a safe distance, of course. She wanted to catch them in full hoodlehoop action, not losing their minds over their princess. She ran until they lost their breath and collapsed, red-faced and panting and giggling in the grass, which was an even better picture than the game, so Sara ducked into a cluster of bushes and drew as quickly as she could. When she was done, she *still* should have had plenty of time to get back, but it turned out that the bushes she'd hidden in were covered in thorns. And while she'd sketched, they'd hooked into her braids. The second she'd tried to stand, the thorns yanked her back by the head. She'd spent an eternity slowly unhooking herself and wincing and sucking her fingers as the barbs pricked her skin, but finally, *finally*, she got free.

And that's when the bells started bonging.

Sara stared at the castle, still so far ahead. She twisted her skirts around her fists one more time, hoisting them just a little higher. She couldn't trip again. Couldn't lose more time. She just had to pass the stables, and then—

Sara saw the boy a second before she slammed into him. He was nothing but a flash of black clothes and light skin coming out of the stables, and she had no time to stop before—

"OOF!"

They both tumbled to the ground, Sara flat on top of him. Which was good, she guessed, because at least her dress wouldn't get any dirtier.

"Hey, get *off*!"

"Sorry-sorry-sorry!" Sara said. She tried jumping lithely to her feet, but the move turned into more of a rolling flop and ungainly crawl. Then she looked down at her victim, sprawled spread-eagle on the grass.

She gasped. "Galric?"

The boy's eyes grew to giant moons and his milky face turned five shades paler. He scrambled up awkwardly, a wild jumble of knees and elbows, then backed away several steps and bowed low.

"Princess Flissara," he said. "My humblest apologies. I never should have spoken to you that way. Or at all. I'm sorry."

"Don't be," Sara said. "You didn't do anything wrong."

And yet she flushed as she said it because of course his father had done the worst possible wrong, and they both knew it.

"You can get up," Sara said. "It's okay."

Galric rose, but he kept his head down so his stringy black hair stayed flopped over his face. He was a few inches taller than Sara, and she knew he was a couple years older.

"I should go," Galric said. "People could be watching."

"The Keepers of the Light?"

Galric flinched so violently Sara had to laugh.

"It's not like they come when I call. Or, I mean, I guess

they would, but I'm not calling." She leaned closer to Galric, her voice dropping to a whisper. "I don't like them either."

Now it was her turn to flinch. It was treasonous for even a princess to say such a thing, and Sara knew better than to blurt out everything she thought, even if she wanted to.

Galric looked around to see if anyone was watching, then said, "I guess when you're a princess you don't have to be scared of anything."

"I wish," Sara said.

And in that second she wanted to tell him *exactly* what scared her. Which was ridiculous, of course. Out of everyone, he was positively the last person she should tell anything. It's just that for as long as Sara could remember, everything she'd said had been supervised. Her family was around, or Primka, her tutor, or Katya, her nurse, or Rouen and the other Keepers, or just whole groups of Kaloonians who hung on her every word and would pick up on anything she said or did that didn't fit into what their Princess Flissara would do.

But here . . . she was just with Galric. And despite his dad's history, he was just a regular boy. She studied his face. He looked curious and attentive. Sara got the feeling that if she did speak her mind, he wouldn't judge. He'd just listen.

She opened her mouth to start . . . but then she shook her head.

"I'm sorry," she said. "I'm late. Weekly Address and all. Already started."

"Yeah, of course," Galric said, backing away. "Go. Just, please . . . don't tell anyone you saw me. I'm not supposed to leave the manure pits during the day, but sometimes I come here for a break and . . ."

He winced and looked around again.

"I promised the groundskeeper I'd never let anyone in the royal family see me. If he knew about this, I'd lose my job, so please—"

"Wait—you'd lose your job for letting me *see* you?"

"Well, yeah," Galric said. "He says I'm too . . . disturbing."

"Because of what your dad did?"

Galric paled, and Sara inwardly smacked herself again. Most people—including Princess Flissara—would tiptoe around a subject as big as the curse instead of blurting it out loud. Sara couldn't take back what she'd said, but at least she could try to make him feel better about it. "But that wasn't you. You were . . . what? One and a half?"

"Something like that." Galric's voice was dull and his eyes had a faraway stare. For just a second, Sara put herself in his shoes, and imagined what it would be like to spend her whole life treated like a criminal for something she didn't even do. Something her father had done so long ago that it had to seem like another lifetime.

She was about to ask him if he even remembered his father when a flash of black zipped out of the stables and jumped into Galric's arms. It was a kitten, and it looked Sara in the eye as if it were formally introducing itself.

"Meow!"

"Nitpick, no!" Galric hissed. He contorted himself to shove the kitten inside his ragged burlap tunic, but the kitten simply poked its face out of the collar and meowed at Sara again.

"I know he's a black cat and he's not allowed," Galric said in a wild rush. "But he's not magic, I swear."

"I didn't think he was," Sara said. "The Keepers would, so you're smart to keep him hidden, but I don't believe everything they say about black cats and left-handed people and twins. I don't think they're all evil."

A thrill ran through her body and she had to catch her breath. That was the closest she'd ever come to sharing her actual truth with an outsider. Had he noticed? She pretended to stay focused on the cat, but flicked her gaze up to see Galric's face.

He was looking right at her.

"Me neither," he admitted.

She smiled and he returned it, and Sara's heart pounded as she wondered how much he really understood. Then he broke her gaze and gently pulled the kitten out of his tunic. He held it out for her to pet. "His name's Nitpick."

"Awww," Sara cooed. She leaned forward so she was face-to-face with the kitten.

He licked her nose.

"So cute!" she exclaimed. "And raspy."

She rubbed her nose to get the strange sensation off her face, but then she leaned close so the kitten could lick her again.

DING!

It was the higher-pitched bell, the one that rang out every quarter hour, and the one that meant she was a full fifteen minutes late for the Weekly Address, and she was still a long way from the castle.

"Blast!" she cried. "Blast-blast-blast! I gotta run."

She started forward, and Galric moved to get out of

her way but somehow sidestepped *into* her way, and she thumped into him and the kitten again.

"Meow!"

"Sorry, Nitpick!"

Sara tried unsuccessfully to step past Galric again and again, but each time they accidentally danced into one another's path until finally she said, *"Stay."* Then she raced past him . . . but somehow a pulled thread on her dress had gotten caught on his tunic belt. It snagged her backward after just two steps.

"Arrrgh!"

She wrapped the string around two fingers and yanked it apart, then took off for the castle, being careful again to knot her skirts around her fists so she wouldn't take another spill. She sped back into the rose garden, where every bush seemed to reach out with its thorns and grab her hair, her dress, and her arms.

"Ow-ow-ow-ow-ow-ow-ow!" she yelled, but kept on running. Breathless, she stormed through the front gate of the castle. The Royal Guards tried to hide their dismay at the sight of her, but they didn't do a very good job.

"Yes, yes, I know, I look amazing."

She had a similar retort for every servant who gasped and groaned and leaped out of her way as she ran past, and even choicer words for every side table, ottoman, and chair she bumped into on her way to the throne room's turret. She stumbled up the long spiral staircase—the royal entrance, which seriously didn't feel royal so much as torturous for her already-screaming legs. She was panting so hard the echo rang in her ears, and she caromed off the walls, so tired she barely kept her balance. Finally she emerged into the throne room, pushed through the purple curtains that hung behind the thrones, and spotted her father out on the wide balcony, addressing the crowd below. Her mom wasn't with him, which was weird, but also a relief. Queen Latonya would *not* take kindly to Sara's current disheveled state.

The Keepers of the Light, however, *were* there. Rouen stood several feet behind the king and off to the side, where the crowd outside couldn't see him, while Grosselor, as always, stood right out there on the balcony with the king, glowing like a second sun.

"As for Princess Flissara," King Edwin said, "I know you were all hoping to see her—"

"And here I am!" Sara shouted, flinging herself out between the two men with so much momentum she folded double over the balcony railing. The crowd gasped, but King Edwin quickly grabbed her around her waist and righted her.

"Thanks, Dad," she said.

"Ah, Princess Flissara!" the king cried, and the entire crowd below echoed the greeting. As King Edwin looked his daughter up and down, taking in the exploding braids, grass-stained dress, and thorn-scratched arms, his mustache tilted upward, and Sara knew he was trying desperately not to laugh.

"My word, Flissara," he said. "When you get lost in a drawing, you really get involved with the scene, hmmm?"

Sara blushed. She knew he knew *exactly* what she'd been up to—or at least the gist of it. And for sure he knew she'd broken about a million rules along the way, but Sara could tell he wasn't upset with her about it. Grosselor, however, would not approve at all, so Sara didn't dare turn and meet his eye.

"Why don't you give our people a few words about your upcoming Ascension Day?" Grosselor asked, loud enough for the crowd to hear. They hurrahed in agreement.

Now Sara had no choice but to turn to Grosselor. Her stomach turned. Yes, he was a hero. A savior even, said most Kaloonians. They revered him. Even people outside the kingdom, like Princess Blakely from Winterglen, gushed about his valor and his—ew—"dreamy good looks."

But he made Sara uneasy.

She didn't let it show. Princess Flissara would show nothing but deference and respect to Grosselor. She smiled like he was her favorite uncle, then moved closer to the balcony's edge so she could see the citizens of Kaloon.

She knew not *everyone* in the kingdom filled the massive cobblestone courtyard for Weekly Addresses—it's not like the chats were mandatory—but it always seemed like they did. From the high balcony, it was difficult to pick out many individuals, but some people always stood out. Like the young woman with the impossibly long curly red hair, who always wore it loose and flowing, and who Sara had found out was Kaloon's only female blacksmith. Or the small child who always sat on her father's shoulders and ate a banana while Sara spoke. Or the dots of bright yellow from the scattered Keepers, whose simple presence ensured that every Weekly Address would proceed peacefully.

"Kaloonians!" Sara addressed the crowd. "Sorry I'm late. I guarantee you there's no place I'd rather be than with . . ."

Her voice died away and she squinted as she saw . . . Galric?

He was in the very back, at the edge of the crowd. His head was down and his hair hung over his face, but he stood on the wooden base of one of the courtyard torches, so he rose higher than anyone else.

"You!" Sara blurted happily.

She pointed, and everyone down below looked around trying to follow her gaze. Everyone except Galric himself, who immediately hopped down from the torch base and disappeared into the crowd.

"Princess?" Grosselor asked, stepping closer to Sara's side.

Sara shivered, but she smiled and moved her pointing finger in a flourish so it indicated *everyone* in the courtyard.

"*All* of you," she said, continuing as if she didn't feel Grosselor's eyes on her. "As you know, next week I'll turn twelve, and the Ascension Ceremony will bring me officially in line for the crown. Thank you so much for all your cards and letters. I've read them all, I promise. And no, Sammy Worthington from Maid Arabelle's class, I'm not scared. Prince Alistair was a long time ago, and we've been perfectly safe since then, thanks to Grosselor and his Keepers of the Light. May the Light keep us all."

The crowd cheered, and Sara forced herself to look adoringly at Grosselor. He swelled with pride, then stepped to the center of the balcony. "Thank you, everyone. And thank you, King Edwin and Princess Flissara. Shall we let them get back to their royal business?"

The crowd cheered again. Sara and her dad had clearly

been dismissed, so they waved to their people, then walked to the royal entrance in the back of the room. Rouen didn't follow them; apparently he was staying in the throne room to hear his leader speak. When King Edwin and Sara had descended half the twisting staircase with no sign of their family's yellow shadow, King Edwin whispered, "Well done, Sara. You made Grosselor very happy."

"Thanks."

They shared a conspiratorial smile. The king was smart enough to rarely speak freely about the Keepers, but when he did he wasn't complimentary. He thought Grosselor enjoyed his power and popularity a bit too much. Mom hated when he talked like that, and always reminded him that without Grosselor and the Keepers, King Edwin's family would have died out in the Dark Magic Uprising, and the king himself would never have been born. That always ended the conversation, but if Sara was in the room, he'd meet her eyes and she'd let him know with a look that she felt the exact same way.

"Where was Mom?" Sara asked. "How come she wasn't at the Weekly Address?"

Her father shrugged. "I'm not sure. She went out riding. . . . I guess she lost track of time."

Sara snorted. "Mom *never* loses track of time. She's *always* back from her ride in time for the Weekly Address."

"Not *always*," the king said, laughing. "She doesn't come every week."

"When was the last time she missed—" Sara's voice cut off as she stepped on the hem of her dress and nearly tumbled down the marble staircase.

"Careful, Sara," her dad said, catching her arm. "No

broken bones before the Ascension Ceremony. Or after, I hope."

"No broken bones," Sara assured him, but she knotted up the bulk of her skirts in a fist and let her dad keep holding her elbow as she carefully picked her way down the spiral staircase of doom.

When they made it down, King Edwin excused himself to meet with advisers, while Sara cut through the longest hall of the castle, lined with tapestries, works of art from Kaloon's greatest creative minds, and portraits of the royal family dating back from forever. As always, the room was filled with workers dusting and polishing, and echoed with the sound of everyone's feet against the wood floor. Sara's own footsteps clomped in her ears as she moved farther down the hall, toward a massive gold statue of Grosselor. It sparkled like the man himself, and raised a triumphant fist while stomping down on the twisted body of the Dark Mage Maldevon.

Sara didn't like the statue. She skirted it and ducked into a smaller corridor. The floors of this rounded, windowless turret room were covered in a thick woven carpet that muffled sound. Sara walked into the middle and felt the gaze of fifteen suits of armor staring at the center of the room as if guarding it. Sara looked around to make sure she was alone, then tiptoed silently to the fourth suit from the door, right-hand side. She peeked behind it, eager to see if the back panel was open and if there were any special secrets left for her.

"Is it Royal Rear End Inspection Day?" Mitzi asked.

Sara quickly darted away from the suit of armor, which made Mitzi laugh. She was the palace head chef and always went out of her way to bring the princess special treats. Sara relaxed immediately, and she grinned when she saw the tray of cookies in Mitzi's hands.

"What did you bring me?" she asked excitedly.

"Cookies, Your Highness. Yummy oatmeal–chocolate chip and peanutty peanut butter."

"You are the *best*!" Sara grabbed a cookie and took a huge bite.

Mitzi beamed, and for about the millionth time, Sara thought it was criminal that Mitzi didn't have kids because she'd be the best mom ever. Oh, sure, Sara loved her own mother, but Queen Latonya was so regal and poised and sophisticated and *correct*. Mitzi, on the other hand, was short, blond, curvy, and always said or did the first thing that popped into her head, no matter how silly it was. Honestly, Sara felt like she had more in common with Mitzi than with her own mother.

"That cookie was *incredible*!" Sara raved. "I could hug you. I'm going to hug you." She threw her arms around Mitzi. "I'm totally hugging you right now."

Mitzi laughed. "And just this morning you said you were allergic to hugs."

Sara froze. "I did?" She forced a laugh. "Huh. Sorry, not a morning person, I guess." She shoved another cookie in her face to shut herself up, then spoke around it. "I should go. Katya'll be looking for me."

"Okeydokey," Mitzi said, "but take the cookies. I made them for you."

"Really? Thanks!" Sara grabbed the tray and sped down the gallery, wincing as she accidentally bit the inside of her cheek. She walked away as fast as she dared, down the long hall, then off to the Grand Staircase, which was blissfully *not* marble and spiral-shaped but carpeted, wide, and straight. She tromped up to the massive gilt-and-wood door of the family residence, which she flung open and accidentally slammed into the wall. She jumped, but somehow managed to keep all the cookies on their tray. When she finally got to her room, all she wanted to do was flop onto her bed and go limp.

Instead she threw open the door and screamed—because she nearly collided with a girl who looked absolutely identical to her in every way.

Chapter 2
Flissa

"Sara!" Flissa cried. She scrunched up her face and took in Sara's disheveled hair, scratched arms, and ruined outfit. "You're quite a mess. What happened?"

Sara opened her mouth to speak, but Flissa could tell by the way her twin sister's violet eyes danced with excitement that the story would only give her palpitations. She put up a hand to stop her. "Actually, I don't want to know. Not yet at least. I need a second to prepare."

Flissa carefully took the tray of cookies out of Sara's arms so she wouldn't drop it, and set it on the floor. Only then did she throw her arms around her sister for a hug.

"I missed you," Flissa said. "I'm glad you're back."

"Huh," Sara said. "I thought you were allergic to hugs."

"What?"

"That's what Mitzi said you told her. *After* I hugged her."

Flissa winced. "I'm so sorry. I forgot to tell you. It seemed like such a nothing moment, I didn't even think to."

Flissa sat at her desk chair like a good student and

looked up at Sara attentively. "Okay, tell me everything that happened to *you* this morning. Everything."

As Sara gave her the quick rundown, Flissa felt the blood drain out of her face.

"Princess Flissara would *not* hang out at the stables with a stranger," she said when Sara finished. "Or a black cat! And I can't believe you let Mitzi find our secret hiding place. I left a note for you in that suit of armor! Now we need to find a whole new place."

"We don't, though," Sara said. "Mitzi didn't see me open the suit; she just saw me checking it out."

"But the cat, and *Galric* of all people! What if he talks? What if he tells people what you said about the Keepers?"

"He won't," Sara said, though Flissa couldn't fathom how she could sound so sure. "Trust me," Sara added.

Flissa sighed. "I do. You know that. We just have to be careful. Ascension Day is coming up, and—"

A high-pitched voice chimed in and finished Flissa's sentence. "And everyone in Kaloon gets nervous when an heir approaches Ascension Day. Ever since the Dark Magic Uprising."

The voice came from Primka, an apple-sized bright blue-and-yellow songbird—and the girls' tutor. She flitted into the room from a hole in the ceiling, then swooped down to rest on the back of Sara's desk chair, or more accurately, on the layers of dresses Sara had draped across the back of her chair.

"So even though you've spent nearly twelve years pretending to be the exact same person, and you *think* you know what you're doing," Primka continued, "the truth is, you need to be more careful than ever. Allow me to offer some pointers."

She did, but Flissa didn't listen. Instead, she met Sara's eyes and they tried not to laugh. Flissa didn't mean to be rude—Primka always gave very sound advice. It was always the *same* advice, though, and both Flissa and Sara knew it as well as the words to their favorite song.

"Oatmeal–chocolate chip or peanut butter?" Sara whispered, gesturing to the cookie tray. "They're both amazing."

Flissa peered at Primka. The bird wasn't even looking at the girls. She was in full lecture mode, flitting around the room as she preached. Flissa turned back to the cookies and considered the flavors.

"They both look so good," Flissa said. She bit her lip. "Let's see . . . oatmeal–chocolate chip is delicious, but the chocolate could melt and get all over my hands. Peanut butter is also delicious, but sometimes if there's too much peanut butter it sticks to the roof of my mouth."

"You could have one of each," Sara suggested. "I did."

Flissa shook her head. "Then I might spoil my lunch. I need to choose."

Flissa hated to choose. Her upper lip broke out in beads of sweat, and she wiped her clammy hands on the sides of her rose-colored dress—a dress that would have been identical to Sara's if Sara's weren't stained and tattered.

"Fliss?" Sara said gently. "It's okay. There's no wrong choice."

"There is, though," Flissa groaned. "What if I take a bite of the oatmeal–chocolate chip and then realize I really wanted the peanut butter? Or I take a bite of the peanut butter and realize I really wanted the oatmeal–chocolate chip?"

"Half of each?" Sara suggested.

Flissa shook her head. "That doesn't seem right."

Now she wasn't just sweaty, she was breathing heavier too.

"I can't do it," Flissa said. "Help me."

"Locket."

Flissa tugged on the chain around her neck and pulled out a delicate gold locket. Sara wore a matching one, of course, and each locket held a miniature portrait of the other twin . . . though anyone who looked would just think Princess Flissara simply liked carrying around a photo of herself. Flissa's locket, however, held something else as well: a thin wood chip. When the twins were only six, Sara had found the chip and asked a royal carpenter to cut it to coin size and sand it down so Sara could draw on it. On one side, she'd painted a tiny portrait of their dad, and on the other side, their mom. The images were childlike, but amazingly accurate given Sara's age at the time. It was Flissa's most prized possession.

Flissa opened the locket and handed the coin to Sara.

"Queen is oatmeal–chocolate chip; king is peanut butter," Sara declared.

Flissa nodded, and the tension eased out of her shoulders. It was easy to choose when the final answer was out of her hands.

Sara flipped the coin in the air and, as always, missed catching it. The twins scrambled after it as it rolled along the floor and into one of Sara's strewn-around shoes.

"King!" they cried in unison, and Sara smiled as she handed her sister a peanut-butter cookie, which Flissa ate without reservation or regret, *after* she returned the coin to its place around her neck.

Primka shook her head and sighed. "You two aren't even listening to me, are you?"

"Of course we are," they answered in unison—then burst out in identical peals of laughter.

Primka sighed, but Flissa saw something like a smile play across her beak and she knew the songbird wasn't seriously upset. "Allow me to redirect your attention to something else," Primka chirped. "Posture and elocution lessons!"

Flissa stood taller. She very much enjoyed posture and elocution lessons. She reached up and tugged her ponytail apart to tighten it on her head (she always kept her hair in a high pony when she was up in their room), then took a running start and did five handsprings, feeling her skirt billow out as she tumbled. As Flissa knew, five was the perfect number of handsprings to carry her the entire length of the thick woven carpet her parents had commissioned for exactly this use. Flissa stuck the landing, then smiled a little as she looked into the floor-length mirror and watched Sara slowly pick her way over every article of clothing, stuffed doll, and art project in progress she had in order to make it to Flissa's neat and tidy side of the room.

Flissa knew the bedchamber had been designed for a single princess, but she thought it would be impossibly sad for one person to rattle around in such a huge space. Divided in half, each side held everything she and Sara could possibly want. Sara had the round, pink-tulle-canopied bed specifically made for Princess Flissara. With so many frills and flowers on the comforter, it would look like a birthday cake if Sara ever picked up her belongings and let the designs show. Instead, she chose to leave the bed stacked with stuff. She wouldn't even put things away at bedtime; she claimed her layers of thrown-around clothes were like an extra blanket, and the sheets of canvas and charcoals at her side meant she could wake up and draw the remnant of her dreams.

Flissa's bed had originally been in another room of the royal quarters, but the twins' parents, with help from the twins' nursemaid, Katya, had managed to move it on their own so no one would wonder why the room needed a second bed. It was wide enough to fit *four* girls, which Flissa thought was far too gargantuan, but she appreciated its bounciness, and had perfected many a flip on its vast expanse. She also liked that the bed butted up against the massive floor-to-ceiling bookcase that ran the entire length of the wall. She kept her favorite books closest to her pillow so she could roll over and grab them at any time of night.

Flissa watched her sister's reflection in the mirror like a hawk and saw every peril in Sara's path. "Not that way, Sara," she said a split second before Sara would have tripped over a high-laced boot and tumbled face-first onto a golden jewelry box. "Take two steps to your left, then climb onto your bed and crawl across. Not all the way—you'll crumble your charcoal sticks—just halfway. Then roll back down to the floor and tiptoe around your holiday crown—you'll be right here."

Sara obeyed. Honestly, Flissa loved her sister more

than anything, but sometimes she didn't understand her. If she were as accident-prone as Sara, she'd keep her space clean and obstacle-free. She did that anyway, really. It pained her to have any of her belongings out of place—what if they got lost or damaged?

Sara clearly didn't share Flissa's worries. As far as she was concerned, no dress was so wrinkled it was beyond a good shake-out, and no amount of tidiness was worth putting in time she could better spend drawing. As for the bumps and bruises she incurred when Flissa wasn't around to guide her through the minefield, Sara just shrugged them off.

Finally, Sara stood tall beside Flissa and blew an errant hair out of her face. "Okay—posture and elocution. Let's do it."

Primka fluttered between and behind them. She studied their reflections in the mirror. "Honestly," she sighed. "It's remarkable anyone believes there's only one Princess Flissara. The two of you look nothing alike."

Flissa and Sara locked eyes in the mirror, then exploded with an identical laugh.

"We look *exactly* alike!" Sara said.

Flissa knew it was true, but she also knew what Primka meant. Flissa and Sara were the exact same height—chest-high next to the suit of armor where they put their secret notes. They had the same wild black curls—curls that would hang all the way down to their waists if they weren't properly rolled and pinned and braided whenever the girls left the room. Their skin was the exact same light brown shade, the perfect mix of their parents. And they had the exact same violet-colored eyes.

They *looked* alike. But as Flissa stared at her sister, still tousled and rumpled from her latest adventure, eyes dancing with excitement for whatever came next, Flissa knew they were *not* the same.

And it made her heart ache.

Primka flitted around the sisters, inspecting them, then batting them with her wings to make adjustments. "Sara, don't slouch—stand up straight and tall, just like Flissa. Flissa, you're not a suit of armor—you can relax a *little.* Sara, a dress is not a welcome mat. Do not step on the hem. Flissa, your hair is not a food group—don't put it in your mouth. And, Sara, as for *your* hair, you look like a horse when you blow it out of your face. Your hair shouldn't be *in* your face to begin with!"

"It came out when I tripped!" Sara said.

Primka sighed and buried her face in her wings. "I understand, child. I do. But Flissa doesn't trip, so you can't either."

"I trip sometimes," Flissa interjected. "I make sure of it, just so it's okay when Sara does."

Sara reached out and squeezed her hand.

"I understand," Primka said, "but it's really not very princessly. It's the kind of thing people expect you to grow out of."

"But I haven't grown out of it," Sara said. "Who cares what people think?"

"*You* do!" Primka said, flapping wildly. "You *must*! If you're ever discovered, it's . . ." She looked around, as if Grosselor himself might be hiding on top of Sara's canopy or under Flissa's bed. She dropped her voice to a whisper. ". . . banishment to the Twists. And if you think your royal blood will stop the Keepers of the Light, think again."

Sara rolled her eyes. "Ugh, the Keepers of the Light. Can't we just get rid of 'em and have magic in the kingdom? It would be fun!"

Flissa paled. "Fun?!"

"No." Primka flittered to Sara's face. "It would not be *fun* at all. It would be dangerous. Very dangerous. You know what happened to Prince Alistair and his family—"

"*Forever* ago!" Sara sighed. "And, Primka, come on—you're a talking bird. You're smaller than my hand, and I've seen you carry books as thick as my head. *You're* magic!"

"And she *hides* it," Flissa said. "It's like Mother always tells us—the system isn't perfect, but it keeps us safe. Yes, there are twins like us with no magic, and those like Katya and Primka who have *good* magic, and yes, for now we have to hide, but until there's a better solution, that's the price to pay to keep dark magic out of Kaloon."

"But—"

"No. You didn't see what I saw, Sara. You don't know what dark mages can do." Flissa wrapped her arms around herself and shuddered.

It had happened when she was eight, but she still thought about it every day. Flissa had been practicing her horsemanship since birth, and after she'd begged for a full year, Queen Latonya agreed that Flissa's skills were strong enough that she could spend exactly two hours exploring Kaloon's hills on her own. As a precautionary measure, the queen hung a shiny silver whistle around Flissa's neck—an alarm she could blow, just in case. Flissa had tucked it into her bodice. She knew she wouldn't need it.

The day was perfect, and Flissa still remembered how

free and grown-up she'd felt. She could still feel the wind blowing in her face, bringing with it the smell of fresh grass, wildflowers, and the pleasantly gamey musk of her first horse, Penelope. Even the chill of the whistle against her skin woke her senses and added to the taste of adventure.

If she'd just kept Penelope galloping, Flissa never would have heard it at all. But when she turned onto a new trail and spied a clear stream, she knew her horse could use a rest and some water. She slowed her to a walk and led her for a drink.

That's when she'd heard the laughter and giddy squeals.

Girls, it sounded like. Maybe her own age? Whoever they were, Flissa could tell they were having a lot of fun.

Flissa imagined Sara in this exact same position; for sure the girls' happiness would draw her like a magnet. She'd probably ride right up to them, hooting and hollering herself, and she'd ask to join their game.

Flissa usually had the opposite reaction. New people made her nervous. New *kids* who were already friends and probably wouldn't want her butting in . . . that was enough to send her riding full tilt in the other direction, hoping like crazy they'd never know she'd been around.

But today was a day for new adventures. She took a deep breath and urged Penelope away from the water and toward the voices. Flissa ran the horse to the top of the next hill, where she could hide behind some bushes and still get a good view. The spot overlooked a grassy meadow, through which two girls in simple dresses ran, giggling so hard they half stumbled with every step. Flissa had been right; the girls did look her age, eight or nine tops. They must have been outside for a while, since their dresses were rumpled, and their braids—one girl's reddish-brown and the other's a startling white-blond—were littered with half-mangled flowers that had been inexpertly poked between plaits. Flissa could imagine the two of them sitting in the tall grass, doing each other's hair and giggling and playing games. It's what Flissa imagined she and Sara would do if they were allowed to run freely through the fields together, and it made her smile.

Flissa smiled even wider when she saw the girls' destination: a massive dandelion gone to seed. It was huge; its fluffy head was as big as the fist the reddish-brown-haired girl made when she reached it first and yanked it out of the ground. While her friend still raced to catch up, the girl closed her eyes, moved her lips in a silent wish, then puckered up and with a single blow sent the entire cloud of seeds flying. Flissa watched the tiny white dancers pirouette through the air, and closed her eyes to make her own wish before they landed.

"That was *my* flower, Anna!" one of the girls shouted between gasps for breath.

Her voice was so upset, Flissa's eyes snapped open. It was the blond girl. She'd stopped running, and now stomped toward her friend, her face twisted in fury. "I called it."

"But I got to it first," the reddish-brown-haired girl—Anna—retorted. "And now my wish will come true!"

Dots of angry red rose in the blond girl's cheeks. "You already got five wishes. You took *every* wish flower! This one was mine! You promised!"

Anna smirked and shrugged. "Snoozers, losers."

"You *know* you're faster! It's not fair, Anna!" the blond girl hollered. "It's not *fair*!"

She stomped her foot, and her friend staggered back a step. Flissa thought she smelled a whiff of lavender, though there was none nearby.

The brown-haired girl was mad now too. "Don't be such a sore loser. Honestly, you're such a baby sometimes!"

The blond girl thrust out her arms, crying out in frustration and rage. For a second, Flissa was transfixed by the large sickle-shaped purple blotch on the back of her right hand.

Then she smelled lavender again. As if the flowers were everywhere. The scent was so overpowering, Flissa could barely breathe.

Then came the screams.

As the blond girl glared, Anna rose high into the air, flailing and screaming. The scent of lavender grew, and Anna spun around and around in dizzying circles.

Flissa couldn't stand it. She kicked her heels into Penelope's flank and bolted out of the bushes. "Stop!" she wailed. "You're hurting her!"

The second she saw Flissa, all the anger drained from the blond girl's face. She looked like a beautiful porcelain doll as her blue eyes widened and her tiny pink mouth fell open.

"Princess Flissara!" she gasped.

Then Anna shrieked, and Flissa looked over just in time to see the girl hit the ground with a sickening thud.

Flissa couldn't breathe. The world spun, and a dark halo crept at the edges of her vision. She felt herself toppling and leaned forward, hugging tightly to Penelope's neck so she wouldn't fall off the horse.

That's when she felt the whistle against her skin.

She yanked it out and blew as hard as she could. She wouldn't stop.

Within moments, Flissa saw the most beautiful thing imaginable: the bright yellow tunics of three Keepers of the Light, bounding into the dell on horseback from three different directions. Flissa didn't see what happened next. Her mom galloped toward her at breakneck pace, pulled Flissa onto her own horse, and held her close the whole ride home. Back in the palace, she'd carried Flissa right up to the Residence and into her own giant bed, where she told Flissa over and over that this was why they had the Keepers, and promised her that everything would be all right.

It wasn't all right, though. Flissa couldn't get the image of the blond girl out of her head—that furious stare as she hurled her magic at her friend. It was there every time Flissa closed her eyes, and she wouldn't leave her mother's bed until she knew whether Anna would be okay.

It turned out she was . . . in a way. Her injuries healed within a week, and King Edwin told Flissa there'd be no lasting damage.

No *physical* lasting damage.

The people in Anna's village, it turned out, didn't believe it when Anna said she and her family didn't know about her friend's magic. The Keepers believed them; they didn't punish Anna's family at all. But the villagers thought Anna had been hiding her friend's secret, thus putting everyone in danger. They vandalized Anna's family home, and they refused to use her father's blacksmithery. Flissa begged her father to try to help, but when his men went to visit the family, Anna's parents were already packing up—the children in tears—to flee the kingdom and try to rebuild their reputation somewhere else.

It wasn't fair. Anna and her family hadn't done anything wrong. It was all the other girl's fault—the one with the sickle-shaped scar—her and her magic.

"I'm so sorry, baby," Queen Latonya had said after the king told Flissa the news. "Just know that the bad girl's gone. The Keepers sent her to the Twists. She won't hurt anyone ever again, I promise."

Even now, years later, Flissa still had nightmares about the girl with the sickle mark on her hand. In her dreams, *Flissa* was the one she tossed around like a rag doll. She was the one who plummeted helplessly to the ground. She was the one tormented and forced to flee.

And the smell of lavender still made her sick.

Sara moved to Flissa and put an arm around her. "Fliss, I get it. I do. There are bad mages. Seriously bad. I'm just saying they're not *all* like that."

Primka fluttered down to Sara's shoulder. "Right," she said. "Some of them are Keepers of the Light. And others, good souls like myself and Katya and the two of you, who make sacrifices and do what we need so we can follow the rules."

"Until a better way comes along," Flissa said, echoing her mother's words on the topic. "One with more shades of gray that still keeps us all safe."

"Right," Sara snorted. "And in the meantime we're sharing a life."

Flissa shrugged. "What's wrong with sharing a life? I think we're lucky. If I didn't have you, I'd have to make appearances, and do Weekly Addresses, and endure county festivals—"

"County festivals are fun," Sara countered. "You get to meet all kinds of people."

"Which *you* love to do. And *I* get to compete in archery tournaments, and fencing matches, and ride up and down the countryside in royal processions. Would you want to do any of those things?"

"Have you *met* me?" Sara said. "I'd get shot by an arrow, stabbed, and trampled."

"See?" Flissa grinned. "Being Flissara is perfect."

"It does seem to suit you," Primka sighed. She flitted behind Flissa and hovered in the air. "Down, please."

Flissa obediently took her hair out of the high ponytail, and Primka began expertly braiding it with her feet while flapping her wings to hover in midair.

"Though it would take both of you to get through a royal ball without disaster," Primka said. "Flissa, you're a symphony on your feet, but you make terrible conversation—"

"With princes and princesses I don't even know or like," Flissa countered.

"While, you, Sara, can light up the room with your chatter," Primka said. "But you'll get your dress caught in the tablecloth and pull an entire banquet to the floor."

"That happened *once*!" Sara objected. "And the banquet meal was liver with onions. Everyone should have thanked me."

"But they didn't," Flissa said. "Now *I'm* the one who gets sent all the time, which means I have to dance with the sons of earls and dukes and touch their sweaty hands. It's horrible."

Sara belly flopped onto a pile of laundry on her side of the room, and Flissa heard something under the pile crack. "Then let's change things up," Sara said excitedly. "Let's not *wait* until a better way comes along—let's *make* a better way come along. Our Ascension Ceremony's next week, right? Once it's over, and we're officially in line for the throne, let's just tell the truth!"

"The truth?" Flissa echoed. "About us?"

"The truth?!" Primka exploded, and from the sound of her voice, Flissa had no doubt that if the bird hadn't had her feet full of Flissa's braids, she'd be flapping in Sara's face. "The *truth* is that Ascension Ceremony or no, the Keepers would know you're in violation of the Magic Eradication Act. You'd lose all your royal rights, and the two of you—plus anyone else who knew the truth, like your parents, and Katya, and *me*—would most likely be executed for actively deceiving the kingdom."

Sara's jaw dropped, and she stared at Primka as if she'd never seen the bird before. "Executed?"

Flissa nodded. "Or sent to the Twists. Which is just as bad."

"Worse," Primka said.

For once in their lives, Sara was stunned into silence, which to Flissa made no sense. It's not like the Magic Eradication Act was news. After all these years, it was still posted all over Kaloon, and their dad even read it out loud every year on the anniversary of Grosselor's triumph to celebrate the birth of the Keepers. Ascension Day wouldn't change anything. The rules were the rules, and they'd known them since they were born. Flissa and Sara were twins. Simply by existing they were in violation of the most important law of the land. So as long as they or anyone they cared about lived in Kaloon, they had to keep their secret and share an identity. It was that simple.

An eerily soft, slow knock at their door broke the silence.

Flissa's heart thudded. Only a few people were allowed in the Residence, and none of them knocked like that.

Sara nodded to Flissa, an unsaid *You take it.*

"Hello?" Flissa called, straining to keep her voice normal.

"Girls?"

It was their father, but there was something about his voice. Flissa couldn't explain it, but she had a horrible feeling that something was terribly wrong. She wanted to keep the door shut and never find out what was waiting for them on the other side, but Sara was already flinging it open.

Their father tried to smile, but it looked more like a grimace. His mustache drooped. And though he tried to blink it away, his brown eyes watered.

He took Sara's hand and beckoned for Flissa to join them.

Flissa's legs felt like noodles, but she somehow made it across the room. Her father took her hand and squeezed it gently.

"I have something to tell you, but I promise you I'm going to find a way to make it better."

Flissa glanced at Sara, but Sara wouldn't tear her eyes from their father for even a second.

"It's your mother," he said. "I found her when I came

back to our room. She told me something happened on her ride. She somehow made it back home, but . . ."

He glanced away and pursed his lips, collecting himself, while Flissa heard the blood whooshing in her ears.

Their mother. Something horrible had happened to their mother.

"Is she okay?" Sara asked.

Their father shook his head the tiniest bit. "She tried to tell me what happened," he said, "but she had so little strength . . ."

Flissa reached out her free hand and took hold of Sara's. She squeezed and waited an eternity for what their father would say next, but her heart was pounding so loudly she wasn't sure she'd even hear him. When he finally opened his mouth, her stomach clenched.

"I believe . . ."

His mustache curled down further and his voice cracked the tiniest bit. Flissa gripped Sara's hand harder as their father set his jaw and released the words she wished he could take back.

"I believe she was cursed."

Chapter 3

Sara

Sara didn't believe it. Their mother couldn't have *actually* been cursed. Curses didn't happen in Kaloon. Sara hated the Keepers of the Light, but the one thing they were good at was keeping harmful magic away from the kingdom, so Mom being cursed was just impossible.

Flissa didn't feel the same way, Sara could tell. Her sister's hand was getting clammier in hers with every step they took toward their parents' bedchamber.

In some ways, Flissa was the bravest person Sara knew. She hopped on untamed horses and rode the bucking beasts until they nuzzled her and ate out of her hand. She played physical combat games against Kaloon's young soldiers and won. She swung on vines over nettle patches and didn't break a sweat.

But a threat to their family? That had her pale and shaking. Sara tried to squeeze some of her own confidence into her sister's hand.

"I don't know if I can do it, Sara," Flissa whispered. "What if she's—"

"She's fine," Sara whispered back. "Or she will be. I know it."

Just ahead of them, their father reached the thick wooden door of the bedchamber, carved with stories of Kaloon's history. Sara had spent hours sitting cross-legged in front of it, drifting into imagined moments from each vignette, but now she only got a glimpse before their dad pushed it open.

Primka zipped in first, and Sara saw her fly up to a hulking figure bent over the bed.

Katya.

Sara hadn't realized she'd tightened her whole body until she suddenly let it go.

"Katya's here," she whispered to Flissa. "It'll all be okay."

Katya wasn't just the twins' nursemaid—she helped the whole family. She'd started working in the palace when *Dad* was born, so their family was like her own. And Katya trusted them with her life—the royal family and Primka were the only ones who knew she had magic.

Whatever was wrong with Queen Latonya, Katya would fix it.

Flissa nodded, but her hand was still slippery in Sara's. Sara squeezed it, then led them closer to the bed.

"Mom?"

Katya turned. Her pillowy face, normally creased with endless laugh lines, was flat and serious. Her constantly dancing blue eyes were now fixed like stones.

One look from that face stopped Sara and Flissa in their tracks.

"Slowly now," she said, her voice gentle despite the

warning on her face. "These are deep, cold waters. Best you don't dive in."

Flissa's hand was suddenly ice. Sara had to squeeze it several times to urge her slowly forward. They moved to the opposite side of the bed from Katya and Primka.

Their mom barely made a lump in the covers, as if she had shrunk into herself. Sara took deep breaths as she inched closer, trying to prepare herself for whatever she might see on Queen Latonya's face, but when she actually saw it, she nearly doubled over. Next to her, Flissa went rigid and sucked in a breath.

Their mother had always been beautiful. Perfect features, with a wide corona of dark curls. Now those curls lay limp and streaked with white. Her cheekbones jutted sharply from her suddenly sunken face. Her mouth hung slack, and her eyes were open but rolled back—they only saw the slim lower crescents of her pupils; the rest was all rheumy white.

Sara stared at her chest to make sure she was breathing.

She was. Barely.

"It's worse than it was when I left her," their father admitted. "At first I thought it was the flu, but—"

"But the flu doesn't age you forty years in just a few hours," Katya said. "You were right to come get me."

Sara leaned closer. "Mom?"

She hoped for any kind of response, even the slightest twitch, but their mother didn't move until suddenly she coughed so violently she thrashed against the mattress. A thick green cloud burst out of her mouth and hovered above her.

"No."

Their father's voice was a thundering growl. Sara and Flissa turned to see him at the foot of the bed, gripping both bedposts with white knuckles. His nostrils flared with rage.

"Sweet merciful heavens," Katya muttered. "Back away, girls. Quickly."

They did without question. Sara watched in horror as her mom's coughing subsided and the green mist seeped back inside her mouth, her nose . . . even her eyes.

Sara's breath caught in her throat. When she found her voice, she shrieked.

"A doctor! We have to get a doctor!"

She turned to run out and get one herself, but she tripped on the carpet. Flissa caught her.

"No," their father snapped. "No doctor."

"What?!" Sara retorted. "Dad, seriously? Didn't you see that green . . . *stuff*?"

"It's not 'stuff,'" her father said tightly. "It's a curse. *The* curse." He turned to Katya. "You see it too, don't you? The same as before."

"I'd recognize it anywhere," the nursemaid said sadly. "I've been seeing in it my nightmares for the last twelve years."

Sara's eyes whipped back and forth from one to the other. "I don't get it. What are you talking about?"

"The *curse*, Sara," Flissa said softly. "The one Gilward put on her when she was pregnant. The one that was supposed to kill her . . . and us too. It looked just like that mist."

"Which means Gilward has struck again," the king said

through clenched teeth. His shoulders tensed as he gripped the bedposts even tighter.

Sara eased her body against the side of the bed, letting it hold her up. She was dizzy and couldn't catch a full breath. If Gilward was back in Kaloon, he could finish what he started twelve years ago. He could kill them all.

Flissa must have been just as worried because her words tumbled out in a wild avalanche. "No," she said frantically. "Gilward's in the Twists. *No one* escapes from the Twists. The Keepers of the Light combined their magic to make it incredibly strong. And the border recognizes and remembers the magical traces of *everyone* exiled there. If an exile tries to use that magic, the border *absorbs* it. That means even the most powerful dark mages working together can't get out of the Twists. They can't! That's what keeps Kaloon safe!"

Sara found strength in her sister's certainty. She stood tall again. "Right," she said. "And I bet lots of things can make green mist. Like . . . I don't know . . . a poisonous plant. Or bad food, maybe. What if the kitchen workers cooked something spoiled and now it's just rotting in her body and the green stuff's coming from that?"

Primka flittered over and waved a wing at Sara's hand. Sara held it out like she'd been taught to do since she and Flissa were tiny. Primka perched on her palm, and Sara raised her to eye level.

"Sara," the songbird said gently, "I know you don't always keep up with your magical history lessons, but Flissa can tell you we *did* cover this. Every mage is different, and each one's spells leave a unique magical trace. This mist, this *specific* mist, is Gilward's. *Only* Gilward's."

Sara looked to Flissa, a question in her eyes. Flissa nodded slightly, then bit her lip.

"I know you're right," Flissa said, "but unless Mom was riding in the Twists, how would Gilward get to her? How could he possibly get out?"

"The Keepers of the Light," their father huffed. He let go of the bedposts and paced up and down the chamber like a lion. "They're the only ones who could get him out."

Every nerve in Sara's body zinged to life. Did her father say he thought the *Keepers* were behind this?

"But that's ridiculous," Flissa said. "The Keepers of the Light keep us safe. They would never—"

"It's Prince Alistair all over again," their dad said, and Sara wasn't sure if he was talking to them or to himself. "Another Dark Magic Uprising. They've been biding their time. Now Ascension Day is coming, and they think they'll do the same thing to me that they did to King Lamar. But I won't allow it!"

He punched his fist against the wall, and it boomed like cannon fire. Sara jumped, and her mind raced to keep up with what her dad was implying. "Wait-wait-wait—you think the *Keepers* helped Gilward curse Mom?!"

"He doesn't," Flissa said quickly. "That would be crazy. The Keepers are on our side. If we really think Gilward did this, we should *tell* the Keepers. Then—"

"No!" their father snapped, true fury in his eyes. "Flissa, I *forbid* you to tell the Keepers a single word about this. Same goes for you, Sara. I meant what I said: Gilward could never get out of the Twists without magical help. I don't know how many of the Keepers are plotting against us, but we have to suspect them all."

Flissa's brow knit together as she frowned. "Even Grosselor?"

"*All* of them," their father said. Then he turned to Katya. Sara saw his face redden, but his voice remained strong as he asked, "How long does she have?"

The large nursemaid peered down at the girls' mother. Katya took a deep breath, closed her eyes, then let her hands hover over Queen Latonya's body, circling them above her head and chest.

When Katya opened her eyes again, she spoke solemnly to the king. "The curse is strong. I can feel it moving through her body. I'd say she has less than forty-eight hours."

"Until she *dies*?" Sara exploded. She turned to her sister, and immediately regretted saying the word out loud. Flissa was stiff and pale, her terrified eyes wide as moons.

Their father raced to their side and bundled them into his arms. Sara hugged him tight and let herself melt into him.

"That won't happen," King Edwin assured them both. "A curse can only be removed by the mage who cast it, so I'll find Gilward. I guarantee he's still in the kingdom. I'll take my finest Royal Guards—ones I can truly trust—and we'll quietly scour the palace and everything around it. We'll find Gilward long before anyone knows we're even looking. And once he removes the curse," the king added through gritted teeth, "we'll find out which Keepers were helping him, and we'll take care of them as well."

"How do you know Gilward is in Kaloon?" Katya asked from the other side of the bed. "What if he's already disappeared back into the Twists?"

“No one would ever voluntarily go back to the Twists,” the king retorted. “It’s a hellscape.”

Primka leaned out from her perch on the night table. “Gilward might go back,” she offered, “if he thought the hellscape was safer than staying in the kingdom with you on his tail.”

She fluffed her feathers to twice their normal girth, as if hiding from her own impertinence.

“I don’t believe that,” the king said. “This—what he did to Latonya—it’s a message. To break me before Princess Flissara’s Ascension Day, just like they did with King Lamar.”

Sara watched her father’s mouth twist in rage. His mustache stuck out in twin pitchfork points, and she heard the smack of flesh on flesh as he pounded his fist into his hand for emphasis. “Gilward is *here*, in *my* kingdom, and I will *not* let him destroy it or my family!”

“Do you really believe the dark mages will come after us on Ascension Day?” Flissa asked, her voice high and small. “And the Keepers will help them?”

Sara watched her dad’s mustache droop sadly as he saw Flissa’s scared and uncomprehending face. He placed a hand on each of their shoulders.

“You will be fine,” he said. “I truly believe you are in no immediate danger until Ascension Day, and I promise you, I will have this well in hand before then.”

Sara believed him. She nodded.

Flissa, she could tell, did not. She was probably too scared.

“Still, I need you to be extra cautious,” their dad continued. “We can’t let anyone know what happened to your mother, and we can't act as if we suspect a thing. Go about your royal duties as always. I'll do the same, but trust that my Guards will always be out there, and I'll join them every moment I can do so without rousing suspicion. We won't rest until Gilward has removed the curse from your mother and this household is completely out of danger. Do you understand?"

"Yes," the girls chorused, and Sara was relieved to see the tips of Dad's mustache perk up as he smiled the littlest bit. Then he raised a single eyebrow and turned to Sara.

"One more favor, and I mean this especially for you," he said. "No breaking the rules. No trips through the palace grounds, no slipping away from the servants . . . do nothing alone. Stay in your room whenever you can, otherwise stay with Primka, or Royal Guards, or servants we trust. Surround yourself with others. Don't avoid the Keepers, but don't ever be alone with one. Not until we know who's on our side and who is not. Understood?"

It didn't take any prodding to get Sara to keep her distance from the Keepers. "Yes," she said.

Flissa nodded solemnly.

"Okay." Their dad smiled and squeezed their shoulders. "I love you both very much, you know that?"

Sara smiled back. "We know."

"We love you too," Flissa said.

Their father smiled wider and drew them each in for a huge hug—first Flissa, then Sara. He always gave strong bear hugs, but Sara felt him hold her a little tighter than usual, and when they pulled away, he sniffled and his eyes were bright.

"Primka," he said, "please take the girls back to

their room. Katya and I need to discuss some plans."

"Of course, Your Majesty," Primka chirped. She fluttered to the girls to lead them out, but Flissa ignored her and moved closer to the bed. She crawled onto it and stretched out, right next to Queen Latonya. Sara ached to join her, and even took a step forward, then she glanced at her mother's eyes—the eggy yellowy-whites with only the eeriest hint of irises that wouldn't look her way.

Sara couldn't do it. She was afraid to get any closer.

Flissa clearly didn't have the same problem. Moving impossibly slowly and gently so she wouldn't disturb their mother at all, she smoothed Mom's stringy, now-even-whiter hair back from her face, then whispered softly in her ear, "I love you, Mother. Sara and I both do. So very much."

She gently kissed the queen's shriveled cheek, and Sara could almost feel the sensation on her own lips—skin so wasted and fragile it could crumble to dust at the slightest touch. She shuddered.

Flissa rolled off the bed without even moving the mattress, then turned to Sara. With only a look, she asked, *You?*

Sara shook her head imperceptibly. She stayed rooted and forced on a smile. "Love you, Mom. We'll see you soon. Love you *so* much."

The queen didn't move. No twitch, no glance, no sign that she had any idea they were there. Sara stared. Would this be her last image of her mom? She didn't want it to be. She tried to picture Queen Latonya sitting at her ivory-and-gold dressing table, combing her curls with short, firm strokes, or filling the room with a glowing smile as she showed off a new riding outfit.

She painted the scene in her head, but she couldn't get their mom into it. It was this wasted, openmouthed shell every time.

Primka fluttered into her field of vision and mercifully scattered her thoughts.

"Come, girls," she said gently. "Let's go."

Neither she nor Flissa said a word as they followed Primka out the door and down the hall. To avoid her thoughts on the way, Sara scanned the first hanging tapestry she saw and picked out a tiny image all the way off to one side: a small child kneeling in the grass, his face hidden in his hands. For the entire walk down the hall, Sara imagined the child's life in detail, and every second of the day that brought him to the moment captured in the artwork. She was still gratefully lost in that world when Primka delivered them to their room.

"I'll come back," Primka said. "I have some questions for Katya and your father. You're good to stay here for now."

She zipped back through one of the many tiny chinks between the wall and ceiling through which she preferred to make her entrances and escapes.

"Sara?"

Sara snapped out of her daydream and looked at Flissa. She still stood in the entrance to the room, wiping her hands on the sides of her dress. Sara stepped closer and saw Flissa's upper lip was beaded in sweat.

"What is it?" Sara asked. "What's wrong?"

"I don't know what to do. I mean, I think I know what to do, but—"

Flissa's chest heaved like she was having trouble taking a breath. Sara's own heart quickened, and she lunged to take Flissa's hand but tripped and sprawled onto the floor. In a heartbeat, Flissa was down there next to her.

"Are you okay?"

"I am now. You're breathing." Sara rolled over and mirrored Flissa's kneel. She took her hand. "Tell me."

Flissa nodded. "I think Father's wrong and Katya's right. I think Gilward is hiding back in the Twists."

Sara's face contorted. "Why?"

"It's the smartest thing to do. And he's smart. He tried to hurt us and Mother before we were born, and he's waited twelve years to do it again. On Ascension Day, just like the first Dark Magic Uprising. That's an enormous undertaking—one he wouldn't risk by making mistakes—and yet he cursed Mother early, to send a warning and scare us."

"Yeah. And it worked."

"Yes," Flissa agreed, "but look at the consequence: Father's on alert and going after him. Gilward had to know that would happen."

"Maybe he did," Sara said, "and he thought whatever Keepers he's working with could hide him. But they won't. You heard Dad. He and his Guards'll tear Kaloon apart until they find him."

"But, Sara, that's the point! Gilward and the Keepers will *expect* that. They'll expect Father will assume Gilward would want to stay close and hidden to prepare for the Uprising. They'll expect him to turn Kaloon upside down. And they'll expect him to think that never in a million years would anyone go back into the Twists unless they had to."

Sara took a second to process everything Flissa said.

She slid off her knees and onto her bottom. "So . . . you think Gilward went back to the Twists and will hide there until Ascension Day."

Flissa nodded, paler now. "And by that time, Mother will be gone. And Father will be heartbroken and tortured because he couldn't save her. So even though we'll all know it's coming, he'll be even less prepared when the dark mages come after us."

Sara's head hurt. Everything Flissa said made sense.

"They're messing with him on purpose," Sara said, thinking it out. "Gilward's luring him out on a mission that's doomed to fail."

Flissa nodded. "Which means Father won't find him in the next forty-eight hours—*less* than forty-eight hours—and . . ."

She didn't need to finish. Sara knew what she meant.

"Then we have to tell Dad—now! He has to change his plan!" Sara leaped to her feet so quickly she stepped on her hem and tumbled immediately back down. Flissa grabbed her arm.

"No," she said. "He won't do it. He won't believe us. He didn't believe Katya when she said it either."

"But if you explain it the way you explained it to me—"

"He still shouldn't go into the Twists!" Flissa cried. She released Sara's arm and wiped her hands on her dress. "If Father's right, and the Keepers are involved, he can't disappear like that. If he does, they'll know what he's doing. They'll go after him."

"But if he *doesn't* go to the Twists, then Mom—"

Now it was Sara who couldn't say the words.

"It doesn't have to be that way," Flissa said. "I think . . .

I *think* . . . I think . . ." She bit her lip and looked up at the ceiling, then said, "The coin. I need the coin. Open my locket, please. My hands are too sweaty, I can't."

"Flissa, why? What do you—"

"Please!" Flissa begged.

Sara didn't hesitate again. She hooked a finger through the chain around Flissa's neck and tugged out the locket, then opened it up and pulled out the coin. "Can you tell me what king and queen are?"

Flissa shook her head. "I know what they are. Just flip it."

Sara flipped the coin. She tried to catch it, but it bounced off her hand and onto a wadded-up gown she'd worn yesterday. Together, Sara and Flissa crawled over to it.

"Queen," Sara said. "So what does that mean?"

Flissa folded her legs. She closed her eyes and took a deep breath. When she opened them again, she seemed oddly calm. Pale, with a livid flush on her cheeks, but calm. One more deep breath, then she finally spoke.

"It means I have to go to the Twists."

Her voice was clear and strong, but the words made no sense to Sara at all.

"You have to *what*?!"

Flissa shrugged. She took the coin back from Sara and slipped it back into her locket. "It's the only thing that makes sense. I'm strong. I can fight. I'm quick on my feet. I've read all about the Twists and magic, and you can still be Princess Flissara while I'm gone, so no one will know. I'll find Gilward, bring him back, and make him take the curse off Mother."

"How?!" Sara exploded. "How would you make Gilward

do anything? He'd just curse you too. How would you even get to him? How would you even get into the Twists? How would you know where to find them? Isn't the entrance a huge Keeper secret?"

"It's a magical entrance," Flissa said. "I've read about it. It moves, and only the Keepers know where the entrance will be and when."

"Uh-huh. And that dress you're wearing is red, not yellow. You're not a Keeper."

"No," Flissa agreed, "but I imagine I could find the entrance by asking someone in the Underground."

"Someone . . . underground?" Sara asked, imagining a world of mole people in tunnels beneath the earth.

"Not *living* underground, *the* Underground," Flissa clarified. "It's in history books. The Underground is a group of people here in Kaloon who don't like the Keepers. They want mages and non-mages to live together again, and work secretly toward that purpose. In the generation after King Lamar, Grosselor discovered the Underground, which he said was filled with dark mages, so he had them publicly executed and kept their bodies on display in the palace courtyard—"

"Ew!" Sara recoiled. "That's *horrible*."

"Yes, but they were dangerous, so Grosselor had to send a warning to stop other dark mages." She frowned and bit her lip. "At least, Grosselor *said* they were dangerous." She shook her head, then continued. "Either way, most of the books say that Grosselor's actions ended the Underground for good, but others say it still exists. Just smaller, and deeper in hiding. And the books say anyone suspected of Underground ties should be turned over to the Keepers immediately." Flissa frowned again. "Which I guess is why they're so deep in hiding."

"Exactly," Sara said. "So how would you find them? It's not like you can just ask around."

"That's true," Flissa agreed. She reached up and twirled the end of a braid. "Maybe I could ask Katya or Primka? They're magic. They'd have a reason to want magic back in Kaloon."

Sara snorted. "You've heard Primka talk. She's *for* the Keepers of the Light. And Katya might not love them, but she always says we have to do what they say. And even if she *was* with the Underground, you really think she'd help us get to the Twists?"

Flissa frowned. "Us?"

"Well, yeah! You really think I'd let you do something this nuts without me?"

Sara watched Flissa's emotions pull her face in a million directions.

"No," Flissa said. "I mean, I want you to go, but it's not safe. And if we're both gone, there's no Princess Flissara. People will notice. Father will notice. And he might come after us and then—"

"Dad will be way too busy looking for Gilward here, and Katya will be taking care of Mom. Primka will notice, but she won't want the Keepers to get suspicious, so she'll tell Katya we're sick or something. And we won't be gone long. We have to be back with Gilward in less than forty-eight hours, right?"

Flissa looked at her hopefully. "You really want to go?"

"I *am* going. If you go, I go. That's it."

Flissa's eyes watered, but she smiled. "I know I

shouldn't be glad—it's too dangerous—but I am. I honestly don't know if I could do it without you."

"I honestly don't know if we can do it *together*," Sara admitted. "How'll we find someone we can ask about the Underground without them reporting us to Dad, or Primka, or the Keepers? And who would have any idea about Gilward or how we could find him? Or how we could get him to come back with us instead of killing us on the spot?"

Flissa didn't answer. She tucked a braid end in her mouth and sucked on it. Sara drummed her fingers on the floor and blew through her lips . . . then she leaped to her feet.

"I've got it! I've-got-it-I've-got-it-I've-*got*-it! I know who to ask!"

"Who?"

"Don't you remember who I met today? *Galric!* Gilward's *son*! Even if he doesn't know about the Underground, he's not like us—he could ask and find out! And if we're with him and we see Gilward, we'll be safe! Gilward won't curse his own son. He'll *listen* to Galric. It's perfect!"

Flissa wrinkled her nose. "Are you sure?"

"Yes!" Sara pulled Flissa to her feet and stared into her sister's eyes. "Don't you see? Galric can help us get into the Twists and make Gilward turn back the curse. He's the one!"

Chapter 4
Flissa

The next two hours were a flurry of planning, mixed with a lifetime of torturous waiting. Per their father's explicit orders, they couldn't leave their quarters except for royal engagements, and Princess Flissara's next appointment was a horseback ride with Princesses Blakely and Ivamore, visiting from Winterglen. In a way, it seemed silly to obey this rule when they were about to disobey a million others, but if they wanted to save their mother, they couldn't arouse anyone's suspicions until the plan was in motion and they were already in the Twists.

As the equestrian of the pair, Flissa had to handle this first step of the plan, even though she wished she could hand it to Sara. At least they had the time to go over again and again what Flissa would say and what responses she might get in return so she'd be prepared. Flissa also took the opportunity to dive under her bed and retrieve some of the books about magic and the Twists she'd found in the library. She flipped through them with Sara and tried to share everything she knew. She wasn't positive Sara was paying close attention to any of it, but the studying made Flissa feel better.

By the time Primka came in to get Flissa laced into her riding boots, pants, and jacket, Flissa was ready.

Except her hands were sweating, and she had to keep wiping them on her wool jodhpurs.

Sara sat on her bed drawing. Flissa couldn't believe her sister seemed so relaxed, but of course that was part of the plan too. Flissa and Sara had to act normal so Primka wouldn't be suspicious.

At least, as normal as anyone would be knowing their mother was less than forty-eight hours from death and a cadre of dark mages was planning a giant uprising that would end their lives.

Sara was fine, though. She seemed thoroughly engrossed in her artwork, and only every so often glanced up to meet Flissa's eyes. An unspoken:

You okay?

Yes. I'm okay.

They probably didn't have to be so careful. Primka herself was a bit of a wreck. She mis-hooked and re-hooked Flissa's clothes ten different times, and kept a running monologue all the way.

"It's good you're going out," she said. "It's important to keep up a good front. Your father has already spoken in secret to the Royal Guard members he can trust, and they're hunting down Gilward here in the kingdom, so it's only a matter of time before they find him. Your father also sent word to Grosselor that the queen is ill and might be out of sight for a couple of days, so that's good. Soon everyone will know, and whoever's behind—well, what happened—will feel like their plan is working. They'll let their guard down, and it'll be even easier for your father and his men to find and defeat them."

Primka knotted the last lace on Flissa's jacket. "There. You look beautiful. No one would ever know anything is out of sorts in the least."

Flissa turned to the mirror. Her hair was tucked into a braided bun beneath her riding cap. Her jodhpurs slid smoothly into her tall riding boots, and her jacket buttoned neatly over a simple cotton top. It was one of the outfits Flissa felt most comfortable in, and she breathed in the image so it might calm the uneasy churning of her stomach.

"Thank you, Primka," she said. "You did a perfect job as always."

"You're welcome. Now please listen for the bells. When the quarter hour sounds, you'll head out of the Residence. I've arranged for Mitzi to escort you downstairs. I know how much you enjoy her company."

Flissa winced, and the pink feathers on Primka's cheeks grew pinker.

"Oh, no." She fluttered in place, clearly upset. "It's *Sara* who enjoys Mitzi's company. I'm so sorry. I don't know what's wrong with me. I would never—"

"It's fine, Primka," Flissa said. "I like Mitzi well enough. She'll be great."

"It's just that I'm upset. Which I know is silly, because of course you're her daughters and you're far more upset, but the idea of a second Dark Magic Uprising—"

Primka's eyes widened. She covered her beak with both wings and plopped to the ground, landing on a pile of Sara's laundry.

Sara leaned down off her bed and scooped Primka up. "You can talk about it in front of us. Dad already did. It's okay."

Primka nodded, wings still over her beak. Then she released them just the littlest bit. "Okay, then. Flissa, don't go anywhere if Mitzi's not there to escort you. Come get me instead. I'll be in— I'm just going to— I'll be—"

"You'll be with Katya and Mother," Flissa said kindly. "Please tell her we love her."

"Yes. Of course," Primka said. She flew to both Sara and Flissa and hugged her wings around their cheeks, then flew out through one of her chinks.

The minute the bird was gone, Sara rolled off her bed and took Flissa's hands. "You ready?"

Flissa nodded. "The manure pits, right?"

"Exactly," Sara said. "Can't miss him. Thirteen, a little taller than us, pale skin, black hair that kinda hangs in his face so he has to flip it back, and brown eyes. Really brown, like suck-you-in brown."

Flissa scrunched her face. She almost thought she saw Sara smile a little as she described Galric. Flissa didn't like it.

"Understood," Flissa said.

The quarter-hour bells chimed, and for a second, Flissa's stomach turned inside out. Sara squeezed Flissa's hands, and Flissa squeezed back. She held on a long moment, then forced herself to walk out the door. She strode down the carpeted hall to the main door of the Residence, heaved back to move its hulking mass, slipped through—and nearly plowed into Mitzi.

"Flissara!"

Flissa jumped and yelped. She knew Mitzi would be there, but not right there in her face. Most people—even the Keepers of the Light—usually gave the Residence doors a wide berth out of respect. From the first mentions of the palace in Kaloonian history, the Residence was off-limits to everyone except the royal family and anyone they specifically invited inside. In Flissa's generation, only Katya had clearance to come freely in and out as she pleased. Primka too, of course, but as far as anyone outside Katya and the family knew, she was only a regular pet bird and didn't count.

"Sorry," Flissa said, painting on the happy smile Sara would use when she saw Mitzi. "You surprised me."

Mitzi frowned sympathetically. "Then I'm the sorry one. Guess I was just excited because I get to walk you down to your horseyback ride." She threw out her arms, then made a concerned face. "Allergic to hugs now, or no?"

Flissa hoped Mitzi didn't notice her blush. She still couldn't believe she'd said that. It was so Flissa-and-not-Flissara of her, but she'd been lost in her thoughts and hadn't been careful.

"You kidding?" Flissa said, channeling Sara as she forced her own arms open wide and threw herself into Mitzi's. While safely hidden by the hug, Flissa allowed herself to grimace at Mitzi's word choice. *Horseyback?* Who talked like that to an almost-twelve-year-old? Flissa didn't understand what Sara loved about the cook at all.

Mitzi loosened her grip, and Flissa painted the grin back on.

"Oh, I almost forgot," Mitzi said. "I brought you a snack." She reached into the deep pockets of her long pleated skirt and brought out a piece of cloth, which she unwrapped to reveal a perfect square of chocolate. "A fudge square. They're for tonight's meal, but I thought you might like one sooner."

Mitzi winked—another thing Flissa never liked—and handed her the chocolate. Flissa popped it into her mouth in one bite, and for just a second, she softened toward Mitzi. The woman might be overbearing and inappropriate, but she absolutely knew how to bake.

"How's your mother?" Mitzi asked.

Flissa choked on the fudge square.

Mitzi patted her back until Flissa stopped coughing, then croaked, "She's fine. Why?"

Mitzi looked confused. "Word is she's under the weather and she might stay in bed for the next few days. Is that not true?"

Flissa swallowed hard and took a couple deep breaths to settle herself. Of course. Primka mentioned that Father had put the word out. Flissa inwardly kicked herself for reacting so badly.

"Yes, yes. Indeed."

Princess Flissara did not say "indeed." Flissa was off her game. She had to be more careful.

"I mean . . . yeah. Just a cold or something, I'm sure, but she'll rest and get better. Thanks for asking."

"No problem. Now let's get you down for some giddy-up time!"

Mitzi whooped, then mimed riding a horse, galloping down the hall as she held pretend reins. Flissa laughed out loud, but she was incredibly glad Mitzi remained just slightly ahead so she wouldn't see Flissa's grimace. Thank the universe Princess Flissara wasn't so much Sara that she'd be expected to pretend-ride along.

The galloping ended at the top of the grand staircase, and Flissa saw Rouen, the royal family's assigned Keeper, waiting at the bottom. His yellow robes were like a beacon.

Normally, Flissa liked when Rouen was around. Despite his craggy, lumpy skin, potato-like nose, and caterpillar-thick brows, he made her feel safe. He was kind, and she knew his primary job was to look after her family.

But now, after what Father had said about the Keepers being the only ones who could have gotten Gilward out of the Twists, even the sight of his robes terrified her, and her whole body chilled when he fell silently into step right behind her.

Flissa stiffened. Did he know about Gilward? Was he part of the plot? Did he want another Dark Magic Uprising? Was he watching her and hungrily plotting her demise?

"How's your mother?" he asked in his raspy voice.

Flissa nearly jumped out of her skin. She concentrated with all her might to make sure not a single speck of her body reacted to the words, and in fact calmly slowed her pace so she could fall into step beside him and show the respect that Princess Flissara would normally display to the Keepers.

"Thanks for asking," she said. "She feels a little sick, but Katya says it's nothing serious."

"Good," Rouen said. "I did assume that, since you and the king are both keeping up your regular schedules. Not something you'd do if the queen were truly ill."

Flissa tripped over her own feet, which she *never* did unless it was on purpose. Luckily, Princess Flissara did it fairly often. Flissa grabbed Rouen's arm to catch herself. When he put his own hand on top of hers, she fought back a scream.

Mitzi whipped around. "You okay?"

"Yes, thanks. Sorry. Just clumsy. You know me."

"Sure do," she said with a wink. "Here, lemme help. Hook on."

Mitzi extended a hooked elbow, and Flissa slung her arm through it. Rouen kept hold of her other elbow, and together they continued down the hall.

Trapped between Mitzi and Rouen, Flissa felt like she was on her way to prison.

Clinging together, the threesome strode through the main hall, then down the long marble corridor with branches leading to both the kitchen and the cavernous room used for balls and formal meals. This massive ballroom was empty save for a clutch of servers cleaning the multitudinous windows and shining the lacquered-wood tables for the next royal meal. The kitchen, however, bustled with activity and the mixed odors of a million different sweet and savory foods. Flissa let herself breathe deeper as she passed, and she swore she could pick up the scent of more fudge squares among the mingled smells.

Finally, Mitzi released Flissa's arm to push open the double golden-grate doors to the rear lawn, and Flissa openly smiled for the first time since before she'd heard the news about her mother.

Her beautiful horse, Balustrade, was saddled up and waiting for her, a groomsman standing by his side.

Balustrade was their tallest horse, and their wildest. He wouldn't let anyone ride him except Flissa, and she still remembered the day she—at only ten years old—had squeezed her legs around him and stayed astride until he realized they belonged together. Now he was the sweetest animal in the world and even let other people feed and groom him because he knew that was required in order to remain Flissa's horse. He *tolerated* those other people, but Flissa was the only one he loved.

"May I?" she asked Rouen.

He nodded and released her elbow. The second she was free, Flissa walked right up to Balustrade's side and leaned against his jet-black flank. She breathed in his musty, horsey smell, and he turned his head to nuzzle her ear.

Flissa looked deep into Balustrade's eyes. He knew she was upset, Flissa could tell. He wasn't magic like Primka, but he knew things all the same. More than anyone could imagine. Like the time Rayella, the head groomsperson, brought the horse to *Sara* at an outdoor festival. Rayella had thought she was giving Princess Flissara a wonderful surprise, but Sara had been terrified that Balustrade would buck her off and give up their secret. But without anyone telling him, the horse somehow knew exactly who Sara was, and what he needed to do to keep their secret. He not only let Sara mount him, but he also moved extra gingerly to make sure she could stay astride.

"I love you, Balustrade," Flissa now whispered. She pulled two sugar cubes from her jacket pocket, which Primka always kept filled for her. Then she moved to his side, easily placed her foot into the stirrup, and swung onto his back. She gently ran her hand over his braided black mane.

"Honestly, Flissara," Blakely said, "we've been *waiting*. Can we go now?"

Princess Blakely was the older of the two visiting princesses. She was seventeen and, according to Sara, far too excited for her elderly father to pass away so she could take over the throne. She wore a dress and sat sidesaddle on her horse, which to Flissa was patently ridiculous. Worse, she kept her hair loose instead of braided, because she wanted the world to see her long blond hair bouncing in the wind. Flissa thought of asking if she'd also want the world to see her long blond hair in a bloody clump after it got tangled in thorny branches and ripped out of her head, but she'd never have the courage to say something like that, and it wouldn't be very Princess Flissara of her if she did.

Ivamore, only nine, was slightly more tolerable than her sister. She wore pants, sat astride her horse, and had the sanity to keep her hair in neat braids while riding. Still, she had the same supremely entitled attitude of her older sister and functioned as if the world were created to satisfy her every whim.

Flissa offered them both a smile. "Sorry, Blakely. It's good to see you."

Flissa nudged Balustrade into motion; the other princesses followed. "I hope your father's well," Flissa said.

"He is," Blakely said as if the words were a bitter pill. "Maybe your mother could go cough on him. I heard she's sick."

Flissa wasn't even thrown. Gossip spread fast, especially when Blakely was around.

"She's fine. Just a cold," Flissa said.

"Really?" Ivamore said. "'Cause *I* heard that creepy mage who cursed your mom was seen riding out of Kaloon as fast as he could."

Flissa choked and coughed to cover it. "Cursed?"

"Back when you were born," Blakely said, rolling her eyes. "Some servant said he was back in Kaloon. Stupid, we know. The guy was sent to the Twists forever ago. But it's always like that. Every time we come into a kingdom, all the little peons try to impress us with the crazy secrets they know. I get the good stuff. Ivamore gets lies from scruffy kitchen boys who have no idea what they're talking about."

"He wasn't scruffy," Ivamore shot back. "He was a *handsome* kitchen boy. And there were two of them who said it, not just one. The other one said he heard the old guy was with a Keeper."

Blakely whipped around to face her sister, suddenly interested. "Which Keeper? Was it Quendrick? He's really cute."

"Ew! He's like a thousand years old!"

"So? They don't age! What about Thraxos, then? He's younger."

"Sure. Like ninety."

Flissa let them bicker as she tried to calm her racing heart.

Someone had seen Gilward in Kaloon.

More importantly, someone had seen Gilward *riding out* of Kaloon. Escorted by a Keeper.

Her instincts had been right. Katya's too. Gilward may well be plotting a second Dark Magic Uprising, but he wasn't sticking around the kingdom between phases one and two. He was taking shelter in the Twists.

And the sooner she and Sara could get to him, the sooner they could save their mother.

"What do you think, Flissara?" Blakely asked. "Which Keeper should I try to snag while I'm here? Grosselor, maybe?"

Flissa hid her disgust behind a big, open grin.

"I think we should ride to the vineyards," she said. "Git on, Balustrade!"

The horse knew her so well she barely had to touch him with her heels before he sped ahead. This was one of the Princess Flissara duties she actually enjoyed, when "diplomacy" meant opening up Balustrade on their acres and acres of land, keeping him in check only enough to make sure the visiting dignitaries weren't embarrassed by Flissa's prowess compared to their own.

At least, that was usually a concern on rides like this. Today she had bigger issues on her mind.

Flissa waited until they reached the far orchards. The apple trees were in full bloom, their petals dripping an inconstant stream of pink confetti. There was plenty of room to ride between rows of trees, and it was one of Flissa's favorite places to canter.

"Care to race?" Flissa said.

"Yeah!" Ivamore said. "Come on, Blakely, let's do it!"

"It's hardly ladylike, if you ask me," Blakely said from her useless sidesaddle perch, "but sure, I guess we can."

"To the high well," Flissa said, purposely naming a landmark that even at full speed would take nearly a quarter hour to reach. Ivamore eagerly accepted the challenge, and the three of them moved their horses into a line. Ivamore counted off: "Three . . . two . . . one . . . *go!*"

Balustrade knew it was a race, Flissa could tell. And she could feel his torture as she coaxed him to stay slow when all he wanted to do was lean in and take the easy lead. Flissa kept him behind Ivamore easily enough, but it was agony for him to remain behind sidesaddle Blakely. Still, he obeyed, and little by little Flissa let the princesses put more and more distance between them, until they'd crested a hill and moved out of sight.

Then Flissa quickly turned off the path and didn't slow until she reached a nearly invisibly slim trail through the forest at the orchard's side. When the path opened up and she knew she was far enough that the princesses wouldn't hear Balustrade's hoofbeats, she kicked him into a canter. Together, they easily navigated the twisting trail, leaped over the stream that bisected the forest, and raced all the way down through the lower plains. She only slowed when she got to the farthest reaches of the palace grounds, where she'd only ridden once or twice. The ground was boggy here, and she carefully picked out the most solid spots.

The smell hit Balustrade first. He reared back and neighed, completely overcome. Then it hit Flissa, and she gagged. "I suppose these are indeed the manure pits."

She could see them from astride Balustrade: three large pits, each surrounded by a rock wall to pen them in. All of Kaloon's livestock waste was funneled here and it made excellent fertilizer, but a long-since-passed head gardener had discovered the manure fertilizer worked best when the pits were stirred regularly, so the manure became a mixed slurry combined with rainwater and mud. If there was a worse job in Kaloon than stirring the manure pits, Flissa couldn't fathom what it was.

Sara was right; there was no way to miss Galric. Not only did he look exactly the way Sara described him, he was also the only living creature around besides Flissa and Balustrade.

That was good. No people meant next to no chance a Keeper would appear.

The skin above Flissa's upper lip broke out in sweat.

Did they really need Galric in order to succeed? Did she have to talk to this strange boy? His father had just tried to kill her mother—wouldn't it be smarter to assume he wanted the queen dead as well?

Flissa weighed the options. She'd have done it out loud if she were with Sara, so her sister could hear and chime in, but now she did it in her head. She could talk to Galric and try to get his help, but he could turn out to be an enemy. He could report the incident to the Keepers. Sara had said she didn't think he would, but she didn't have the most discerning sense of character. She found something to like in almost everyone.

But if she didn't talk to Galric, if they didn't get his help . . . how would they find the Underground? What possible hope did they have of convincing Gilward to remove their mom's curse?

But what if Galric was magic too? What if he'd *helped* his father escape the Twists? What if Flissa tried to talk to him and he put a curse on her?

Or what if he was the key to saving her mother's life?

Flissa yanked the locket from under her shirt and opened it up, squeezing the coin in her palm. "King, I talk to him; queen, I go home."

She tossed the coin and watched it spin in the air before she snatched it expertly and smacked it on the back of her hand. Slowly, she revealed its face.

A drawing of King Edwin.

Talk to Galric.

At least she could do it with a friend. "Come, good Balustrade," Flissa said softly, and though he clearly didn't want to, the horse trudged toward the manure pits.

Galric didn't see them coming. His back was to them. He stood on one of the rock walls and leaned against a massive wooden rod that extended deep into the pit—his stirrer stick, no doubt, though it didn't look like he was doing a lot of stirring. He didn't budge as Flissa approached, and her heart fluttered faster as she imagined him working out the intricacies of a brutal curse in his mind.

She waited, hoping he'd turn her way so she didn't have to start things. She even made Balustrade stamp in place, and blow through his lips, but she got no reaction. Finally, from right behind Galric, she said, "Hello?"

"Wha—?!"

Galric spun around so quickly he lost his balance and almost fell backward into the manure pit. Waving his arms wildly, he grasped for the slack of Balustrade's reins.

"No!" Flissa shouted.

Balustrade had bitten the last person who'd grabbed him like that, then bucked for an eternity until Flissa had calmed him down. And that was on the fields he loved. She couldn't imagine what her horse would do when he was already riled up by the horrible stench of the manure pits.

But Galric had already fallen too far to stop. He seized on the reins, yanking Balustrade's head forward—

—and the horse merely blew through his lips, as if irked by a fly.

Galric hoisted himself back to standing, then pushed his forehead against the horse's and held Balustrade's face in both his hands.

"Sorry about that, Blusters," Galric said. "Thanks for helping me out."

Outrage now eclipsed Flissa's fear. *"Blusters?!"*

"Princess, hey." Galric said it with a casualness Flissa didn't like. She also didn't like that he had hopped off the rock wall of the pit and was now scratching Balustrade just above his muzzle, the spot only Flissa knew he liked.

"What are you doing to my horse?" Flissa demanded.

Galric smiled. "I told you, I hang out at the stables when I can, so Blusters and I are good friends."

"Stop calling him that. His name is Balustrade, not . . ." Flissa couldn't even bring herself to say it. ". . . *that.*"

Galric grimaced. "I dunno. *Balustrade*'s so fussy, you know? Like those braids in his mane."

"His braids are *beautiful*."

Galric shrugged, and Flissa's jaw dropped. If the coin hadn't told her to follow through with Sara's plan and talk to him, she would have turned and galloped right back to the castle. Instead she sat taller, turned Balustrade away from Galric—and tried not to notice the horse turning his head to look back at him.

"You shouldn't take such liberties with the princess's horse," Flissa said stiffly. "Or with the princess."

Galric stopped paying attention to Balustrade and squinted up at her. "Are you okay? You're acting weird."

"I'm not," Flissa said quickly. "I'm acting like myself."

"Okay," Galric said doubtfully, "but you were really different this morning."

This was not the conversation Flissa wanted to have right now. She needed to say her piece and get away before the combination of the odor and this boy's strange bond with *her* horse became too much to take. She opened her mouth to begin, when she noticed a strange lump undulating on the boy's chest.

"Is your shirt moving?" she asked.

"MEOW!"

A small black kitten leaped out of Galric's shirt and up into Flissa's arms. She caught it instinctively, then gasped and dropped it when she saw what it was. Galric caught the kitten before it hit the ground.

"Don't drop him—what are you doing?!"

Flissa felt like she'd been slapped. No one ever yelled at her. Again she almost rode away, but her mother's desiccated face flashed in front of her eyes, and Flissa thought she'd pass out. She leaned forward and rested heavily on Balustrade's neck.

"Hey," said Galric, his voice gentle now. "I'm so sorry, Princess Flissara."

He reached up and touched her hand, but she drew it away as if his had been dipped in the manure pits. He pulled his own hand away just as quickly.

"Sorry again. I just— You already knew about Nitpick, so I was surprised— You still won't tell the Keepers about him, will you?"

Now Flissa remembered. Sara *had* said Galric had a black cat—a *mage's* pet, strictly outlawed in Kaloon—but Flissa hadn't imagined she'd have to touch the creature.

She took a deep breath to settle herself, but it only made things worse. Now she could taste the manure scent on the back of her tongue.

"I need your help," she said softly so the sound wouldn't travel, "and I need you to tell me the honest truth. Can you do that?"

Galric gripped his hands together, as if that were the only thing stopping him from reaching out to her again. "Anything. Yes. Are you okay?"

"I am not," she admitted. "But I sincerely hope you can help make it better. What do you know about your father?"

Everything about Galric changed. His face went dark, and his eyes got small and cold. His hands balled into fists. "Same as you, I guess," he said dully. "He did something horrible and got banished to the Twists when I was around one. Left me with no one."

"So you're not loyal to him?" Flissa pressed. "You don't support what he did?"

Galric scrunched his face like he smelled something far worse than the manure pits. "You seriously came here to ask me that?" Then his eyes widened. "This whole thing's a setup, isn't it? This morning, now—you're working with the Keepers of the Light, aren't you? Well, there's nothing to get on me, and you're not taking Nitpick!" He shoved the kitten back in his shirt and ran.

Flissa shook her head—why had Sara thought she

could handle this?—then she kicked Balustrade into gear and easily turned the horse into Galric's path.

"Stop," she said. She dismounted so she could look Galric in the eye. She needed him to see how important this was. "Please. I'm not working with the Keepers. It's the opposite. I need to know—are you part of the Underground?"

Galric looked around warily, and Flissa spoke quickly so he wouldn't run.

"I'm not setting you up. Please-please-please believe me. I need to talk to someone with the Underground because I need to get into the Twists."

Galric grimaced like Flissa had just juiced a giant lemon on his face. "*Into* the Twists?" he asked. "What do you want, a tour? Can't you just ask Grosselor for that?"

"No," Flissa said. "It's nothing like that. It's a matter of life and death, and I don't know anyone else I can ask."

Galric stared at her for what seemed like forever, but he must have seen the true pain in her face, because he softened. "I'm not with the Underground," he said, "but I know people. I don't know if I can take you now, but maybe in a couple hours—"

"No," Flissa said. Much as she wanted to start saving her mom immediately, she and Sara had to run their plan with acute precision, or they'd get caught and all would be lost. "It has to be later tonight. And it's best if I meet you in the castle. Do you know it inside? Have you been there?"

"In the castle?" Galric laughed ruefully and ran his hand through his hair. "Yeah. I worked in the kitchen when I was little. Before everyone said I looked too much like my dad and I could scare the royal family if I stayed. But sure, I spent a lot of time there."

"Do you think you could get in without anyone seeing you? And hide in the hall by the Residence until everyone's asleep . . . like midnight?"

"Sure," Galric said. "I could hide in the secret passageway. But—"

Flissa was sure she'd heard him wrong. "The . . . *what*?"

"Secret passageway," Galric said. "You know, that row of engraved columns there. The one with King Lamar's name on it opens. It's a door to a secret staircase. You knew that, right? I mean, you *live* in the palace."

Flissa had passed the row of engraved columns every day of her life. She'd had no idea one of them was a door to a secret passage, but she wasn't going to tell Galric that. She stood taller. "Of course."

Flissa caught Galric starting to smirk, but he had the sense to stop the look in its tracks.

"Great," he said. "So we can meet there, but not at midnight. It's not that late. There's a midnight watch that goes around, and most of the staff is still awake. Two o'clock would be better. But you already knew that, of course."

"Indeed," she said tightly.

The truth was that midnight seemed impossibly late to her. She and Sara were always in bed by ten, even on festival nights, and she hated to wait that long when each passing hour meant less time to save their mother. But if they got caught, then the whole plan was useless anyway.

"Princess Flissara?"

The voice was faint, but it was unmistakably Princess Blakely's. Flissa instantly swung back onto Balustrade.

"Two o'clock," she said quietly. "In the passageway. I'll see you then."

She urged her horse on with her heels, and he raced away with Flissa as fast as they could go.

Chapter 5
Sara

"And then what happened?" Sara asked.

Flissa had been back for two hours, but Primka had zipped into the room the second she'd arrived, fussed and fluttered to get Flissa out of her riding outfit, hovered in the royal washroom as the twins washed their faces, dressed Sara in her ball gown for dinner, did Sara's hair, and fretted over whether it would be a good or bad idea for them to see their mom. Just when it seemed like she'd leave them alone, *Katya* came in. She *did* take them in to see Mom, which was horrible because she looked so much worse than before, and it only made Sara crazier that she hadn't had the chance to talk to Flissa about their plan.

When Katya had Primka take them back to their room and the bird finally left them alone, Sara flopped onto Flissa's giant bed, grabbed a pillow, and screamed into it. Then she yanked Flissa's arm, pulled her down on the bed, and demanded information as fast as Flissa could spill it.

"Well," Flissa said, "after I heard Blakely's voice, I rode off as fast as I could, splashed Balustrade through the river to get the manure pits off his hooves and my boots, then ran through the jasmine grove to take away the rest of the smell, and then I caught back up with her and her sister."

"Where did you tell them you went?"

"I'm fairly sure Ivamore had no idea I was even gone," Flissa said, "but I told them I saw a particularly colorful butterfly and rode after it and got lost."

Sara laughed. "You would *never* do that. *I* would if I knew how to ride a horse, but you? No way."

Flissa smiled the littlest bit. "I was thinking of you when I said it."

"So now we just, what . . . wait for two in the morning?" Sara asked. "That's so *late*."

"I know. But if Galric's right, we can't get out any earlier if we don't want to be spotted. Besides, Princess Flissara still has a banquet tonight, right?"

Sara flopped back on the bed. "Ugh! Yes." She affected a snooty tone and announced, "'The royal dinner honoring our guests from Winterglen, Princesses Blakely and Ivamore.'" Then she shrugged. "Maybe Ivamore will tell me more about the Gilward rumor she heard."

Just then, the clock chimed and Primka soared into the room from one of her ceiling nooks. "Dinnertime! Go on, Sara. There's a Royal Guard waiting to escort you downsta— Sara! You can't lie around in your dinner gown, you'll get all rumpled!"

"Sorry!" Sara said. She grinned at Flissa as she darted out of the room. A Royal Guard was indeed stationed by the door to escort her down, but Sara knew he couldn't be one of her dad's most trusted soldiers—they were all out scouring the kingdom for Gilward.

When they reached the ballroom, Sara couldn't help but

smile. It was beautiful: floor-to-ceiling windows with sea-blue draperies pulled open to reveal the night sky, creamy-white walls, and gold everywhere—carved into designs on the walls, in the sprawling table centerpieces, and all over the harpsichord that sat in the corner so everyone could enjoy their meal with music.

As princess, Sara sat at the head of one table of honor, while the king and queen each headed their own. With Queen Latonya "under the weather," Princess Blakely's father was given the honor of sitting at the head of her table, while Blakely and Ivamore flanked Sara at her own.

As she moved toward her seat, Sara looked at her father. He was already seated, putting on an amazing performance by laughing uproariously with a group of earls and dukes. Grosselor, as always, sat next to him. He was the only one not laughing. He remained upright and pious in his yellow-bejeweled tunic. He wasn't eating either. The Keepers of the Light had their own separate dining room. They came to all the royal meals, of course, but stood around the outskirts of the room like dashing statues—bright yellow eye candy to keep everyone feeling safe and happy.

For just a second, Sara's dad caught her eye, and she saw the intense combination of rage, fear, and strength simmering beneath his happy exterior. It struck her right in the heart, and she burned with pride. She couldn't even imagine how he was holding it together. He was surrounded by Keepers of the Light, any—or *all*—of whom could be the ones who helped curse his wife and were now planning to take out his whole family in a second Dark Magic Uprising, but he laughed and joked like everything was fine. He was determined to do whatever it took to put the Keepers at ease so his Guards could catch them unawares and destroy the plot in its tracks.

Unfortunately, he was on the wrong path. But Sara would take his strength and use it on her own journey.

"Flissara!" Blakely called, waving Sara to her chair. "Come quick—it's important!"

Sara forced herself *not* to plop down in her seat, but to instead take her ladylike—and Flissara-like—time to perch on its edge with excellent posture. Blakely leaned close and lowered her eyelids. "See?" she said. "I outlined them in kohl. Beautiful, right?"

"Gorgeous," Sara said. And it was. The black outline around Blakely's eyes made them stand out in a mesmerizing way.

Blakely grinned. "Ivamore's too little, but I could do yours. Want me to?"

Sara very much did, but Flissa would never go in for such a thing.

"No thanks," she said, "my father wouldn't approve."

But in her mind she imagined a Kaloon where twinhood *wasn't* illegal. A Kaloon where she could scream "YES!" to Blakely's offer and even get tips from her to find her own style and look, separate from Flissa's.

"Suit yourself," Blakely said. "Which Keeper should I bat them at first? How about that one."

Blakely winked at Eberwulf, one of the few Keepers who was almost as young as he looked. He smiled and nodded back, and Blakely practically swooned.

"I wish we had Keepers of the Light in Winterglen," she sighed. "It must be amazing to have actual *heroes* around all the time."

Sara's stomach turned, but she forced a smile. "Heroes. Yes. It's wonderful." Then she changed the subject and turned to include Ivamore. "So . . . heard any good gossip lately?"

She was hoping to get more details about Gilward and who exactly spoke to Ivamore about him, but they only wanted to talk about the party they attended last week in Shellsbury, and all the drama that went down there. Normally Sara would have hung on every word, but today she was just uncomfortable and impatient. She felt like every Keeper in the room was staring at her like cats eyeing a juicy mouse.

Like most royal meals, this one was three hours long, and for Sara it was a giant forever jumble of pretending to listen, pretending to laugh, and pretending to have fun. The only thing she did in earnest was eat, because Mitzi and the other chefs made the most enticing delicacies in the world. When she stuffed herself silly, she considered crying sick so she could run back up to Flissa and get back to planning, but the last thing she wanted to do was make Dad worry about her. If he worried, he'd have her watched like a hawk, and there'd be no way she and Flissa could ever get out to save their mother.

As the long banquet went on, Sara kept an eye on her dad. The night was wearing on him. Dark circles bloomed under his eyes, and the tips of his mustache drooped downward, but Sara was sure only she noticed. He acted like his same, boisterous self, eager for everyone to join in his fun.

Hoping to take some pressure off him, Sara dialed up her energy and worked the room, taking time to chat with everyone she could. "Lady Shuttlehorn, so good to see you!" "Duke Muncy, did you make me a batch of that shortbread?" "Duchess Jacobia, I heard your daughter's quite the equestrian now!" It was all the tiny conversations she usually loved because they gave her glimpses into other people's lives, but tonight it was all by rote. She especially made sure to smile at every Keeper she passed, same as always. Whenever she caught her dad's eye, he smiled approvingly, which made it all worthwhile.

Sara stayed in the dining room until the last guest from her table had retired. Only then did she wrap her arms around her dad to hug him good night—not too long or too tight, as people were watching—and she forced herself not to tense up as Rouen fell into step with her to escort her back to the Residence.

"Tell me about your mother," Rouen said in his sandpaper voice once they were out of earshot of the ballroom. "How is she *really*?"

Ice ran through Sara's veins, and she stumbled, then quickly recoiled when she bumped against the solid rock of Rouen's body. He took her elbow to steady her and wouldn't let go.

"You know how she is," Sara said. "She has a bad cold. That's all."

"A *bad* cold?" Rouen asked suspiciously.

Was the "bad" part wrong? Had she just messed everything up?

"Cold, bad cold . . . whatever it is, it's bad for her because she missed an amazing banquet, right? I mean, the food was so good, and . . ."

Sara just kept talking about the banquet, hoping to allay any suspicions, but the minute she and Rouen were all alone in the hall outside the Residence, he whipped in front of her and leaned in, his face so close she could see the creases between every lump and crag. "It's my duty and my privilege to protect the royal family, Princess Flissara," he said, his voice low and intense. "If you need anything, or you have information that can help me do my job, promise me you'll tell me."

Sara's insides shook, and she was suddenly sure of it: *He knew.* He knew what had happened to her mom, and the only way he could know is if he was one of the Keepers behind it. Now he wanted Sara to confirm the strike was successful and the second Dark Magic Uprising was working as planned.

She felt nauseous, but she forced a smile and answered him lightly. "Sure. I promise. But everything's fine. Can I just go back to my room, please?"

Rouen stared into her eyes a moment longer, then stood without another word and walked her a few more feet, folded his hands, and lowered his head—the custom for allowing royal family members their privacy as they walked to their door. Sara was sure he didn't keep his head down. She could feel his eyes on her back, and it took every ounce of restraint not to look at the row of columns to her left—especially King Lamar's, where she and Flissa would be meeting Galric in just a few hours.

Sara heaved open the door and quickly shoved it closed behind her. She stood with her back against it, just breathing, before she walked the plush carpet to her and Flissa's room.

Flissa sat at her desk, eating off a giant tray that held a platter with great slabs of everything Mitzi and the cooking staff had served. She ate with one hand and held a book with the other, and didn't even put down her fork when she needed to turn the page.

"The meal is delicious," Flissa said. "Katya brought it to me this time. She had to make a tray for Mother. For appearances. I'm not terribly hungry, but it's wise to eat and keep up our strength."

Sara nodded. Usually Primka brought a sack of food to whichever twin didn't go to a meal. The kitchen was always so crazy around mealtime, it was easy for the bird to flit in and gather things unnoticed. But with Queen Latonya down with her "cold," it would only make sense that Katya would put together a full royal platter.

Flissa's face darkened. "You're upset, I can see it," she said. "What happened?"

Sara told her about Rouen. When she was done, Flissa frowned.

"It's possible he's involved," she said. "But it's also possible he's heard rumors from other Keepers. Maybe he's not in on it at all. Maybe he's honestly worried about us."

"Or maybe they're all in it together. *All* the Keepers," Sara said.

Flissa shook her head. "I just can't believe that. The Keepers of the Light have protected Kaloon for generations. It certainly seems like one of them has turned against us—maybe even a few—but all of them? No."

Sara didn't agree, but she also didn't want to argue about it. Galric was coming at two in the morning to take them to the Underground and then the Twists, and they had to get ready.

"You were reading," Sara said, nodding to the book on Flissa's desk. "Anything helpful?"

"A lot, I hope." Flissa grabbed a small leather-bound book from her desk. "I made a list of things I think we'll need."

A rucksack topped the list, one for each of them, and Flissa had already pulled them out—buckle-down pouches with straps they could wear on their backs. Flissa wanted to bring all her books about the Twists, but that would make the sacks too heavy. She settled on her two favorite volumes, one for each sack. Sara complained that Flissa picked the two heaviest of the bunch, but Flissa said knowledge would be their most powerful ally on the journey, and having it was worth a little extra sweat.

"Fine," Sara relented. "Change of clothes? Pajamas?"

"By the time we leave, we'll have only around thirty-four hours to get into the Twists, find Gilward, convince him to heal Mother, and come back," Flissa said solemnly. "I don't believe we'll be doing a lot of sleeping or changing."

Instead, Flissa thought they should use the rest of the rucksack space for food, but none of the leftovers on Flissa's massive platter would travel well. "And we shouldn't bring anything with too strong an odor," she said. "Nothing that would attract the attention of beasts."

"Beasts?" Sara repeated

"Beasts," Flissa confirmed. "Both regular and magical. The books describe them in many different ways, but trust that we don't want to see them if we can avoid it."

Sara said she'd take food duty. She waited until just

before bedtime, when Princess Flissara might be hungry again after the banquet. She put on her nightgown and robe for appearances, and padded out of the room in her slippers. This time she couldn't help but stare at the columns along the wall, each embossed with the name of another royal ancestor. The names started even before King Lamar and stretched down far beyond where her parents and she and her sister would someday be.

Where her parents and *Princess Flissara* would be. One princess. Whether the Keepers were good or bad, as long as they held sway in Kaloon, the world would never know Sara and Flissa as two individual people.

Was that even possible? Could they actually keep up the charade the rest of their lives? Sara had tried to bring it up to everyone she could: Flissa, Primka, Katya, her parents. Flissa never wanted to talk about it, and everyone else just told her not to worry, everything would be fine. Her dad always came the closest to a real conversation. Whenever she asked, he said, "Your mother and I have plans."

That's it. He never said what the plans were, and she'd been asking off and on since she'd turned eight—but they had plans.

Did the plans mean sharing a life forever?

What if she fell and got a scar on her face? What if one of them got really fat or really skinny? What if they fell in love, or wanted to have kids one day? How would that possibly work?

Sara had moved to the column with King Lamar's name on it and absentmindedly ran her fingers over the letters as she thought. When she heard a voice, she yelped out loud.

"You're out late, Princess."

Rouen stepped out silently from between two columns farther down the row. Sara shut her eyes and cursed herself for not being more careful. "I'm hungry," she said. "I'm going down to the kitchen for a snack."

"No need," Rouen said. "I'll save you the trouble. What would you like?"

Something that won't get the attention of magical beasts, she thought, but she only answered, "I'll know it when I see it."

"I'll bring up a selection," he said. "In the meantime, you should go back into the Residence. The royal nurse is there with the queen, yes? Katya?"

Sara frowned. The way he said Katya's name, it sounded like he wasn't sure who she was, which was weird. The question had to be a trap. Maybe Katya's presence this late would tell him how sick the queen really was. If Rouen was one of the Keepers plotting against them, that's something he'd very much want to know.

Rouen leaned slightly forward and licked his lips, eager for an answer.

"I don't know," Sara said. "I wasn't in my parents' room."

"Of course," Rouen said blandly, though his whole face fell and he rolled heavily back on his heels. "I'll get you your snacks."

He didn't move, though, and Sara realized he was waiting for her to go back to her room.

"Thank you," she said. "Knock when you have them, please."

Standing tall and pretending she didn't feel the weight of Rouen's beady-eyed stare, Sara carefully strode back down the hall. She slipped into the Residence and leaned against the closed door. She didn't dare move. When Rouen came back, she wanted to answer right away so he couldn't count food delivery as a royal invitation to enter. If he did, and he saw her with Flissa, the Keepers wouldn't need a Dark Magic Uprising to take down the royal family. Grosselor could do it in the name of Kaloonian law.

Sara ran her fingers over the door's carvings and counted her breaths until she finally heard Rouen knock. Quickly and carefully, she opened the door just enough to squeeze through, then shut it again behind her—on her robe. She pretended not to notice.

Rouen stood right in front of her, his arms wrapped around a giant white wicker basket bursting with pink ribbons and flowers and covered by a pink cloth. He looked ridiculous holding it—like a giant canary clutching a baby bassinet.

"When I told Mitzi the snacks were for you, she went a little overboard," Rouen said drily. "Would you like me to take some back down?"

"That's all right," she said, stifling a giggle. "I like having choices."

Rouen handed her the basket. She tilted heavily as it pulled her to the floor.

"Need some help?" he offered.

"No," Sara snapped. "I'm good, thank you."

He didn't move. He stood and watched as Sara put the basket down and struggled to open the door, which was stuck with her robe caught inside. When it gave, it swung open far too wide, and Sara had a horrible vision of Flissa standing right there, lured by the noise to check on her.

She wasn't. The Residence hallway was empty. Sara picked up the picnic basket and heaved it inside, then kicked the door shut with a satisfying slam. Walking like a drunkard, Sara hauled the massive basket in to Flissa, who took it out of her arms like it was weightless.

Flissa removed a note from Mitzi and read it aloud. *"Enjoy the snicky-snacks!"*

"Awww! She's so sweet!" Sara said.

"Really?" Flissa said. "'Snicky-snacks'?"

"It's cute! What'd she get us?"

Flissa rummaged through the giant basket. She smelled each item, and agonized over what would and wouldn't be strong enough to attract a ravenous magical beast. In the end, she left all meat, fish, and cheese behind, but plucked out the scones, several tea cakes, three small loaves of hearty bread, and several small jars of butter, nut butter, and preserves. She wrapped the baked goods in two old shawls, one for each of them, and put them into the rucksacks, which they hid under Sara's bed, beneath a big pile of laundry. They shoved the picked-over basket into the back of Sara's closet behind some unused canvases.

"See?" Sara told her sister. "It's good to be messy. If the whole room was like your side, we couldn't hide a thing."

Flissa rolled her eyes, but Sara knew she'd made her point. By the time Primka arrived to tuck them in, there were no visible signs of their plan at all.

"Your father wanted to tuck you in himself," Primka assured them, her voice low as she pulled Flissa's covers up to her chin, "but he's with his Guards, searching for Gilward."

Sara met Flissa's eyes, and she knew they were both thinking the same thing. She also knew Flissa would never speak up and say it, so she did. "Primka, Princess Blakely told Flissa she heard a rumor about Gilward. That people saw him riding out of Kaloon."

Flustered, Primka fluffed her feathers. For a second, she was twice her normal size.

"People hear all kinds of things," Primka said. She wouldn't meet Sara's eyes as she pulled up her covers. "Doesn't make them real."

"Katya thought Gilward might have run away to the Twists," Flissa added. "Do you?"

Primka busied herself dousing every light except their tiny night-lamp. When she finally spoke, it wasn't an answer at all.

"I'm sure the king knows what he's doing. Don't give up hope."

"We're not," Flissa said, with such an edge to her soft voice that Sara immediately looked at Primka, to see if she'd noticed. Either she hadn't, or she didn't understand what it meant, because she flitted to each twin and ran her wing gently down a cheek, like she did every night, then fluttered up to the ceiling.

"I love you both very much," she said, her voice nearly cracking. "I just want you to know."

And then she flew away. Flissa looked stricken and ghostly in the dim glow from their night-lamp.

"Primka never talks like that," Flissa said. "She doesn't believe Father's going to find Gilward. She doesn't think Mother's going to make it."

Sara knew Flissa was right. She swallowed the lump in

her throat to sound strong for her sister. "He doesn't have to find Gilward," she reminded Flissa. "*We* will."

Flissa nodded.

Now came the hardest part. The waiting.

Sara hated waiting, and she especially hated waiting when she had to be silent so Primka or Katya wouldn't come in and try to get them back to bed. Or worse, think they were too upset to sleep and decide to stay in the room with them.

Sara kept twitching and rolling over. Weird as it was, she was *excited*. For the first time ever, she was leaving the castle at night. Without a chaperone. *With* her sister. Just thinking about it made her want to leap for joy—but then she'd remember her mother struggling to live and she'd feel small and guilty and awful.

Until her imagination took over and her heart started leaping all over again.

When the clock struck one, Sara jumped out of bed . . . but got tangled in her covers and thumped to the ground.

She froze inside her blanket cocoon—had anyone heard?

She held her breath.

No one came.

She felt Flissa kneel silently beside her. She untangled her, then handed Sara the traveling clothes she'd picked out while Sara was at dinner. They'd both wear the exact same thing: their most comfortable silk pants and shirts, plus ankle boots and a traveling cloak. Each cloak had a large hood. It would stop prying eyes from a distance, and if the worst happened and they got caught, Flissa could stay covered and run away. Sara-as-Flissara would get in trouble for being out at night, alone, but their bigger secret would stay under wraps. Flissa had made Sara promise that they would stay hooded at all times, even when they were alone with Galric. Sara thought it was kind of silly. If Galric kept a black cat and knew people in the Underground, it was a pretty safe bet to assume he could be trusted to keep a secret, and he'd already said he agreed with Sara that twins weren't evil. Still, Flissa worried, so Sara agreed.

The two changed in the near darkness, then stood very still and waited. When the palace clock chimed fifteen minutes to two, Sara reached out, took Flissa's hand, and squeezed.

Time to go.

They shrugged on their rucksacks, and Sara followed Flissa's lead. They pushed through their bedroom door and paused, listening for sounds.

Nothing from the hall to their parents' room. No footsteps, no flapping of wings. Nothing at all.

Sara squeezed Flissa's hand again.

Flissa moved forward. Slowly, to accommodate Sara's searching half steps.

They got to the thick wooden door that separated the Residence from the rest of the castle.

They had no idea what was on the other side. Rouen could be out there, waiting. Galric could have been mistaken, and the late watch could be out on duty now. Anyone could be in that hall, really, and no matter who it was, if they saw two Princess Flissaras leaving the Residence, Sara and Flissa wouldn't have to worry about sneaking into the Twists—they'd be thrown there, and they'd never get back out.

Sara moved ahead of Flissa. She grabbed the metal knob. It felt cool against her palm. She turned it slowly, so slowly, so it wouldn't make a sound. Then she cracked it open as silently as she could. The second she had enough space, she poked her head through—and choked on her own breath.

The Royal Guard was so close she could almost lean out and touch him. Sara recognized Abrel right away. He was the king's most trusted Guard, and extremely powerful—almost as large and strong as the door itself. It was a miracle he hadn't heard it swing open. She could only imagine it was because he was concentrating so hard on potential threats from outside the Residence, not inside.

For a second, Sara was surprised Abrel wasn't off looking for Gilward, but then she realized of course her dad would leave his best Guard to watch his daughters and ailing wife through the night. She felt like an idiot for not thinking about it before.

Sara felt Flissa tugging on the back of her cloak, looking for answers, but Sara didn't dare move. If Abrel even turned around, it was all over.

But how would they ever get past him to meet Galric? And what if they couldn't get to Galric at all? Would he come looking for them? Sara shuddered, imagining what would happen if Abrel saw Gilward's son slipping into the hall from a secret passageway.

Flissa tugged harder on the back of Sara's cloak. Sara didn't know if Flissa wanted information, or if she was signaling Sara to go back in and give up, but it didn't matter. Sara remained perfectly still.

The palace clock chimed two.

Sara almost cried out as Flissa yanked harder on her cloak, and she toppled backward. Flissa caught her before she could fall, but when Sara glared at her in the dim light from the hall, she saw the stony determination on Flissa's face. She also saw Flissa's locket hanging open, and the coin pressed between two fingers.

Flissa had a plan, and the coin had told her to move ahead with it.

Sara stepped aside as Flissa put back her coin and tucked the locket away, then shrugged off her rucksack and pulled out one of the glass jars of preserves. Swiftly and silently, Flissa pushed the door open a little further, cocked back an arm like she would before throwing a javelin, then hurled her whole body forward, flinging the preserves with all her might before immediately ducking back behind the door.

Silence . . . then the faraway sound of breaking glass.

"Who goes there?" Abrel snapped.

When no answer came back, Sara heard him race across the hall and pound down the stairs.

Sara's jaw literally dropped open. "You threw that all the way over the staircase?!" she whispered.

"Let's go," Flissa whispered back. "Hurry."

She pulled her hood over her head, reached out and pulled Sara's up as well, then grabbed Sara's arm and ran. She didn't stop until they were both at King Lamar's column.

Chapter 6
Flissa

"It's like throwing a javelin from one side of the banquet hall to the other!" Sara whisper-hissed once she and Flissa had ducked behind King Lamar's column. "And you made it over the railing so it smashed downstairs! That's, like, perfect aim!"

"Shhh!" Flissa hissed.

She didn't care how low Sara kept her voice, the last thing she wanted was to talk. The two of them were out of the Residence. Together. With other people around, and a Guard who could come back any second. She wanted to get out of the hallway. *Now.*

She tapped gently on the column, and for the briefest second, she hoped nothing would happen and she and Sara could go back to bed and forget the whole plan.

Then a panel in the column popped open. Flissa ducked inside, yanked Sara in after her, and pulled the door closed.

"You brought someone else?!" Galric exploded.

Flissa and Sara were at the top of a steep spiral stone staircase, and Galric was a few steps down, gaping at the two hooded girls.

"Shhhh!" Flissa hissed. Then she pointed down the staircase.

Galric paled, clearly remembering they weren't alone in the palace. Without another sound, he turned and started down the staircase. Flissa, meanwhile, maneuvered Sara so she was between herself and the wall, and could hold on to both for stability. Even with that, it was a treacherous descent, with spirals so tight even Flissa felt dizzy. Only the dimmest glow from far-apart torches lit the way—just enough light to see how stunningly far they still had to go. Flissa felt Sara's hand tighten on her arm as they spun down together, and her legs ached in sympathy for Sara's with each steep step.

Finally, Flissa's feet thumped down onto a lumpy dirt floor, and the start of a long stone-walled path. There were more torches here, so it was easier to see. Galric was waiting, pacing. His shoulders hunched, and his dark, stringy hair hung in his face. He cradled Nitpick in his arms.

"You brought the cat!" Sara cooed. She let go of Flissa and stumbled forward on the uneven floor. Galric instantly released Nitpick and lunged to catch her before she slammed to the ground.

"Thank you," she said. She tilted up her head to smile gratefully at Galric . . . which made her hood fall back off her head.

Flissa closed her eyes and inwardly groaned. The hoods were supposed to stay *on*. Now Flissa had to keep covered no matter what so Galric wouldn't see their identical faces.

Galric peered at Sara curiously. "You like Nitpick now?"

"Well, yeah," Sara said. "I always liked Nitpick."

Flissa stomped the floor. She felt like Balustrade, but

since her voice was as identical to Sara's as her face, it was the only way she knew to remind her sister there was a reason Galric might think Princess Flissara didn't like the cat.

Unfortunately, Sara wasn't the one who noticed the stomp. Galric did. He ran his fingers through his hair. "I didn't realize you were bringing someone else," he told Sara. "The person I know with the Underground . . . I only said I was bringing one person. It's dangerous with more."

"I understand, and I'm sorry," Sara said. "But this is my most trusted servant. I can't get along without her."

Galric shifted uncomfortably. "Yeah, okay . . . but you could have told me. I mean, we're in this together, so we have to tell each other stuff."

Under her hood, Flissa rolled her eyes. She wanted to say they were *not* "in this together." She was his princess, and he was doing her a favor because she'd asked.

"You're right." Sara smiled warmly. "I'm sorry. I should have said something."

Galric smiled back, and Flissa could see all the tension release from his long limbs.

"It's okay," he said. "I shouldn't have gotten upset. I mean, you're the princess. I just got really nervous before when you didn't show up right at two, and—"

This was taking forever. Flissa stomped her foot again.

Galric looked at her and frowned. "Is she okay?"

"She's mute," Sara said. "Sad, really. Interesting story, though. We found her on a processional through one of the outer reaches—"

Flissa buried her hooded face in her hands. If Sara told one of her stories, they'd be standing in this same spot for a lifetime. Holding the hood down tight, she stomped *both* feet, close enough to Sara that she jolted.

"Another time," Sara said. "We should keep going."

"Right. Of course," Galric said, but he threw Flissa a confused look before he started walking again.

Sara fell into step next to him. "Does anyone else use these tunnels? I mean, is it okay we're talking out loud?"

"As far as I know, no one does," Galric replied. "I mean, they *did*, at some point, but I've never seen anyone down here. I only found the tunnels because I heard the rumors when I was a kid, so I looked for them."

"Rumors?" Sara asked.

"In the kitchen. That's where they sent me to work after . . . well, when I was old enough. All the older kids talked about this scary dungeon below the castle with magical torches that never went out. They said the Keepers of the Light—when they started, back in King Lamar's time—magically carved the place out so they'd have a place to take and torture anyone magical."

Flissa frowned. That's not how she'd heard the story. She gently took Sara's hand so Sara would fall into step next to her, just behind Galric. That way Flissa could speak and Galric would still think the voice was Sara's.

"Anyone with *dark* magic," Flissa clarified. "And it wasn't exactly 'torture.' After the Dark Magic Uprising, Kaloon's safety depended on Grosselor finding *everyone* magical and getting them to the Twists. So he did a lot of questioning. Some of it got intense, yes, but it was all for the good of Kaloon."

Galric spun around, and Flissa shut her mouth. He looked at Sara, a little perplexed, and suddenly Flissa thought about Primka, and what she'd said about the two of them not being identical at all.

Galric frowned at Sara, then started walking again. "Yeah," he said. "That's what they say. All for the good of Kaloon."

Flissa didn't like Galric's tone. She wanted to say more, but then the group turned a corner and emerged in a large cavern. Craggy rocks with rust-colored tips stood up in spikes from the floor.

"These are so pretty," Sara said, running her hand over one. "I like that the tops are different colors than the rest of the rock."

"It's blood," Galric said. "They say Grosselor and his original Keepers used their magic to get inside their prisoners' heads. If they didn't like the answers they got to their 'intense' questions, they'd make the prisoners jump on the spikes and impale themselves."

He turned and looked pointedly at Sara, whose jaw hung agape.

"But, you know . . . all for the good of Kaloon."

Flissa didn't know how Sara responded, because for a moment she wasn't there. She was eight years old again, watching that dark mage girl with the sickle mark on her hand hurl her friend Anna into the air as the girl kicked and flailed and screamed.

But that wasn't Grosselor's way. The Keepers *protected* Kaloon from mages like that. It was their whole purpose, the whole reason it was worth following the Magic Eradication Act to the letter, flaws and all.

Flissa took a deep breath and pulled herself tall.

Galric was spouting rumors. He didn't know what he

was talking about. He didn't spend his childhood studying history like Flissa. He spent it running around the royal kitchens, living off whatever scraps of food and bits of news the palace staff could spare. Had he scurried around enough to know hidden spots in the castle that Flissa never knew existed? Sure. Did that mean all of his so-called knowledge was valid? Not in the least. Most rocks varied in color. The red on these spikes was doubtless natural, and the blood story just a myth passed down to give gullible children nightmares.

Flissa didn't realize she'd been lost in her own thoughts until she looked around and saw they'd moved beyond the floor spikes and were walking across a long cavern. Flissa thought they had to still be under the castle somewhere, but she couldn't imagine how far under—the rocky ceilings towered above her, twice as high as the ones in the banquet hall.

"What is *that*?" Sara asked.

Flissa followed her sister's gaze. She was pointing most of the way across the chamber, where a chasm as wide as a dueling field split the floor. Tendrils of purple smoke wafted up from inside it.

Flissa knew exactly what it was, and she squirmed inside because she'd read about pits like this, and they were indeed tools of the Keepers of the Light. The purple smoke came from a magical fire inside the pit: Forever Flames. They offered all the pain of being burned alive with none of the actual burning. In the Keepers' earliest days, when things were dire and they needed to use extreme measures to free Kaloon from dark magic, they could force suspected dark mages into the flames and leave them inside as long as they wanted, to torture them until they broke and admitted their villainy.

"Not sure what it is," Galric said, and since he was looking at them, there was no way Flissa could explain. "But I know it's bad news. Only way out of this place is over it, though, so . . ."

He walked to the wall next to the chasm's edge, and Flissa saw a series of thick ropes there, pulled back against a rocky outcropping like half a curtain. Galric took one in his hands, then looked at Sara. "We swing. I put in the ropes myself when I was ten, the year before they moved me to the manure pits. I dared myself to do it. It was pretty crazy, but . . . they're sturdy."

He tugged on them to prove it, and Flissa followed the ropes to their origin—a spot on the ceiling, high above the center of the pit. Galric had tied the ropes off to a thick, strong, ring-shaped rock. Flissa could see how he must have done it—she could trace the perfect climbing path along the walls and craggy ceiling—but he wasn't lying when he said it was crazy. Flissa honestly didn't know whether to be impressed by his bravery or concerned by his lack of common sense.

Sara eyed the chasm dubiously. "Do we really have to swing over this? You're sure there's not some other way around?"

Galric laughed. "I might not get out much, but even I saw you joust the Duke of Ellsbrough. When you jumped off Blusters and swung from that branch to kick his lance out of his hand? This is nothing compared to that. As for your friend, though," Galric continued, glancing at Flissa, "I don't know. Do you think this'll be too hard for her?

'Cause if it is, I mean, it's a pretty straight shot back to the staircase. She could get there easy, and it's still late enough no one would see her come out of the column."

Flissa seethed. If she could speak without risking their secret, she'd tell Galric he was incredibly rude for speaking about a "servant" like she wasn't in the room; that he was wildly mistaken and it was *she*, not Sara, who had performed in that duel; and that if he ever called Balustrade "Blusters" again, she was going to swing off a tree branch and kick him in the stomach.

Or maybe she wouldn't say all that. But she'd be tempted, for certain.

"She isn't going anywhere," Sara said. "We stick together. She can handle this." Sara stepped a little closer to the pit and peered in, then looked at the ropes. She moved closer to them and gave one a little tug. Then she smiled proudly at Galric. "And so can I."

In one motion, Flissa moved across the floor, hooked Sara's arm, and swept her far enough away from Galric that she could whisper without him overhearing. "In no universe are you swinging over that pit."

"What?!" Sara whispered. "Flissa, we flipped the coin. We're doing this."

"This isn't about the coin, this is about your *life*. You won't make it across. It's too far. You'll fall."

"I won't! I'll be fine," Sara insisted.

"You can't know that," Flissa said. "You don't know what it's like. You don't do things like this. *I* do things like this."

"But that's the thing—we're both here. We don't have to split things up now. We both get to do everything."

Impossibly, Sara grinned. Like this was a game. "It's kind of exciting, right?"

"No!" Flissa shot back. "There *has* to be another way out."

"He already told us there's not," Sara said, "and we're running out of time. Dad's not going to find Gilward. We know that. Getting to the Twists is our only hope to save Mom, so if we have to swing over this pit to do it, that's what I'll do. Mom's life depends on it."

"*Your* life depends on *not* doing it!" Flissa heard her voice get louder, but she couldn't stop herself. If anything happened to her sister . . .

Sara took Flissa's hands and peered under the hood to look her in the eye. "I can do this. I'll be fine."

Flissa looked into Sara's confident eyes and knew she wouldn't win this fight. She couldn't bring herself to say yes, but she finally nodded. "Be careful," she whispered. "More careful than you've been about anything you've ever done."

"Deal." Then she spun and started walking toward Galric. "Let's do this thing."

"Great," Galric said. "Meet you on the other side."

He grabbed one of the ropes, took several steps back, then raced top speed to the edge of the chasm, where he leaped up and swung all the way across. "Your turn, Princess!" Galric called from the other side. "Then your friend."

"Okay!"

Sara grabbed the rope, and Flissa's head spun. She ran to Sara and clutched her arm again. "I changed my mind," she blurted desperately. "You don't understand what's in that pit. You can't do this. I can't let you. There has to be another way."

Sara gently pulled her arm away. "There's not," she said. "And I'm good. I'll be careful. Trust me. I can do it."

Flissa reluctantly backed away. With her heart in her throat, she watched Sara run to the ropes. In Flissa's head, Sara missed and tumbled into the magical flames again and again, but in real life she gripped the rope and leaped with all her might—

—straight up. She leaped straight up instead of out, so the rope had no momentum. It swung her to the exact middle of the chasm, then hung there, limp. Sara dangled helplessly, high above the pit of magical flame, bathed in purple glow.

"I was wrong!" she yelled. "I can't do it! I can't!"

She screamed as her sweaty hands slipped and she slid two inches down the rope.

Instantly, everything else faded away and the only thing in Flissa's mind was saving her sister. "I'm coming!" she cried. She raced to the wall of ropes, grabbed one, and didn't even bother to race back for a head start. She just leaped, then swung her body to gain speed. When she reached Sara, Flissa wrapped her legs around her sister so her momentum would carry them both to the other side.

"Let go!" Flissa screamed when they reached the far edge.

Sara obeyed; then Flissa hurled herself off her own rope and wrapped her arms around Sara, becoming a protective turtle shell. When they thumped to the ground, Flissa rolled them over and over, dissipating the impact so they wouldn't get hurt. The second they stopped, Flissa crawled up to search her sister's face. It was streaked with dirt, but Flissa didn't see any cuts or scrapes. Sara smiled.

"I'm good. It was kinda fun."

"But your bones? Your muscles? Nothing's pulled or strained?" Flissa asked. "The fire didn't burn you at all?"

Sara smiled wider and shook her head.

Flissa still had a million questions, but then Galric's voice quavered next to them.

"Y-y-y-you," he stammered, and Flissa turned to see he'd gone ashen white. "T-t-t-*two* of you!"

Uh-oh.

Flissa reached up and checked. Sure enough, her hood had fallen off.

Their secret was out.

Chapter 7
Sara

The look on Galric's face hurt Sara way more than the fall. He was pale to begin with, but now he was pure paste.

"Twins?" he asked.

Sara jumped to her feet and moved toward him, but he backed away.

"Yes, we're twins," she said urgently. "I'm Sara, and this is Flissa, but you *can't tell anyone*."

Galric's mouth gawped open. "Two?" he squeaked.

"I think we broke him," Flissa said.

Sara tried again. "Galric—"

"You're magic!" he cried. "And you wanted me to get you to the *Twists*?"

Sara looked at Flissa. They'd both caught him using the past tense.

"You're *still* getting us to the Twists," Sara said. "You have to."

"Or what? You'll put a curse on me?"

The whole curse thing hit a little too close to home for Sara, and she didn't know how to respond. Flissa didn't have the same problem.

"Yes, Galric, we're twins. But we're *not* magic. One does not always mean the other."

Galric's eyes flitted from one twin to the other, and he cowered a little, as if that curse might come flying his way after all. "It does to the Keepers."

"Agreed," Flissa said. "That's why we hide. And we're fine with that, because even if it means the Keepers are too cautious, it's better than living in a world with so much secret dark magic that the Keepers have to expose people to the horrors of Forever Flames to find out where it all is!"

"'Forever Flames'?" Sara asked. She peered back to the pit and the purple smoke still wafting out of it. "Hold on—what did I just swing over?"

Flissa ignored her and kept talking. "And be honest, Galric. You hide too. You knowingly house a black cat. If the Keepers knew, they'd think *you* were a mage. In the time of King Lamar, you'd end up right there beside us experiencing the torment of eternal fire. And even today you and your cat would be sent immediately to the Twists."

"Seriously," Sara interjected, "'*the torment of eternal fire*'? We should not have been swinging over that thing."

"So tell me," Flissa continued, keeping her eyes on Galric, "are *you* magic? Is Nitpick?"

Hearing his name, Nitpick poked his little head out from the neckline of Galric's shirt. He meowed and leaped toward Sara, who fumbled him around before finally hugging him close. He used his sharp claws to climb onto Sara's shoulder and curl into a tiny purring ball.

"Awwww," Sara cooed. "See, Galric? Nitpick still likes us."

She leaned her head to feel the kitten's soft fur on

her cheek. When she looked back at Galric, his eyes had softened.

"Yeah, he does," Galric said. "And he's good at judging people. Even magic people."

"We're not magic," Sara said quickly. But then she reconsidered what he'd said. "Wait—you know magic people?"

"Well, yeah. I told you I know people . . . er . . . I told . . . *one* of you I know people . . . um . . ." Then suddenly his eyes opened wide. "Ohhhhh. Flissa . . . Sara . . . Flissara!"

Flissa raised an eyebrow. "That just came together for you?"

"Kinda, yeah," Galric said. He smiled sheepishly, and there was something so sweet about it that Sara couldn't help but smile back.

"Seriously, though, you get it, right?" Sara asked after a moment. "You'll keep our secret? You'll help us get out and to the Underground, just like we planned?"

Galric ran his hands through his hair. He looked slightly defeated, and Sara was worried he'd say no.

"Yeah, I'll keep going. I mean, I guess it doesn't really change anything . . . except *everything*. . . . I just wish you'd tell me *why*."

"We will, I swear," Sara said. "We'll tell you everything." Flissa elbowed her, and Sara knew it was because she wanted to tell Galric as little as possible. "But the most important thing I can tell you is we don't have a lot of time, so can we please just keep going?"

Galric looked back and forth between them so many times it made Sara dizzy. Then he sighed. "Yeah. Come on. This way. Here, Nitpick."

The kitten leaped off Sara's shoulder and into Galric's hands. He tucked him back into his shirt and led them to the far end of the chamber, where five paths branched off. Each had a stone archway barely taller than Galric himself, and they all looked identical to Sara, but Galric beelined for the second archway from the left, which led them down a dirt-floored, rock-walled corridor. The path was very slim, and Sara was so lost in thought that she had trouble walking straight. She'd veer slightly to the left or right, and Flissa kept tugging her arm so she wouldn't accidentally bump into the torches scattered along the wall.

It was Galric that had her preoccupied. He stayed silent, which made her nervous. He'd said he'd keep helping, and that was good, but did he like her less now that he knew she was a twin? Sara knew she shouldn't care either way—they weren't on this trip to become friends—but she still did. She kept her eyes on his back, as if it might offer some clue about what he was feeling.

"The twin thing," Galric finally said, never breaking stride or looking back at them, "is that because of my dad?"

Now Sara understood, and she both relaxed and felt terrible at the same time. He hadn't been quiet because he didn't like her anymore, he'd been quiet because he was afraid his dad had done something terrible to them. *More* terrible to them than what he'd already thought.

"No," Sara assured him. "Our nursemaid, who delivered us, says we were twins all along. That's why the curse didn't kill us. The bad magic had to go through Mom first, and then it was all spread out between Flissa and me, so we were okay."

The tension in Galric's back eased a little. "Good." He stopped walking. "We're here."

Galric looked up, and the girls followed his gaze. There was a circular space in the rock ceiling—the beginning of a tube that extended up, up, up to a circle of moonlight shining through tree fronds outside. To Sara it looked magical—like they were at the bottom of a wishing well.

"Amazing," she said. "Where does it come out?"

"Nowhere near the castle," Galric said. "None of the Guards will see you, and it's pretty well hidden from the Keepers. As well as anything can be hidden from them, I guess."

Sara saw Flissa light up and grin as she stared at the long vertical passage, and it made Sara smile too. She could practically see her sister's arms and legs twitching to go.

Flissa spun to Sara so quickly, her braids smacked her cheeks. "You can do this. It is exponentially easier than the rope swing. I see plenty of hand- and footholds, and even outcroppings where you can pause and take a rest."

She twirled a braid and looked pleadingly at Sara. "Would you mind terribly if I started up?"

Sara laughed. The climb looked awful to her, but for Flissa it was like a giant wrapped present.

"Go," she said. "I'm fine. If I need help, Galric's here."

Flissa frowned a little at that, but then she smiled and scrambled onto the wall, moving faster and with greater agility than Sara had on flat ground. Within seconds she'd climbed all the way to the top, and sat perched on an outcropping just under the open circle of sky. She stared up at it for a moment, then turned and gestured for Sara and Galric to join her.

"Let me guess," Galric said, staring up at Flissa in awe. "She's the one I saw joust the Duke of Ellsbrough."

"For sure," Sara agreed. She looked back at the impossibly high wall. "So how exactly do I start up this thing?"

Galric offered to climb next to her and point out hand- and footholds along the way. Flissa had been right: The climb wasn't difficult, even for Sara, and with each pull of her arms and push of her legs, she felt stronger and more accomplished.

"This is amazing!" she said. "I've never done anything like this!"

"You're doing great," Galric agreed. "Just don't look down."

Sara looked down.

The floor loomed miles below, and as she stared, it telescoped even farther away. Her heart leaped into her mouth, and she gripped the wall so tightly she couldn't feel her fingers.

"I'm gonna fall," she gasped. "I'm-gonna-fall-I'm-gonna-fall-I'm-gonna-fall!"

"Why did you look down?" Galric cried.

"You said 'look down'!"

"I said '*don't* look down'!"

"The words 'look' and 'down' were in there!" Sara said. "Blast-blast-blast-blast-blast, *I'm gonna fall!*"

Galric scuttled closer to her. "You won't," he said. "I'm right here with you, and I'm gonna help you, okay?"

Sara nodded.

"Focus on the sound of my voice. Got it?"

Sara nodded again.

"Good," he said. "Now put your left foot on this ledge and push your weight down. You can do it."

Sara did what he said. It worked.

"Yes, yes, good. Now your left hand on this rock and pull. Okay? I'm right here."

Sara listened again. She pretended her body wasn't under her control at all; it just listened to directions and did what it was told.

"This is good," Sara said nervously as Galric patted the next spot for her right hand. "Keep doing that, but talk to me. Distract me. I don't want to think about what's down there."

"Sure, if that'll help. Right foot here and push. What do you want to know?"

Sara thought, then nodded. "Okay, I always wondered this. I never thought the Keepers were the most—I don't know—sympathetic people, especially when they think someone might be magic." She paused as she stretched up, and Galric pointed out a stone for her left foot. "So how did you end up staying in Kaloon when your dad was sent to the Twists?"

If the question made Galric uncomfortable, he didn't show it. He just kept pointing out hand- and footholds. "Someone convinced them not to," he said. "Still not sure how. But it's not like the Keepers left me alone— Okay, this one's a big stretch. Reach all the way up here, okay? Good."

"What did they do?" Sara asked, all kinds of imaginary scenarios already playing out in her head.

"At first? I mean, I was really little, so I don't remember all of it, and it's all kind of jumbled together with what other people told me about it after. I know the Keepers took me away. For a few months, I'm told, but it's just flashes for me. Let's bring it a little to the left—there's an easier path that way."

"Did they take you here?" Sara asked, sidling to the left. "Is that why you know it so well?

Galric laughed. "I'm pretty sure the Keepers haven't used this place in generations. Remember, I told you I found it when I worked in the kitchen."

"Oh, right. Grab up here?"

Galric nodded, and Sara grabbed and hoisted herself higher. Galric kept pace.

"So where did they take you instead?"

"I don't know. But I remember bits and pieces of what happened. The thing that sticks out is this box they had, a metal box. Just big enough for me to crouch in. They'd lock me in, with just my head sticking out, everything else crammed inside. Now grab the rock on your left, the big sticky-outy one. Yes, good."

Sara couldn't believe he was talking about this like it was nothing. It sounded awful. "Why?" she asked. "Why would they do that to you?"

Galric shrugged. "I guess the idea was— See, that was a great one! I didn't even have to tell you. Now grab that indentation for your right hand— If I were magic, and they made me miserable enough, I'd use magic to get out. I wouldn't be able to help it. And they were right. If I'd been magic, I *would* have used it to get out. I'd have done anything to get out of there. Right foot there, left arm there, then pull your left foot to that ledge."

Sara climbed, but her head was a million miles away

with poor not-even-two-year-old Galric. "That's awful—and they kept you for *months*?"

"Not in the box. Pretty sure that was just an every-now-and-then thing. I just hated it so much it's the only part I remember. But when the Keepers let me go, the woman who took me in said I was so afraid of small spaces, I didn't even want to go inside. She put out hay bales for beds, and we pretty much lived outside for a couple weeks." He looked up, then smiled at Sara. "You're so close. Just a few pulls more. That stone right there."

Sara took a smaller step than he suggested. She knew they had to hurry, but she didn't want the conversation to end. "Someone took you in?"

Galric smiled, the warmest smile Sara had seen on him yet. "Yeah. She said she'd watch me, even take responsibility if I ended up doing anything magical. My guess is she's the one who stopped the Keepers from throwing me in the Twists in the first place, but she never said."

"So then the Keepers stopped bothering you?"

Galric laughed ruefully. "No. When I was little they popped up all the time. Would grab me out of nowhere while I was playing with other kids and keep me for a few days. Test me. The box thing. Just to make sure I wasn't magic and didn't belong in the Twists. Didn't take long before the other kids weren't allowed to hang out with me anymore. Too scary. But, you know, the older I got, the less interested the Keepers were, so that was good. They still grab me sometimes, but now it's only maybe once a year. And I'm used to it now. The tests don't even hurt anymore."

Sara had stopped climbing. She just looked at Galric as he busied himself studying the wall, seemingly unfazed by the terrible things that had happened to him—that *still* happened to him.

"I'm so sorry, Galric. If I'd had any idea—"

Galric met her eyes now. "What could you have done? Who's really in charge in Kaloon, the royal family or the Keepers of the Light?"

Sara immediately opened her mouth to defend her family's honor, but she didn't say a word. Galric was right, and Sara knew it better than anyone. She was a princess of Kaloon, but she'd been hiding from the Keepers of the Light since birth.

"I wish it were different," Sara finally said.

"Me too. Right foot there, and—"

"You made it." Flissa's voice cut in, and Sara looked up to see her sitting on a ledge just a few feet away. "I knew you could do it. Here."

She reached out her hand. Sara grabbed on and let her sister pull her to the ledge by her side. Together, they looked up at the night sky. "I wish we didn't have to go," Flissa said. "I wish we could stay here all night."

Sara agreed. Tucked under the lip of the ground, they were safe from prying eyes, but still out in the world together, something neither of them ever imagined could actually happen.

"But we can't, right?" Galric said. He scrambled up the last stones, reached up for the edge of the hole, and hoisted himself out. "You said you don't have much time."

"Exactly," Flissa said. She hoisted herself out of the hole too; then she and Galric both reached in to help Sara. She let them hoist her up; then she rolled onto a bed of soft grass tucked under a giant weeping willow tree whose branches hung all the way to the ground. The curtain perfectly camouflaged the secret tunnel, as well as the three of them. Moonlight shone through the leaves, and Sara stayed on her back looking up at it. She'd never been outside this late—she'd never been *awake* this late—and even though she was in her own kingdom, everything felt strange and surreal.

She rolled to her feet and parted the curtain of fronds. They were on a hill, and below them the towns and villages of Kaloon spread wide under a gorgeous starlit night. The sweet air kissed Sara's face, and she took a deep breath to drink it all in. Then she saw the castle and gasped. It looked far away and enchanted, outlined by the lights of a million sconces. She had never in all her life seen it this way, the way everyone else in the kingdom probably knew it best.

"It's beautiful," Sara sighed. "Flissa, our kingdom is beautiful."

"It is," Flissa whispered behind her, "but it's also dangerous for us to be out together, so please stay hidden. There are Guards, Keepers—"

"And your own subjects," Galric cut in. Flissa shot him an angry look, but he put out his hands in defense. "I'm sorry, but it's true. Kaloonians love Princess Flissara, but if they see you're twins and you've been fooling them forever? Not good. They'll get mad. Or scared. Or both. Most of them would turn you in, and I bet some of them would go after you themselves. And did you bring weapons?"

"Weapons?!" Flissa asked incredulously. "We are not using weapons on our subjects, no matter how frightened they get or what they do."

Galric rolled his eyes. "Not for here, for the Twists. That whole place was built from Keeper magic. Do you even know what that means? Do you know what they're capable of doing?"

"I know what they can do when they're forced to," Flissa said tightly.

"Yeah, okay, sure, when they're forced," Galric said, though Sara knew after his own experiences he saw the Keepers very differently. "But that's when they made the Twists, when Grosselor was 'forced' to make a really bad place to keep people he didn't like, or who threatened his power, or—"

Flissa frowned and shook her head as he spoke, and now she jumped in. "I don't know who taught you Kaloonian history, but I know some books that—"

Sara jumped in and tried to shift the subject. "We don't need weapons because Flissa *is* a weapon. She's been studying forever. She knows all kinds of combat: hand to hand, fencing, broadsword—"

Flissa blushed under Sara's praise, but Galric shook his head. "Uh-uh. I've seen her on the jousting field, and she's amazing, but the Twists aren't a game. No one's gonna blow a trumpet and warn you they're coming. They'll act fast."

To make his point, he reached for Flissa's wrist. She immediately grabbed and twisted his arm, using his own momentum to flip him onto the ground. He thumped down, and Flissa placed her foot on his chest. "You were saying?"

"Weapons covered," Galric croaked. "Can I get up now?"

Flissa shrugged. "Maybe."

She let him lie there a moment, then removed her foot so he could stagger to his feet. He coughed a few times.

"Okay," he said when he'd caught his breath. "Let's go see my friend and get you to the Twists."

Chapter 8
Flissa

Flissa's upper lip had been beading sweat for the last half hour. She knew because she'd been following the chimes of the clock bells, which she could still hear even though the palace was long since out of view.

She'd always known she dreaded making decisions. That's why it was so wonderful to have Sara. Flissa could always rely on her—or her coin—to make the right choice, the one she was sure the universe wanted for her. Now it was Galric making the choices, and Flissa couldn't help but feel like each one led them closer to their doom.

That wasn't entirely fair, she knew. Since they'd left the willow, Galric had been quite savvy. He never seemed to doubt his way, and he'd kept them hidden among the shadows and the trees. But now they all crouched together at the edge of a copse, staring down a steep hill at a wide, sparsely treed village that Galric said they had to pass through.

"The good thing is most people are asleep," he said.

"What about their animals?" Flissa asked. Looking

down, she could see the wood-slatted backyards with chicken coops and dogs. "What if they wake up and make noise?"

"They won't," he said.

"You cannot possibly know that," Flissa said. "What if they bark or crow and then the people wake up and see us?"

"Or what if there's Keepers in town?" Sara added.

"Do you see any yellow robes? I don't see any yellow robes," Galric answered.

"We wouldn't see them," Flissa reminded him. "Keepers hide."

Galric ran his hands through his hair. "This is the only way I know how to go."

"So what are our choices?" Flissa asked Sara, feeling the sweat prickle all over her body. "We follow Galric, which could mean discovery; or we don't follow him, which means we can't get to the Twists. Either choice could end our mission."

Sara looked at Flissa meaningfully. They both knew what the end of their mission meant. "Do I need to flip the coin?" Sara asked.

Flissa pulled on the chain and held the locket in her hand. "What do you think?"

Sara shook her head no, then turned to Galric. "Go ahead. Lead the way."

Their first job was getting down the hill *to* the village, and Galric had an idea for the best way to stay low and move fast. He took Nitpick from his shirt; then Flissa and Sara followed his lead as he lay flat on the ground, arms and legs outstretched to make himself as long and thin as possible, and rolled. Flissa made very little sound as she swooshed through the grass, but somehow Sara found every uneven patch, and each *oof* and *oh* and *thump* echoed like a cannon in Flissa's ears.

When they reached the bottom, they all lay perfectly still until they were sure no one was coming, then crawled to the edge of a water trough behind a cottage and crouched there, waiting to make their next move. Flissa turned to Sara, who was a mess. Grass stuck out of her braids, her cloak, her pants, everywhere. And she was grinning. Was she actually having *fun*? She opened her mouth to say something, but Flissa put a finger over her lips. It was far too dangerous to speak.

The village was laid out haphazardly, with a large central gathering house, plus twenty cottages and their yards dotted between that and the woods that began on the other side. A dirt path bisected the village, and Galric did his best to keep them as far from it as possible. They darted from cottage to cottage, ducking behind wells, carriages, and chimneys. Each time, Flissa took Sara's hand and picked out the clearest path, the one without any obstacles.

As they crouched behind a chimney and caught their breath, Flissa's heart quickened. They were almost out. Two more cottages and they could make a break for the woods.

Galric pointed to a doghouse up ahead, and Flissa and Sara nodded. Then he signaled to run, and they all sprinted forward. Flissa thought she'd picked out the perfect path, but somehow a root found Sara and she tumbled forward, smacking *into* the doghouse. A large dog came bounding out, barking at them at the top of its lungs.

"Aaaa!" Galric shuddered and ducked behind Flissa and Sara.

"Seriously?" Sara laughed as she whispered. "Its tail is wagging. It just wants to play."

"That doesn't help matters," Flissa said through gritted teeth. "He's *loud* and he'll wake people up. Calm down, boy," Flissa cooed softly to the dog, hoping to channel some of the same animal mojo that had allowed her to tame Balustrade. "Quiet now."

She was still making eye contact with the dog when Sara grabbed her arm in a vise. "Get down!" she hissed.

Flissa heard the desperation in Sara's voice and obeyed immediately. The last thing she saw before she disappeared behind the doghouse was a swish of bright yellow fabric coming around the corner of the next cottage.

A Keeper!

Flissa, Galric, and Sara huddled together, not daring to breathe. Flissa was sure she heard the pounding not just of her own heart, but of the others' as well. Would the Keeper hear it too?

"What is it, Rufus?" the Keeper asked the dog. "What do you hear?"

Rufus stopped barking, but his snout was pointed directly at them. Only a corner of the doghouse kept them out of the Keeper's eyeshot. They heard her feet crunch over the ground. Closer . . . closer . . .

Sara looked plaintively at Flissa, but Flissa knew there was nothing they could do. If they ran, the Keeper would see them, and even if they could run faster than her, they couldn't outrun her magic. Depending on her strength, she could make a tree fall in their path, or open up the ground to swallow them. She could even just freeze them in their tracks, and it would all be over.

"You've found something there," the Keeper mused, "that's for sure."

Five more steps, Flissa calculated. That's all it would take before the Keeper would see them.

Four.

Three.

"MEOOOOOOW!"

Nitpick leaped out of Galric's shirt and raced around the corner of the doghouse. Galric lunged for him, but Sara and Flissa both held him back, and Sara smacked a hand over his mouth so he wouldn't call out. Rufus the dog started barking the second he saw the kitten, and zoomed after Nitpick.

"A black cat!" the Keeper called. "Get it, Rufus!"

She chased after Rufus and Nitpick, leaving the pathway to the woods completely clear. Only then did Sara remove her hand from Galric's mouth.

"We have to save him," Galric said. "He's just a kitten!"

"A *smart* kitten," Flissa shot back. "Nitpick did that on purpose. To protect us. And if we don't get away immediately, his gesture will be in vain."

"He'll be okay, Galric," Sara assured him. "Nitpick's fast, and small, and he's a black cat in the dark. He'll get away."

Galric nodded, but his eyes watered and he turned away so he could wipe them with his sleeve. "Okay. Let's get out of here."

They ran full speed, and Flissa and Galric each grabbed one of Sara's hands to keep her on her feet. They sprinted until they were deep inside the woods, then trudged on until they were well beyond the villages and out toward the very edge of Kaloon, where there was nothing but scrub and dust.

Flissa's feet hurt, but of course she would never complain. She could only imagine how Sara felt—she wasn't used to this kind of exercise. For the first time, Flissa was actually looking forward to reaching Galric's mysterious friend. It would be nice to sit for a moment before they continued on their quest.

Just when they'd traveled so far Flissa was sure there *was* no mysterious friend, she saw a ramshackle home that looked like it had been cobbled together from bits of barns, old carriages, and sculptures gone awry. It had no lawn, but instead sat on a large, uneven patch of raked dirt. Despite the predawn hour, chickens waddled around clucking and pigeons perched on the drooping clothesline. As Galric led them to the door, Flissa saw it was practically falling off its hinges.

"Does someone actually live here?" she asked.

"*I* did," Galric replied. "When I was very small."

"The woman who took you in?" Sara asked. "*She's* the one who knows how to get to the Twists?"

"If anyone does, she will," Galric said. He walked up to the door, but as he raised his hand to knock, Flissa's palms started to sweat.

"Wait!" she said. "Sara and I need to hide. We can't let anyone else in Kaloon know about us."

Galric shrugged. "You can hide if you want, but it won't matter. You surprised me, but I bet you won't surprise her at all."

Flissa doubted that very much. "Hoods up, Sara."

As Galric knocked on the door, Flissa pulled up her hood. Sara tried to do the same, but she still had branches in her hair from their roll down the big hill, and the hood snagged on its way up. She struggled with it as Flissa heard a scrape of something heavy, then thumping footsteps. Flissa tried to pull Sara's hood down herself, when the door opened to reveal the silhouette of a woman so large and formidable it was impossible to think there could be another just like her. Flissa's brain completely stalled out as she struggled to force this vision to make any kind of sense, but Sara just blurted, *"Katya?!"*

"Keep it down," Katya hissed. "You want all of Kaloon to know you're here? Get inside. Hurry. And don't you even think about waiting to flip that coin, Flissa. Your mother doesn't have that kind of time."

Galric scrunched his face, confused. "Their mother? The queen?"

Katya rolled her eyes and lurched out of the house, freeing the door for them. She pointed back at the entrance. "In. Now."

Flissa was completely baffled. She looked at Sara, but she only shrugged and walked in. With no idea what else to do, Flissa followed.

Inside the house was just as much of a mishmash as the outside. The single living space was stuffed with chairs, sofas, and daybeds of every color, fabric, and pattern, and the kitchen just off to the side emanated a stranger variety of delicious food smells than the palace kitchens could ever dream up.

Katya lumbered in, then called back to Galric. "Boy, shut the door behind us."

He did, while Katya plopped into an overstuffed rocking chair.

"Sit," she said. She waved an arm, and two puffy chairs slid across the floor and into Flissa's and Sara's backs, sweeping the girls off their feet. A chirp of birdsong rang out, and Sara sat up straighter in her chair.

"Primka?" she asked.

"Sounds like her, doesn't it?" Katya asked. "It's how we first became friends. I needed a bird to cover up my magical signature, and she needed someone to disguise her as a pet."

"And she sounded exactly like your magical signature?" Sara asked. "That's amazing!"

Katya laughed, rocking her chair so hard its joints squeaked. "Sweet merciful heavens, no! You should have heard the unearthly squawk on her before. Like fingernails on a slate. She had to practice for ages to chirp like me, I promise you that."

Now Sara laughed too, but Flissa's eyes goggled out of her head. She jumped to her feet. "How are you laughing?" she exploded to Sara. "Katya knows magic. *Real* magic. Far more than we ever suspected!"

"And all you saw me do was move some chairs around," Katya said lightly. She waved her hand, and with a Primka chirp, Flissa's chair slid into her, knocking her back off her feet.

"There's plenty about me you don't know," Katya said. "And I'm not tellin' you about it now because time is short."

She waved a hand toward the kitchen, and in a flurry of birdsong, a rickety tray of tiny sandwiches, scones, and tarts rolled across the room to them. Galric quickly grabbed a tart and popped it into his mouth.

"Mmm, lemon," he said. "My favorite."

"Wait-wait-wait," Sara said. "You grew up with *this*? And you freaked out when you saw we were twins?"

"Well, sure," Galric said as he plopped down on the nearest couch. "This stuff is basic magic. Twins . . . that's just creepy."

Only now did Flissa notice the wallpaper. It wasn't on every wall. In fact, each wall seemed to have its own decorations, none of which had anything to do with one another. One was painted blue, in a pattern of crashing waves, and the pattern was so convincing Flissa almost thought she heard the roar of the ocean. Another wall was papered in a geometric pattern of circles that seemed to move every time Flissa looked away, then go still whenever she looked at them head-on, which had to be an optical illusion. But the other papered wall . . . it showcased row after row of carousel animals—horses, monkeys, even lions, each with its own animal rider, but the animals actually moved along the wall, lazily bouncing up and down.

"Katya?" Flissa asked. "Are you aware that your wallpaper is in motion?"

"Of course!" Katya said. "Gives me something fun to watch when I'm here. Look—I can turn up the surf sounds and smells. It's very relaxing."

She waved her hand toward the blue wall. A single chirp rang out; then the waves undulated faster. Their crashing sound was more evident now, and sea air filled Flissa's nose. It was a scent she normally enjoyed, but right now it made her slightly nauseous. She met Katya's eye. "I have a vast number of questions."

"No doubt. And as I said, we have time for almost none of them. But I'll get a few things out of the way. I do have more magic than can safely be performed at the palace, and I have activities that are more wisely practiced elsewhere, hence this home, which I've maintained while serving the royal family loyally since your father was small. As for this boy," she said, waving dismissively at Galric, who grinned as if she'd just given him the greatest compliment of his life, "it was obvious to me the instant I saw him that he couldn't summon up magic to save his life, and I couldn't bear to see him sent to the Twists."

"So it was you who saved me," Galric said, the grin even stronger. "I always knew it."

Katya rolled her eyes. "Yes, it was a big mystery, with me taking you in and all." She leaned forward and spoke conspiratorially to Flissa and Sara. "Not very bright, this one."

Flissa frowned, trying to connect the dots in her head. It wasn't working. "So many things don't make sense," she said. "If *you're* Galric's friend who has information about the Twists, why didn't you just tell us? And why in the universe did Galric act so surprised by our secret when clearly he would have known the truth from you?"

"Bite your tongue, my dear princess, because you are mistaken. I have never breathed a word of your secret to anyone, including Galric. As for telling you about the Twists, I didn't bring them up in front of you as a hint. I wasn't trying to tell you to go there. It's far too dangerous.

But after what happened, when I got word through the grapevine that a nameless someone approached Galric and needed help getting into the Twists, I put the pieces together. I'm pretty smart that way."

"Okay," Flissa said, still puzzling it out, "so why didn't you come to us *then*?"

"Did you not hear the part about this idea being very, very dangerous? You needed room to change your mind. And in the meantime, I was looking into alternative plans. I can't go to the Twists myself because your mother needs my care to buy her time—"

"Buy her time?" Galric echoed, his eyes wide. "What happened to the queen?"

Katya held up a finger. "In a moment." Then she turned back to the girls, and her face clouded over. Her voice lost its dancing lilt and went solemn. "Unfortunately, so far all my ideas have come up short. So while the last thing in the universe I want to do is send the three people I care about most into danger . . . right now I really don't see a better way. And I'm very proud of all of you for being willing to do it."

Flissa glowed. Despite all her misgivings about this new side of Katya, the woman's pride warmed her, and she couldn't help but smile. They'd made the right choice.

"Um . . . did you say we're *all* going into the Twists?" Galric asked.

Flissa blushed. Sara gawped at her. Katya looked amused.

"You didn't *tell* him?" Sara asked.

Flissa fidgeted in her seat. "I thought I did—didn't I?"

"No," Galric said. "You said you needed me to get you

to someone in the Underground who could get *you* there."

"That's what you said?" Sara said.

"I didn't mean to leave it out! And I *did* mention the Twists, but then I heard Blakely shouting and I had to leave, and there just wasn't another really good time to bring it up, and . . ."

Flissa's voice petered out as she reached up and played with her braid. Finally she looked sheepishly at Galric. "Think you might want to accompany us to the Twists?"

Katya pursed her lips, fighting off a smile, then shifted her enormous girth to lean forward in her seat and look at Galric. "Allow me to lay things out as clearly as possible. The queen was cursed. The magical signature was your father's, and both my logic and Kaloonian rumor points to him escaping back to the Twists. The king, however, thinks otherwise. He believes Gilward's escape is the rallying cry for a second Dark Magic Uprising, which he thinks will take place on Princess Flissara's Ascension Day."

Galric's eyes were so wide Flissa thought they might pop out of his face.

"A second Dark Magic Uprising?" He gawped. "Is that what you think?"

"I do. That's why I believe he's still in the vicinity. But unlike the king, I *don't* think your father would be foolish enough to stay in Kaloon itself while he waits for it to start. I believe he took refuge back in the Twists, where he's lived for so many years. I believe he hopes to stay safely tucked away there while the queen perishes, making the king so weak with grief that he'll be completely ineffective against your father and his magical allies in Kaloon, whoever they may be."

This was clearly a lot to take in, and Flissa could see Galric's mouth working as he tried to figure out where to start.

"You said the queen would . . . perish," he finally said. "Is the curse that bad?"

"She will die in approximately twenty-nine hours unless the curse is removed," Katya said so matter-of-factly that it made Flissa ache. "And since a curse can only be removed by the mage who cast it . . ."

"You need to get my dad back from the Twists," Galric said. "But I don't know anything about the Twists. Or my dad. I have no idea how to find him."

"I believe I can take care of that," Katya said. "At least, I hope so. Your main purpose is to stop your father from killing the girls on sight. And to help them convince him to come back to Kaloon and remove the curse."

Galric's face darkened. "Why would he listen to me?" he asked dully. "He doesn't even know me. And it's not like he cares what I think. If he did, I'd have told him not to cast a stupid curse and get thrown in the Twists in the first place."

Katya smiled sadly. "He made bad choices where you're concerned. And he missed out on a wonderful son."

Galric looked up, shocked, when she said the word "son," and Flissa wondered if she'd ever called him that before.

"But I believe you'll have more sway over him than you think."

Sara reached out and put her hand on Galric's arm. "Will you please come with us? I know it's a lot to ask, but I don't think we can do it without you."

Galric looked at Flissa. She nodded, though in the back of her mind she was already trying to work out plans without him, just in case. Next, Galric looked down at Sara's hand on him. He gave a long exhale and hung his head. Then he smiled.

"Yeah, I'll go," he said. "Honestly, I was gonna offer anyway. I thought maybe you could use some help. But seriously," he added, looking straight at Flissa, "you've gotta tell me things. We're a team. For real now. Right?"

Flissa wasn't sure they were actually a team, but she and Sara certainly could use his help, so she nodded. "Yes. I understand."

"Oh!" Katya exclaimed like she'd been bitten. "Your mother is stirring. Stay right there."

"Our moth—" Flissa began, but the words dried up in her throat when she saw Katya's massive rocker somersault in a stationary circle, then pop back into place, completely empty. Katya was gone!

Sara's mouth dropped open. "She just went back to check on our mom, didn't she? *Magically!*"

Galric smiled. "Ask her."

WHOOSH! Katya's rocker spun around again, righting itself with Katya back in place.

"Whoo!" she said, fanning her face with her hand. "Always quite a journey." Then she looked lovingly to Flissa and Sara. "Your mother's resting comfortably. I'm keeping the pain away. That's all I can do."

"Amazing," Sara said, beaming. "You traveled back to the Residence in that chair, didn't you?"

"*In* the chair isn't exactly accurate, but yes, I did. You saw how far away we are. You don't think I can lug these big ol' bones back and forth to the palace all the time on foot, do you?"

Flissa looked at Katya as if seeing her for the first time. "Does Mother know how magic you are?" she asked. "Does Father?"

Katya laughed so hard her chair creaked at the joints. *"No,"* she said emphatically. "Though I don't think he'd mind if he did. His parents, though, they'd have had me executed a million times over."

She must have seen the horrified look on Flissa's face, because she chuckled warmly. "Oh, come on now—it wasn't their fault. They were true believers. They'd been raised to think all magic outside the hands of the Keepers was evil. They didn't know any better. Your mother too. Honestly, I didn't let your parents know I had *any* magic until you and your sister were born. Up to then I was just a nurse, and Primka just my pet. But I knew they'd be more open to it once they saw their babies were illegally magic as well."

Sara got that dreamy look she always had when her imagination was hard at work, and Flissa knew she was picturing the scene. Then Sara frowned. "But if Mom and Dad were so against magic—were they upset when we came out the way we did?"

Katya's face turned deadly serious. "Don't you think that for an instant. Your parents loved you both instantly. They didn't care if you were twins, or magic, or if you each had two heads—which you didn't," she quickly added when she saw Flissa ready to ask. "They loved you for you and always have. And the fact that you were different . . . it just made them appreciate that 'different' doesn't have to mean 'bad.' And when I told them I was different too . . . you ask me, they were both just relieved to have someone in their circle who really understood."

"So, was it your idea to make us Princess Flissara?" Flissa asked.

Katya laughed, but it sounded a little sad. "No. I thought we should announce the truth to the kingdom. Your parents have always been so beloved, and your birth was so anticipated. . . . I was sure it would be the perfect time to rally the people and teach them that so-called magical signs were meaningless. I thought we could show Kaloon that magic itself wasn't always bad, even if it wasn't in the Keepers' hands."

"But Mom and Dad didn't agree," Sara said.

"No." Katya smiled ruefully. "They were afraid Kaloonians weren't ready for that kind of revelation. Didn't think they'd support it. No matter how beloved your family was—and *is*—your parents were afraid the Keepers of the Light would point to your twinhood as a true sign of magic, and illegal according to the Magic Eradication Act. They were afraid the whole family would be banished to the Twists. Or worse—that the two of you would be banished, and your parents would never see you again."

Katya looked off into the distance frowning a little, as if seeing the terrible alternative future the king and queen had imagined. Then she shrugged.

"They were probably right. And given how successfully Primka and I had been hiding in plain sight all these years, they thought the same would work for you." She smiled wide now—the kind of smile she always gave them when they'd fallen and hurt themselves badly and needed quick cheering up. The kind she gave when she was secretly worried about them. "And it *did* work. But now we have to get you ready for the Twists. And while there are plenty of twins there, they don't try to be exactly like one another, so . . ."

She waved her arm in a sweep across the room, taking in both Flissa and Sara. Birdsong chirped, and Flissa saw Sara's whole outfit change! Now her sister wore sturdy brown close-cut pants, with a long-sleeved black blouse, fresh boots, and a jet-black hooded cloak that came down to her waist. Sara's long hair was no longer knotted with twigs and grass, but plaited into two neat buns set sleekly on top of her head.

"Sara?" Flissa said, and by the look on Sara's face, Flissa knew she'd transformed just as dramatically.

"Looking glass," Katya said, waving a hand behind her. Flissa expected a mirror to conjure itself out of thin air, but this time Katya was talking about an actual mirror on her far wall. She and Sara ran to it, and Sara practically glowed. She touched her bare neck and shook her head, as if checking to see if her braided cap of hair would move. It didn't.

"I love this!" she gushed. "My hair won't get caught on anything now."

Flissa looked at herself. She was now in black leggings, similar to her jodhpurs, tucked into the most comfortable boots she'd ever worn. On top she had a light green shirt under a deep forest-green cloak that hung down to the middle of her thighs. Her hair was braided into a single thick plait that started at the back of her neck and hung down over her right shoulder. The whole look was beautiful and comfortable, the right colors to camouflage into the wild, and the right fabrics to easily move however she wanted. It was perfect—but it made Flissa's stomach roll.

"We don't match," she said.

"I know!" Sara agreed with far too much enthusiasm. "Because we don't have to *be* each other. It's crazy, right?"

Tears sprang to Flissa's eyes. Did *everything* have to change all at once? Yes, she and Sara had an unusual experience living as one princess, but it was also beautiful, and Flissa loved it. Now suddenly their mother was cursed and dying, their nursemaid was a powerful mage, she no longer felt positive about the Keepers or whether magic was good or bad, and the person she loved most in the world, the other half of her, her twin, was *thrilled* that they looked less alike.

It was too much to take.

The room spun. Flissa hoped it was some kind of magical travel device like the rocker, and she'd appear back in her bed, before any of this had happened.

Then her legs crumpled under her.

Chapter 9
Sara

Sara didn't see it coming. One second she and Flissa were side by side, checking out their new looks in the mirror, and then Flissa was toppling. Sara clumsily held out her hands to catch her, but she got the angle all wrong and thumped to the ground with Flissa on top. Flissa reacted like she'd been struck by lightning. She buzzed to life and leaped off Sara with almost inhuman speed. Then Flissa was the one helping *her*, pulling her to her feet.

"I'm so sorry," Flissa said. "I don't know what happened. I was fine and then—"

"You're exhausted, of course," Katya said. "Ridiculous to imagine you could stay up as long as you have and not be asleep on your feet. It's a wonder Sara and Galric haven't fallen down flat as well. Here."

She waved a hand and three cookies chirped as they drifted in from the kitchen. One wafted to each of them, Flissa, Sara, and Galric.

"They're all the same flavor," Katya said with a nod to Flissa. "No need to choose."

Sara looked at hers. It was like a chewy gingersnap—

molasses-brown, with a little give to the puffy top. "What is it?"

"The best I can offer," Katya said. "What you need is a good night's sleep, but since time is of the essence, this'll at least make you feel like you got close."

Galric popped his into his mouth in one giant bite. Sara shrugged and was about to do the same when Flissa stopped her.

"Sara, wait."

Sara looked over and saw her sister's upper lip beaded with sweat.

"We don't know what these will do," Flissa said. She glanced at Katya, then shielded her mouth with her hand and whispered, "They're *magical* cookies."

"I'm magic, Flissa, not deaf," Katya said. "The cookies are not harmful. I've been your nurse your whole life. Have I ever given you bad advice?"

Flissa racked her brain for a good solid instance, but Sara was already biting into the cookie. "Mmmm! It's good—almost as good as Mitzi's! Except, you know, magical."

"Thank you, Sara," Katya said. "Now, Flissa, you can eat the cookie or not, but you'll do your mother no good if you're falling down on the job."

Flissa moved the cookie from one hand to the other so she could wipe her palms on her leggings.

"Whoo!" Galric hooted. He hopped to his feet and bounced on his toes. "It really works! I feel great, not tired at all."

Both sisters ignored him. Sara stared at Flissa, who looked so frightened and uncertain. For the first time ever, it frustrated Sara. Eating the cookie should be an easy call. *Katya* had made it. The woman had spent a lifetime in their corner, and now here they were together with her in this wonderful, enchanted house with the dancing walls and the sounds and smells of the ocean and the clothes that appeared on their bodies with a wave of her hand. It was astoundingly amazing! Whatever magic Katya had was obviously good. Why couldn't Flissa just trust and enjoy it?

Still, she knew what Flissa needed, and she kept her voice patient.

"Give me the coin."

Flissa eagerly pulled out the locket and handed the coin inside to Sara.

"King, you eat the cookie; queen, you don't."

Flissa looked on breathlessly as Sara flipped the coin. Sara tried to catch it, but it bounced off her hand and rolled under Katya's rocker. Sara dropped to her hands and knees and quickly crawled after it. She reached deep under the rocker and slid it close, being careful not to let it turn over on the way. When it was close enough for her to see, she pushed her face close between the rocker and the floor to peek.

It was queen. Flissa wouldn't eat the cookie.

Sara reached under the rocker, and as she pulled the coin out, she flipped it with her fingers. She worried her hands would betray her and the coin would skitter across the room, but it didn't. She placed her hand flat on the newly flipped coin and slid it out into the open, then sat back on her heels so everyone could see it as she removed her hand to reveal the face: "King."

It was the first time Sara had ever lied about a coin flip.

Flissa looked relieved. "Together, then. My first bite, your second."

They both took huge bites of the cookie. Within seconds of swallowing, Sara felt her whole body wake up. She hadn't even realized her feet and legs were sore until they weren't anymore. Her eyelids felt more open, and even the frenetically cluttered room around her looked brighter and more vivid. She stood taller and took a deep breath of air that filled her whole body down to her toes.

Flissa laughed out loud. "I feel like I could race against Balustrade and win!"

Katya raised an eyebrow. "I wouldn't recommend that, but I'm glad you have energy. You'll need it. You'll also need these." She stretched a hefty arm high into the air and reached into . . . well, nothing as far as Sara could see, but then she heard a chirp, and when Katya clutched her hand into a fist, two tiny velvet drawstring bags—one black and one green—dangled from her closed hand. Katya handed each twin the bag that matched her cloak. The bags were no bigger than plums, each attached to a delicate, thin gold chain just the right size to drape around their waists.

"What is this?" Flissa asked.

"A change of clothes, for starters," Katya said, "just in case. Plus bedrolls in case you need to stay the night, warm fur coats, hats and gloves, a toothbrush, and of course I loaded in all the supplies you had in those rucksacks."

Both Sara's and Flissa's hands whipped back to feel for the rucksacks. Neither one of them had realized they'd disappeared when Katya changed their clothes.

Sara held the bag to eye level. It was almost like

holding a flower bud. She smiled. "A magic bag. To hold everything we could possibly need."

"I don't know about everything you could *possibly* need," Katya admitted, "but I did my best."

Sara couldn't wait to dive inside. She quickly opened it up and pushed in her hand . . . then her forearm. Soon she was impossibly shoulder-deep in the tiny bag, leaning this way and that as she rummaged through the inside.

Flissa looked pale. "Stop. It looks like you've lost your arm. It's horrendous!" She wheeled on their nursemaid. "Katya, that *has* to be dark magic."

"It'd only be dark magic if it actually *ate* her arm," Galric said. "Sara, did it eat your arm?"

Sara wasn't paying attention to them. She was too amazed by all the different textures and materials she felt. There was slick and velvety, and something massive and puffy, and something small and metallic that chilled her hand. Yet anytime she tried to grab something, it slipped out of reach.

"I can't grab anything," she said.

"You have to ask for it first," Katya said. "And you don't need to throw your whole body into it; you could fall in entirely and someone else would have to pull you out."

Sara quickly stood taller, yanking her arm back out of the bag until only her wrist was inside.

Flissa folded her arms. "See? Dark magic."

Sara ignored her. She scrunched her brow, concentrating hard on the item she wanted. She thought of everything they'd put in her rucksack. "Find me . . . Flissa's book!"

SMACK! The spine of the book smacked into Sara's palm, and the pouch opened wide so she could heave it out to show everyone. It wasn't an easy feat one-handed. The book was heavy. "Katya, this is perfect! And—ugh." Her arm drooped under the weight of the book. "The best part is things aren't heavy inside. But how do I get it back in?"

"Ask," Katya said. "Just like you asked to get it out."

Sara crinkled her face and held the book to the mouth of the pouch. "Um . . . back inside?"

WHOOSH! The book slipped back inside the tiny pouch.

"Wow!" Sara whooped. "This is amazing!"

"It is more convenient than the rucksack," Flissa reluctantly admitted. "Thank you, Katya."

"How about me?" Galric asked. "Don't I get a bag?"

"You're lucky you don't get a swat. The girls have enough supplies in their bags for all of you." Katya pushed her massive girth out of her chair. "Now come here, let me look at you."

Galric, Sara, and Flissa obediently moved into a line in front of her, and Sara noticed Katya's already-wide face had puffed up, and her eyes looked red and swollen. For just a moment, Sara felt like she was four years old again, and imagined how sweet it would be to curl up on Katya and fall asleep on her couch-like lap.

"I won't have the three of you getting hurt out there, understand? I need you to look out for each other."

"I'll look after the princesses," Galric said. He sounded so serious that Sara turned to look at him. His skin was paler than ever, and he trembled a little, but he stood tall and Sara saw his jaw clench with determination. It felt nice to know he wanted to protect them.

Flissa snorted. "We don't need 'looking after,'" she said. "We're not helpless. And remind me—which one of us pinned the other when we got out of the castle?"

Galric blushed and his shoulders wilted. Sara felt bad for him. He hadn't meant to insult them; he just wanted to help. They were lucky he wanted to come at all—without him they had no way to get Gilward to listen to them.

"I'm glad you're with us, Galric," Sara said.

He smiled gratefully, and Sara tried not to feel bad when Flissa gave her a hurt look Sara had never seen before. She wanted to say something to make it better, but Flissa turned back to Katya.

"What will you tell Father?" Flissa asked. "What will you tell everyone around the palace when they see neither Princess Flissara nor the queen is present for anything on our schedules today? Will they suspect you had anything to do with our disappearance? Will you be in danger?"

And that was the thing about Flissa, Sara thought, as she gaped at her sister in awe. Not five minutes ago Sara had been frustrated with her for being small-minded about magic and not appreciating all Katya had done, but now here Flissa was worried about the woman's safety when the thought hadn't even crossed Sara's mind.

Katya's smile was like a hug. "Your father won't be a problem. Between worrying about your mother and helming the search for Gilward in Kaloon, he won't notice anything's wrong. Whatever I tell him you're doing he'll believe me. As for palace rumors, those run rampant no matter what, so expect to come back to stories that Princess Flissara has run off with the princesses of Winterglen for some wild adventure or another."

"And the Keepers?" Sara asked, partly because she was genuinely worried and partly because she wanted

Katya to know that she thought about these things too.

"I won't lie, they'll get curious and start sniffing around. But I've been getting the better of them for a long time, and I don't intend to stop now. You, however, need to be especially careful. If what happened to your mother is the harbinger of a second Dark Magic Uprising, the Keepers involved—however few or many that may be—will want to make sure nothing messes up their plan. If they have any worries about Gilward's safety in the Twists, they'll surely come crawling about."

Flissa nodded. "I've read about that. As part of their continuing peacekeeping mission, the Keepers have to periodically visit the Twists and make sure everyone there knows who's in charge."

Katya winced the tiniest bit at Flissa's flattering description of the Keepers' motives. She opened her mouth to speak, and Sara leaned forward eagerly. She wanted to know more. She wanted to know every reason Katya joined the Underground to fight against the Keepers. But there wasn't time for that, not now. Instead of explaining, Katya ticked off final instructions.

"Remember," she said, "be vigilant. Keep your identities secret, all three of you. You never know when a Keeper will be listening. In the Twists they don't always wear yellow robes to help you spot them. And, Galric, you'll want to stay close to the princesses because you'll stick out most of all."

"Me?" Galric asked. "Why?"

"Because unlike the twins, you have no hint of magic in you. They pick up on that kind of thing in the Twists. It makes you an easy mark."

Flissa frowned. "Katya, Sara and I have no magic in us either."

"I disagree," Katya said. She put a hand on each of their shoulders to stop them, then leaned down and looked at them closely, first one and then the other, back and forth. She was so close Sara could see the small white hairs on her chin. "Magic is in the very fiber of your being. It seeped into you before you were even born."

"But it's not like it did anything to us," Sara said. "You always said because there were two of us, the curse was spread too thin to hurt us."

"That *is* true . . . isn't it?" Flissa said.

"It didn't hurt you, no. But of course there were repercussions," Katya said gently. "Think about it. Identical twins. One girl with incredible strength of body, able to leap and climb and fight and triumph against any adversary or obstacle. And one with strength of spirit who never doubts herself and never hesitates to make a decision and go with her gut."

Sara felt weird hearing them described that way. It was true enough, but the way Katya said it, it sounded bad, like each of them had stolen something from the other one. Or had had something taken away.

"Okay, but, what you're saying . . . that's just who we are," Sara said. "That's not a curse."

"It's not a whole curse," Katya said. "The full curse on a tiny unborn baby . . . I don't think you could have survived. But a curse broken up, spread out, weakened between you both . . . it left its mark."

Sara didn't know what to make of that. She felt strange inside, like she suddenly wasn't sure who she was. She tried to catch Flissa's eye, but Flissa was frowning at a spot on the floor. Then she shook her head. "You can't say that. You're just picking parts of our personalities and saying they're from the curse. There's no way you can know who we are isn't simply who we are. You said it yourself—the curse had to go through Mother—and it wasn't strong enough to kill her—then spread out between the two of us. What you always told us is still true: We are who we are. It's that simple."

Flissa looked at Katya as defiantly as Sara had ever seen her, and Katya didn't argue with her.

"You might be right," she said. "Come back home safe and we can talk all about it. But now your mother needs you. Get to the Twists, find your way through the Brambled Gates, then make your way to the marketplace. There you want to find Dorinda. She's a glassblower. Extra pinkie on each hand. Raven hair. One glass eye. She'll help you find Gilward."

Extra pinkies were signs of magic. Sara thrilled to think of a magical person on their side in the Twists to help them out.

"'The Brambled Gates'?" Galric asked. "Do you have some kind of map to that or something?"

"There are no maps to the Twists," Katya said. "It's a magical place. The entrance manifests in Kaloon in various spots, and for limited periods of time. Only the Keepers know where and when the gates will arrive. And magical creatures. They're naturally attuned to the mass motion of that kind of power."

"Okay, but none of us are Keepers, so does that mean you're giving us a magical creature?" Galric asked.

"I already did. And he has proven himself a most heroic companion."

Galric smiled so wide he practically glowed, and Sara couldn't figure out why until she heard chirping and followed the sound to the carousel wallpaper, where one section had stopped its up-and-down movement. Instead, all the moving creatures pushed to the side as one creature and rider grew larger and larger, until Sara could see it was a life-size black kitten with a small bright-blue-and-yellow-feathered songbird on his back. Then the cat leaped out of the wallpaper and raced into Galric's arms while the songbird fluttered into the air. The magic wallpaper stopped moving, but the chirping continued.

"Primka!" Sara cried.

"*You're* the magical creature who will lead us into the Twists?" Flissa asked.

"Oh, no." Primka laughed lightly. "I've been covering my skills far too long. I'm not even sure I have what it takes to get to the Twists anymore without getting us hopelessly lost. Nitpick's younger and far more in touch with his instincts. He'll get us there."

"Nitpick?" Galric asked. The kitten had leaped into his arms immediately and now kneaded the skin of his neck with his kitteny paws. "Nitpick's not magic."

"Actually, that's one area in which the Keepers of the Light are correct," Katya said. "All black cats have magic, to varying degrees. Nitpick's doesn't go much further than an uncanny sense of human character, but he's magic enough to get you to the Brambled Gates."

"Wait—really?" Galric said. "So if he's magic, does that mean you can talk to him? What is he saying?"

"I don't want to tell you—it'll swell your head," Katya said. "Just trust that he's happy to see you." Galric smiled and held the kitten in front of his face. "I missed you too, Nitpick." He kissed the kitten on the top of his head.

Sara thought it was seriously cute how in love Galric and the kitten were with one another. She sidled closer so she could be part of the group. "Me too, Nitpick," she said, scratching the cat behind his ears. "I'm glad you're back with us."

"I am as well," Flissa said, but she made no move to come closer and pet the cat. "Thank you for saving our lives."

"Meow!" Nitpick said.

"It's six in the morning," Katya said. "The sun is already starting to come up, and I don't know where Nitpick will take you to find the Brambled Gates. The sooner you leave the better—the fewer Kaloonians awake, the fewer you have to hide from."

"And the sooner we help Mother," Flissa said. "If your original diagnosis holds true, we have twenty-eight hours or we're too late."

Sara froze. Twenty-eight hours. That was little more than a day. And a full day, no sleep. In a place filled with unknown wonders and terrors, to find a man they knew next to nothing about. And they could only hope his son—who the man hadn't seen in twelve years—would have some pull over him. Maybe it was the cookie Katya had given her, but Sara didn't feel hopeless, even though she knew she probably should. She felt energized. She wanted to go. She wanted to succeed.

"Twenty-eight hours," Katya agreed. "And I believe I've told you everything I can to help. If I forgot anything, Primka will fill you in."

Sara couldn't believe it, and Flissa looked just as surprised. They both turned to Primka.

"You're really going?" Flissa asked hopefully. "You're not just here to see us off?"

"Of course I'm going," Primka said. "It's my job to watch over you. You think I'd let you run off into the Twists by yourselves?"

Sara tried not to let her disappointment show. The shine of wondrous adventure, just her and her sister and their new friend and a magical cat, was dulled a little by their tutor coming along.

"Hugs, all of you," Katya demanded, and spread her arms wide to embrace them all. Sara closed her eyes and enjoyed Katya's scent of citrus and talcum powder, as well as the roar of the ocean that so soothingly filled the room. Katya clung to them all for a long time, and when she let go, her face was red and blotchy. She shooed them along with her hands.

"Go. I hate goodbyes. Go so you can come back with Gilward right away. And don't you worry about your parents. I'll keep tabs on them both."

Sara met Katya's eyes. She felt like she should say something meaningful, something about how happy she was to know Katya better now, and how excited she was to hear all of her stories once Mom was better and everything was back to normal. But for once, Sara didn't have the words. So she just smiled, squeezed Katya's hand, and walked out the front door.

Chapter 10
Flissa

It was hard to leave Katya's. As strange and disorienting as her magical home had been, it still felt like a home. And even though Katya had revealed she was far different than what Flissa had always known, she was familiar at the same time. Now they were following Nitpick through what had to be the ugliest part of Kaloon, filled with nothing but large boulders and endless swaths of sun-dried, brittle grass. It crunched under their feet as they ran from boulder to boulder, taking as much cover as they could, but every step felt like a clarion call to the Keepers of the Light.

Flissa looked up at Primka, soaring above them—high enough that she'd just look like a regular bird if anyone noticed her, not the chaperone to a suspicious traveling party. Having her there made Flissa feel better. She liked knowing all the responsibility wasn't just on them. If they made mistakes along the journey to Gilward, Primka would fix them.

The sun was rising higher, glaring in their faces. Flissa would have been happier with a nice long trudge through a jungle—something with enough cover that she could walk side by side with Sara and bend their heads close to talk about everything. But Flissa realized the image in her head was wrong; she imagined the two of them as bookends, a matched set. But if they bent together now, someone could look at them from behind with their different clothes and hairstyles and not even know they were twins.

The four of them crouched behind another boulder now, with Primka up above. As he did before every mad dash, Nitpick looked at Galric and the princesses first, as if making sure they were paying attention. Then he stared ahead at their goal—another large boulder that swam in the distance, its edges wavy in the bright sunlight.

Flissa nodded. She understood. Galric and Sara did the same.

Nitpick tore off like a bullet. Flissa followed, challenging herself to keep up with the nimble animal, despite the sun's blinding glare.

That's why she didn't see the flash of yellow robes before it was too late.

Flissa barely had time to register what was happening. She caught a glimpse of color out of the corner of her eye, then felt a massive weight on her body as the Keeper tackled her to the ground and harsh grass scratched against her cheek.

She didn't think. Didn't feel any pain. She did exactly what she'd done in training. She planted her hands and her top foot on the earth, then pushed back and rolled the Keeper off her. She jumped to her feet first, and while the Keeper was still on his knees, she kicked him as hard as she could in the chin. His head snapped back and he stayed like that a moment, as if looking up at the sun, then he toppled, unconscious.

Flissa immediately whipped around, knowing a Keeper wouldn't be out here on his own, and saw exactly what she feared. A woman in a yellow tunic and tights faced away from Flissa, her arms thrust in front of her. Galric and Sara faced her, frozen mid-stride. Their faces looked stricken, and Flissa caught the smell of peanuts in the air.

"NO!" Flissa screamed.

The Keeper wheeled around, and Flissa ran toward her as fast as she could. She was about to tackle her, but the second before she could, Galric heaved something over his head and brought it down hard on the Keeper's head. She crumpled to the ground, motionless.

"Blast!" Flissa gasped. "Did you *kill* her? What did you hit her with?"

Galric was white-faced and shaking. He stared down at the Keeper and didn't answer.

"Your book!" Sara said, the words gushing out quickly. "When she turned away, her spell broke and we could move. It was the only heavy thing I could think of!"

"She's alive," Primka said, and everyone turned to see her perched on the unconscious Keeper's chest, her wing splayed out on the woman's throat. "So's the one you kicked in the head, Flissa. I checked."

Galric and Sara stared at her, agog. "You kicked a Keeper in the head?" Sara asked.

"I didn't think about it," Flissa said uncomfortably. "He didn't use magic. He tackled me."

"You are amazing!" Sara cried, and threw her arms around Flissa for a massive hug.

Galric grinned. "Guess your guy's magic's not as strong as this one's. He couldn't get you when you were running. Either way, glad we brought weapons."

Flissa ignored Galric, and she couldn't return Sara's hug. She felt sick to her stomach.

"Sara, we beat up two Keepers of the Light," she said. "It's illegal. And they saw us. *Both* of us. When they wake up—"

"They'll have massive headaches and won't remember a thing," Sara said. "Or even if they do, there's no way they got a good look, and *no one* would think Princess Flissara would be all the way out here."

Flissa's stomach churned harder. "I don't know . . ."

Primka flapped between them. "This is a fascinating conversation, but the Keepers won't stay unconscious forever. We need to get to the Brambled Gates before they wake up and follow us. That means *now*."

No one objected. They ran to Nitpick, who was still waiting at the next boulder.

"Hurry, Nitpick," Galric said. "We need to move. All the way to the Brambled Gates. No more stopping."

But Nitpick wouldn't budge. He sat next to the boulder, rear end on the crunchy grass, and stared straight ahead.

"Nitpick," Galric urged. "Come on. We have to keep going."

Nitpick flicked his ear to show he'd heard, but he remained stone still.

Flissa's heart thudded. She looked over her shoulder at the two yellow spots on the ground—the unconscious Keepers. Were they starting to move? If their group was caught now, after what they'd done . . .

"*Please*, Nitpick," Flissa begged. "We can't just stand here!"

Primka fluttered down and landed on Flissa's shoulder. "We can't," she said. "But I think the kitten knows what he's doing."

Flissa smelled it before she saw it. The scent of fire and rotten eggs. Then a black spot appeared in front of them, floating at eye level in midair. With a low, rumbling groan, it spread, growing larger and larger until Flissa realized it wasn't a flat spot at all. It had depth. It was a hallway, an opening into another place. The blackness stretched back and back, and as it kept growing, Sara and Flissa reached for one another's hands and gripped tight.

When the groaning ceased, the black spot had spread into something impossible. In the middle of the flat, crunchy-grass desolation of the outskirts of Kaloon, an area that sweated under the bright early morning sun, there was now a patch of something else. A chunk of the world as wide as a team of oxen, and as tall as one grown man sitting on another's shoulders, had transformed into a thick forest. A network of twisted, thorny branches—each with the girth of Balustrade's muscular body—snaked around each other like a tangled skein of yarn. But beyond them Flissa could see an entire forest, dark as dusk.

"The Brambled Gates," Primka said. "Our Nitpick here didn't just know where they were, he knew where they were going to be."

"So did the Keepers," Galric said as he realized. "That's why they were out here standing guard."

Sara let go of Flissa and moved to the side, peering behind the entryway. "It's flat," she said.

"That doesn't make sense," Flissa said, but she moved to join Sara and check it out for herself. "I can see inside. It goes back and—"

She didn't bother finishing, because now she saw what Sara saw. When she leaned behind the rectangle of twisted branches, it wasn't there at all. It was as if the portal were a particularly lifelike three-dimensional piece of art, except she couldn't even see the back of the canvas. There was nothing in the back except the dried grass and boulders she'd seen since they'd left Katya's. But when she moved to where they'd stood before, there it was: a slash in this reality, and a living, breathing alternate place. And it *was* alive inside, there was no doubt. Flissa saw leaves swaying in a light wind she didn't even feel out where she was. She saw insects flitting around, and the movement of light and shadow.

"So that's the Twists," Sara said, and though she sounded casual, Flissa heard the light tremor in her voice. "I guess it lives up to the hype. Dark, spooky—"

"And defying all laws of how reality should work," Flissa finished.

"So what do we do?" Galric asked, not taking his eyes off it. "Do we just . . . walk in?"

A low moan echoed off the boulders, and squeezed Flissa's heart. She whipped around and saw the female Keeper, the one Galric had hit with the book, slowly climbing to her knees.

"Yes!" she wailed. "We go in!"

The low rumbling started again, and the edges of the rectangle started to cave in and round out. Flissa quickly realized what was happening.

"The entrance is collapsing," she said. "We don't know how fast it'll close."

She risked one more look over her shoulder. The Keeper had staggered to her feet, but she was bent over, hands on her thighs, her scraggly blond hair hanging down in a curtain.

It was only a matter of moments before she came after them.

"Now! Now! Now!" Flissa cried.

They all dove into the entryway, and Flissa felt the temperature plummet the second she crossed its threshold. She looked for Nitpick to lead the way, but he raced forward and leaped through a small hole made by two of the entwined branches.

"Nitpick!" Primka cried. "Don't get too far ahead! Wait!" She flew to catch up with the cat, then called back to the princesses and Galric. "Hurry! This way!"

A moment later, Primka was gone, and the portal was still shrinking.

"There's no way to get through," Sara said, tugging at the branches around the hole through which Nitpick and Primka had disappeared. "The branches are too tangled. Unless you're a kitten or small bird, every opening's too tiny!"

Flissa looked back over her shoulder. She'd thought they would be safe once they stepped into this jungle, but now she knew they weren't. She could still see Kaloon's flatlands and a figure all in yellow starting to stagger their way.

She whipped her attention back to the brambles.

At first glance, Sara was right—they were too thick to

possibly squeeze through—but as she stared at the tangled network, she saw it—the one way to get past these knotted, thorny branches into the dark forest beyond.

The rumbling grew louder. The portal was closing, and Flissa had no idea how far inside they had to be before it shut entirely. If it closed while they were still clinging to these outer thorny gates, would they be spit back out to Kaloon and the waiting Keepers, or would the closing portal clamp down on them like slamming gates?

Honestly, Flissa wasn't sure which sounded worse.

She spun to Sara and looked her in the eye. "Follow me and do *exactly* what I do." Then she looked to Galric. "You said you wanted to look after us? Now's your chance. Stay behind her and help her through if she needs it. Make sure her clothes don't get snagged on anything or her foot doesn't fall through a rotted part of the branch—nothing to stop her, okay?"

Galric nodded. He looked scared but determined. "Promise."

The rumbling was so loud now that even though Flissa saw Galric's lips move and knew he was saying something else, she didn't hear it. She took one more peek at the staggering Keeper—closer now—then shimmied up the tangled roots like they were a ladder, so quickly that she was halfway up before her brain registered the fact that the branches felt like no tree she'd ever touched. They felt warm. And kind of soft. More like tentacles than branches. Flissa's stomach churned, and she was glad Sara had never done a lot of tree climbing. Maybe she wouldn't notice.

"What's wrong with these branches?!" Galric shouted

loud enough for her to hear over the rumbling. "They're all fleshy and warm!"

"Ew!" Sara shouted.

Flissa rolled her eyes. So much for Galric taking care of them. "Just climb!" she called down. "The portal is closing and the Keeper is on her way! We need to at least get through this first layer of branches *now*!"

She stared down at them until they got close to her. She took one last look out at the fast-approaching Keeper. Her hands were outstretched, and Flissa caught the faintest whiff of peanuts in the air, but nothing happened, so they must have been beyond her magical range.

For now.

Flissa quickly slid her body through a long, narrow space between two branches. From here Flissa couldn't see what was on the other side, and the warmth and malleability of the limbs made her feel like she was slipping between two giant lips. She squeezed her eyes to try to get that image out of her head as one leg slipped through, then another. She hung from her hands, both legs dangling and reaching for purchase until she looked over her shoulder and saw that the ground was only four feet away from her shoes, and looked flat and mossy, so she let go.

It was the right choice. The ground had give, like the padded floors on which she practiced hand-to-hand combat. Flissa looked up immediately and saw Sara's leg sticking out the same hole she'd just gone through. "You're doing beautifully, Sara!"

"Flissa?!" Sara's voice sounded panicked. "You're there, right?"

"I'm here, right below you. Hold tight and slide your other leg through."

"This feels really weird and warm, Flissa. I don't like it."

The scent of peanuts was stronger now.

"Just hurry. You'll be fine. I'm fine. But *hurry*!"

It made Flissa crazy that she couldn't see what was happening out there. She had no idea how close the Keeper was, or if the other Keeper had joined her. Flissa bounced a little, trying to contain herself as she watched Sara's left leg dangle lower . . . then her right leg followed . . . then finally Sara was there in her entirety, hanging from the lip of the trees. Flissa got up and reached her hands high. She tapped Sara's legs.

"I'm right here, see? Just drop down."

"I'm scared."

Now Galric's face peered through the hole. "Here. Let me help. Take my hands."

Galric's face disappeared and his hands came through. Sara took one, then the other, and Flissa couldn't even imagine how Galric was contorting himself against the other side of the wall to do it, but he lowered Sara far enough that Flissa could grab her around the waist.

"Got her!" she called.

Galric let go and Sara's full weight fell into Flissa's arms. She lowered Sara easily to the ground; then Sara threw her arms around Flissa for a tight hug. Tears filled Flissa's eyes. The whole world might be spinning and changing around them, but they were still the most important people to one another. That stayed the same.

The smell of peanuts was suddenly overpowering.

"Galric!" Sara screamed.

He slid through the opening, his legs hanging limply as he thumped to the ground next to them, just as the rumbling sound stopped. Sara immediately dropped down next to him. "Are you okay?"

"She got my legs," he moaned. "I couldn't move them." Gingerly, he stretched out one leg, then the other. "I can move 'em now," he said breathlessly. "I'm okay."

"It's because the portal closed," Flissa said. "We're in a totally different place from her now. Her magic isn't strong enough to keep working."

Flissa's voice drifted away and she felt dizzy. Thank the universe not all mages had equally strong powers. It was only luck that they hadn't just lost everything.

Sara helped Galric to his feet. "At least we finished our first job," she said. "We're in the Twists."

"We're in the Brambled Gates," Flissa clarified, "a magical border between the Twists and Kaloon. They say it's filled with obstacles that will destroy anyone who isn't sanctioned by the Keepers of the Light."

"Any chance that's just a legend?" Galric asked uncomfortably. "I mean, it's not like you hear from anyone who actually made it out, right?" Then his face clouded. "I guess that kinda supports the 'destroy' thing, though. . . ."

Flissa looked around to get their bearings. They were in a forest, but not like one she'd ever seen. Trees seemed to grow in all directions—not just up, but straight across too, and at all different heights. Any ground not covered in branches was coated in that same thick moss that had broken Flissa's fall. Scattered leaves dotted some of the branches, and they swayed in a light breeze that felt cool against Flissa's skin. She was glad she had her cloak.

The most disorienting thing after their walk under the bright morning sun was the darkness. Everything was cast in blue-black, like twilight. Even Sara and Galric looked colorless next to her. Flissa assumed the sun was blocked out by the tree canopy, but when she looked up, there was no canopy at all. Just more interlaced branches in front of some kind of stretched-out membrane with a vague bluish glow.

Honestly, it looked like skin.

Flissa shuddered.

"There's light that way," Galric said. He pointed through the forest to a hint of what certainly seemed like daylight. It was far—maybe three jousting fields away—but there was a clear pathway—perhaps a safe way through?

"Check this out!"

Flissa turned in the direction of her sister's voice.

Sara had discovered a single-leaf plant that sprouted out of the ground. It had a thick stem, and its green leaf was as large as a person, and curled like a cupped hand. She wandered off the path to look closer.

"Not sure we should leave the path," Galric said, but Sara didn't break stride. He looked at Flissa helplessly, and Flissa stifled a smile. Galric clearly hadn't realized there was no denying Sara's curiosity. She gave him a shrug and they followed.

"It looks like a chair!" Sara said when they caught up to her. Then she touched the edge of the leaf. "It *feels* like a chair—like, really, really strong. I'm gonna sit in it."

Flissa's palms broke out in sweat. "I don't think that's a good idea."

"It's a great idea!" Sara countered. "How often are we gonna be in the Brambled Gates with giant chair plants? Once. Twice if you count coming home. Lemme sit real quick, then we'll go."

She sat.

Immediately, sharp teeth jutted out of the leaf, and it closed tightly around her. Sara screamed in horror and kicked her legs.

Galric froze, his eyes and mouth open wide, but Flissa acted without thinking. For the first time, she reached her hand into the bag Katya gave them, and she shouted a word she didn't know existed.

"Scimisword!"

The hilt of a weapon slid into her hand, and in a single motion, Flissa pulled it from the pouch and swung it, hacking the plant off at its base. It screamed an unearthly squeal, then thumped back to the ground, openmouthed. Sara would have fallen with it, but Galric reached out and grabbed both her hands, pulling her to her feet.

Sara coughed and gasped. Her face was red and blotchy, and there were singed spots on her cloak. One of her braided buns had a sunken edge, like it had melted into itself. A burning smell emanated from her body.

"Let go of her," Flissa snapped to Galric. He looked offended.

"I'm not hurting her!"

"Just do it!"

He stepped away, and Flissa looked around at all the branches. She saw one not far from Sara dangling high in the air. That was the one. Flissa threw her weapon. It swung through the air and sliced the thick branch in two.

It reacted like a tortured animal, spasming and squealing like the plant had, but the branch spewed a river of water. Flissa bear-hugged her sister and ran them both under the bracingly cold flow.

"What are you doing?!" Sara spluttered when the water stopped flowing. "I'm soaked!"

"That's the point," Flissa said, gasping for air herself. "That plant was digesting you. You were covered in acid. If we hadn't washed it off, it would have kept eating through you, slowly, until it was too late to do anything about it."

Sara stared at her, mouth hanging open, water dripping off her nose and hair. Then she started to cry.

"I'm so sorry, Flissa," she sobbed. "I should have listened. I'm sorry."

Flissa's heart broke. She pulled her sister into her sodden arms. "It's okay. You didn't know. *I* didn't know until I saw it happen. I'd never read about anything like that. It's not your fault." She pulled back to arm's length and looked her in the eye. "We just have to be really careful here. It's incredibly dangerous, and we're just in the gateway. We haven't even made it all the way into the Twists."

Sara sniffled and nodded.

"Mother needs us to be strong."

Sara nodded some more. She ran her sleeve over her face, then laughed because it was just as sopping as the rest of her.

"We can do this," Sara said. Then she giggled again. "You're really wet."

Flissa laughed too. Her cloak was so soaked it felt like a million-pound weight on her shoulders. She pulled it off and wrung it out, and Sara did the same with her own.

Then Flissa looked at her pouch. "Will it make everything else in there wet?"

Sara shook her head. "I don't think so. It's huge in there." She held a corner of the cloak to the mouth of her pouch. "Back inside," she said, and the pouch sucked the cloak in. Flissa did the same.

Galric approached, holding Flissa's sword as far in front of him as he could reach. He looked at it like it might bite him. "Sorry I froze up on you back there," he said sheepishly. "Great swordwork, though. What is this thing, anyway? You said 'scimisword'?"

Galric had good reason to look intimidated by the weapon. It was half as tall as Flissa and Sara, with an exquisitely sharp, wide blade with a slight curve. Flissa herself was stunned by it, and even though she could feel the blade in her hand and knew it belonged there, she felt chills and took a step away.

"I said it, yes," Flissa admitted. "But I never heard the word before. I have never seen a weapon like this in my life."

"And how did you know the branch would gush water?" Galric asked. "Every branch I ever cut into oozed sap, that's it."

Flissa shook her head. "I don't know."

"Maybe Katya was right," Galric said, amazed. "Maybe you and Sara have some magic in you after all."

Chapter 11
Sara

Sara snorted. "If we were magic, I'd be smart enough not to get myself in stupid trouble."

But even as she said it, she remembered what Katya had said—that she and Flissa were who they were *because* they'd been touched by magic, and it had messed them up from birth. Even though her soaking-wet cloak was in her bag, she suddenly felt so weighed down she might as well have been wearing it.

What Sara really needed was time for her and Flissa to sit down and have a long talk. Flissa had sounded so sure that Katya was wrong about how the curse affected them as babies—maybe she could convince Sara too. But that would have to wait until after they got home, when Sara wasn't so busy constantly coming up with bad ideas that could get them all killed.

Galric held the mysterious scimisword out to Flissa, who looked at it like it was a very appealing poison.

"Take it," Galric said. "Whatever it is, you're great with it. And I bet we'll need it again."

Flissa stared at the blade, then nodded and took it by

its hilt. She raised it and let it settle into her hand, then touched its tip to the tiny velvet pouch on her hip. "Inside," she said, and the sword whooshed away.

"Now we just have to find our way out," Galric said.

Flissa frowned. "Weren't we going to take the—"

She turned, and Sara followed her gaze. Where there had once been a clear path through to the light on the other side of the Brambled Gates, now there was nothing but a tangled network of snaking branches that stretched all the way up. Sara could still see the light at the end where they wanted to go, but there was no longer a way to get there.

"Should we yell for Primka and Nitpick?" Sara asked.

Flissa shook her head. "They ran ahead. If they got out, they'd only risk getting hurt if they came back for us."

Sara shuddered, remembering the acid leaf. She would never want to put Primka or Nitpick in that kind of danger.

"They're small and they're smart," Galric said. "When we get through, we'll find them on the other side. Flissa, you think you can find a path?"

Sara smiled. She liked that Galric trusted her sister to guide them, and she could tell that Flissa liked it too.

"Follow my lead and stay close," she said. "Remember, even if something looks harmless, it probably isn't."

Flissa stood on a thick root, pulling apart a curtain of vines for them, when the first branch attacked. Sara saw it whip forward of its own volition, its sharp tip aimed right for Flissa's temple.

"Duck!" she cried, and Flissa didn't hesitate. She crouched down as the branch zipped past, exactly where her head would have been. Sara's heart thumped triple time, and she lunged to Flissa to make sure she was okay, but her boot caught on a root and she thunked to the ground.

Right in front of her, a thick, craggy branch snaked toward her face. Galric yanked her to her feet before it could attack. Clinging to Galric, Sara watched the branch slither past.

"Don't mess with us!" Flissa yelled to the forest. She was back on the log, brandishing the scimisword. Her face twisted with fury. She looked like the hero of a fantasy tale, and Sara's heart nearly burst with pride. "I have cut you down before, and I will do it again."

Still holding her sword high, Flissa turned to Galric and Sara. "I think it's safe to say two things. One, we know how the path went away. This forest is very much alive and moving, and two, it is very much unhappy with me for slicing into it. The good thing is, I'm sure it doesn't wish to be sliced again, so as long as we stay vigilant, we can get through. Sara, this way!"

Flissa again pulled back a curtain of vines, and when they started wrapping around her arms, Flissa merely flicked her wrist and the incredibly sharp sword sliced several of them away. The other vines released her immediately. "Come on."

But Sara shook her head. She didn't have a sword, or Flissa's coordination. One plant had already tried to eat her. If another attacked, Flissa might not get her away fast enough. "I can't."

"You *can,*" Flissa said, her eyes flashing. "You said it yourself, how many times are we going to be in the Brambled Gates? Now we're here, and we'll show them who's boss."

"I'll come with you," Galric said. "I'll be right next to you. Come on."

Galric held Sara's hand, and they climbed onto the log. It tried to roll under their feet as they walked, but Flissa touched the edge of her blade to it and it quickly stopped.

"Tell me," Galric said as they balanced down the log and through the curtain, Flissa right behind them, "how does the Princess Flissara thing work? Do you guys split up specific princess duties, or just kinda go with whoever's in the mood for what?"

Sara knew what he was doing. Just like when they were climbing out of the pit beneath the castle, he knew she'd be less nervous if he kept her distracted.

"This way," Flissa said. She climbed to the top of a tall pyramid of knotted roots and branches.

"What do you think?" Sara replied to Galric as she followed in Flissa's footsteps. "You've been with us for a while now. Think you know who you saw when?" A thin root wrapped itself around her ankle and she called, "Flissa!"

Flissa sliced her blade across the top branch. "Stop it!" she yelled to it. "You mess with them, you mess with me!"

The branch retracted. Sara took a deep, shaky breath.

Galric urged her forward as he answered. "Well, before yesterday, I only saw you do those speeches on the palace balcony. Or waving from some processional through town. I guess that could have been either one of you."

"Processionals are more Flissa's thing," Sara said, "especially if it's just riding through on her horse. I usually do speeches, though I always try to Flissara it up when I'm talking."

Galric laughed. "Flissara it up?"

"Well, yeah," Sara said. "Flissa's usually a little more formal than I am, and I like to say whatever pops into my head, so Flissara's kind of in the middle. It's the same reason Flissara trips sometimes, even when Flissa's playing her. It's on purpose."

They were at the top of the pyramid now, right next to Flissa. "And it's not easy," Flissa said. "I believe it's far simpler to tame a stallion than to realistically fall when you don't actually need to."

"I believe it," Galric said.

"I'm also the one who does fairs and festivals," Sara said. "I like hanging out with our people."

"It's hardly as if I *dislike* our people," Flissa said. "I just can't bear the gossip. It's awful in the towns, but even within the palace, it's bad. And Mitzi's the worst. Like I care the Duke of Rafleston said he wants to marry us one day."

Sara couldn't believe it—how had Flissa never told her this? "Mitzi told you that?!"

"Yes," Flissa said, starting down the other side of the pyramid. "Which is ridiculous because the duke is nineteen years old."

"And *gorgeous,"* Sara said, following her down. "I wonder if Mitzi let that slip to Princess Blakely. She'd lose her mind. *She* wants to marry Rafleston. Talks about it all the time."

"So, what," Galric said. "You like this guy or something?"

Sara followed Flissa to a large hollow stump—a single tunnel in a wall of tangled branches.

"I don't know about this." Flissa bit her lip. "It's the

clearest path through, but I don't like that it would surround us. It could be a trap . . . but it could also get us out faster than any other way . . . but if it's a trap that doesn't matter . . ."

Sara couldn't see Flissa's upper lip clearly in the dim forest light, but she knew it was damp with sweat. "The coin. You flip it. I don't want to lose it here."

Flissa nodded. She tugged out her locket, and in the split second her attention was elsewhere, a bullet of a spiny-thorned branch shot through the air. Sara screamed, and Flissa looked up and flicked her sword at lightning speed to deflect the barb.

"Nice try," she called to the forest, and tucked the locket back into her shirt. "Can't flip the coin. Let's find another way out, just to be safe."

They were very close to the edge of the forest now. Its light seeped through the branches. All Flissa had to do was find the right spot, and they'd be into the actual Twists. Even after the carnivorous, vindictive forest, the idea gave Sara a thrill.

"So, this Rafleston guy," Galric said. "You're, what, royally promised to him or something?"

"What?!" Sara said.

"Ew!" Flissa said, never taking her eyes off the forest around them. "What is wrong with you? Is that how you think royalty works?"

Galric blushed. "I don't know! How would I know?"

"He's just some duke," Sara said, "and no, we're not 'royally promised' to anyone. I mean, we're not even twelve yet. And we're pretending to be one person. Not even sure how that could work."

Flissa must have heard the edge to Sara's voice, because she glanced her way just long enough for a vine to take advantage and wrap around Flissa's ankle. She immediately sliced it with her scimisword and kept moving, and Sara moved to a less distracting topic.

"You didn't answer my question, though," she said to Galric. "Do you know who was who when you met us?"

"You were the one I met first," he said. "By the stables."

Sara's heart soared. She'd wanted him to get it right. She couldn't explain why, but it was really, really important to her that Galric knew her for *her*. But she had to know for sure if he did, so she played it coy. "You think?"

"Sure. You slammed right into me and fell."

"Oh," she said dully. Of course. The klutzy thing. That didn't even count. It was too easy.

"Plus we've already established that Flissa was the one who was supposed to tell me I was coming along to the Twists and didn't," Galric said pointedly.

"Please do not give me a hard time while I'm protecting you, Galric," Flissa called without turning around.

Sara had forgotten that they'd already established who was who. She was starting to regret this whole line of questioning—it was only making her feel bad.

"Never mind, then," she said, hoping her voice didn't sound as deflated to Galric as it did in her own ears. "It was a silly question."

"It was a good question! And even without that stuff I could answer it. I mean, yeah, the falling thing helps me know for sure and all, and Flissa'd have to be the one who rode up on Blusters—"

"Balustrade," Flissa corrected him.

"—but now that I know you, I could tell you apart more by the way you were, you know?"

Sara scrunched her face, but inwardly her heart skipped. "How was I?"

"I don't know, just—impressive, I guess. I mean, you seemed really interested in who I was and what I had to say. And you didn't even know me, except that my dad was the guy who cursed your mom. I mean, honestly? I thought the minute you figured out who I was you'd throw me to the Twists."

Sara giggled. "I would never throw you to the Twists."

"Actually," Flissa said. "We most certainly did. Here's our way through."

She pointed with her sword. It was a clear path out, canopied by curved branches—an archway leading them right where they wanted to go. "I don't know if this is a trap or the Brambled Gates are simply tired of defending themselves against us, but I can get us through either way. One of you on either side of me. We can do this."

They walked three across, and Flissa had her scimi-sword brandished the whole time, but the forest didn't make a move. Maybe the Brambled Gates figured that if anyone wanted to get *into* the Twists that badly, they should be allowed to do it.

The second before they took the last step out, Flissa froze. "The cloaks," she said. "There are Keepers in the Twists, remember? We need to put on the cloaks and wear the hoods. You first. I'll get mine when we're out and I can lower my sword."

Sara put her hand in her pouch. "Cloak!" she called, and grinned as it smacked into her grip. "It's dry. And warm, like it was out on the line."

"Good," Flissa said. "The rest of me is still soaked, so it'll be nice to have a dry cloak."

Flissa waited until Sara had slung it over her shoulders—backward, at first, but then she spun it around—and fastened it, then they all took deep breaths and prepared for their first step out of the Brambled Gates and into the Twists.

Chapter 12
Flissa

Flissa leaped out in a fighting stance, then gasped and winced in the harsh glare from the sun. She kept her scimisword brandished as she squinted and blinked, and gradually the world became clearer. She pivoted left and right, but didn't see any yellow-robed figures. Or anyone else, for that matter.

"Keep an eye out," she told Galric and Sara, who flanked her. With them on guard duty, Flissa returned the scimisword to her pouch, then called out her cloak and put it on. The combination of the hot day, her wet clothes, and the warm cloak made her feel like a human rain forest, but she supposed there was no way around it. Safety first.

With her eyes now fully adjusted, she glanced around and gaped in awe.

After the dim sameness of the forest, it was as if she had stepped out of a black-and-white world into one that was full color. Katya had told them to look for a marketplace, but there was nothing even remotely like that around. Instead she saw a wide vista of lush grasses, surrounded by mountains. Flissa wasn't positive, but she thought she saw little homes dotting the mountains too. A river flowed through everything, disappearing between mountains and out of Flissa's sight. But the most remarkable thing . . .

"The colors," Sara said breathlessly. "Are you looking at the colors?"

"They're incredible," Flissa said.

The sun was purple, and it sat in a lemon-yellow sky. The grass was orange. Not a burned, dried orange, but the orange of the fruit, vibrant and healthy. And while the water flowed blue, it was the most stunningly clean, clear blue Flissa had ever seen. She thirsted with the need to dive in and feel its refreshing chill drench her body. Only the boulders scattered about seemed like ones they'd find at home, but they were larger and in bulbous, rounded shapes that looked like fantastical creatures themselves.

"I thought the Twists were supposed to be horrible," Sara said. "This is . . . magical!"

"I think that's just it," Flissa said. "There's so much concentrated magic here, it affects everything. Whether the Keepers wanted to make the land strange and beautiful or not, that's what happened."

"Okay, but yes, listen to what you just said," Sara noted. "If magic was bad, lots of magic would make everything awful. But it didn't. It made it beautiful. Just on its own, that's what it did. So maybe that means magic is actually *good.* And good mages like Katya use it that way. But when bad mages use magic, they're using it wrong."

"Or maybe it just proves the *Keepers'* magic is good," Flissa said, "since their magic built this place."

"Magic might be good, but the Keepers aren't," Galric said firmly. "We should—"

Sara gasped and grabbed Flissa's arm. "Dragons! Oh my universe, Flissa, dragons, for-real dragons. Dragons!"

Flissa followed her gaze. Countless magical beasts—dragons, it seemed, though since she'd always assumed those were fiction she couldn't be sure—came around the side of one of the mountains and gathered alongside the river to drink. Some were the size of the entire palace, with tiny wings that had to be only for show. Others were as small as Primka, and fluttered around the larger beasts, landing on their backs and snouts and flittering in and out of the water. Still others flew on wings that sprouted from their shoulders, their bodies hanging large and limp below them, but when they landed, they ran nimbly on their two back legs, with their front hands poised in the air like a spaniel begging for a snack. And the colors—like everything else in the Twists, the colors on the animals spanned the entire rainbow.

"Remind me of the plant that ate me," Sara said, "because I really want to go pet them."

"No petting," Galric and Flissa said at the same time. But then they heard another voice.

"I don't even know about the plant and I don't want to," said Primka as they all looked up to see her flutter toward them. She held Nitpick by the scruff of his neck with her feet, but swooped low so she could drop the kitten into Galric's arms.

"Meow!" he said, and purred as Galric hugged him close.

"He won't admit it, but he was awfully frightened," Primka said. "I told him he shouldn't worry and of course you'd find a way to make it through, but you know how kittens are. There was just no comforting him."

Nitpick cocked his head questioningly. "Meow?"

Flissa laughed. She had no doubt it was Primka who'd been worried about them, and she was glad to be reunited with someone who could take charge again. Flissa was more than happy to give up that mantle.

"Katya said we have to get to the marketplace," Flissa said to Primka. "Do you know the way?"

"I do," she said. "I flew up high so I could see. There's a path on the other side of the river, and it gets small enough that we can cross. It happens to be far downstream from the dragons, so we can keep our distance, but—"

A low, impossibly loud rumble made them all look up. A mountain in the near distance shuddered, and as the rumble grew even louder, dust rose off it and hung in the air like a wispy cloud.

Flissa's instincts screamed danger. She knew they should run, but she couldn't tear her eyes away. The entire mountain was shaking wildly now . . . until suddenly its huge bulk *imploded into itself*, collapsing down to nothing but rolling dust.

Sara grabbed Flissa's arm. "Flissa," she said breathlessly. "That mountain . . . it had *homes* on it."

Flissa was too stunned to respond. She had been thinking the same thing. There were people on that mountain. And now it was dust.

Spreading dust. The cloud from the imploded mountain spread in a wide circle, moving toward the dragons. Flissa saw them snort and sniff and roar, then—

"Earthquake!" Galric cried.

Flissa felt it too. The ground shaking under their feet.

"It's not!" Sara cried. "It's the dragons!"

Spooked by the dust cloud, the sea of dragons had scattered in all directions, with the entire herd of two-footed beasts headed directly toward Flissa, Sara, Galric, Nitpick, and Primka. They moved blindingly fast, wings pointed behind them, green scales shining and red bellies flashing.

"They're coming this way!" Flissa wailed. "What do we do, Primka?"

"RUN!"

Primka took off, and Flissa grabbed Sara's hand to pull her along as fast as she could. "Galric!" she cried, but he already knew what she wanted.

"Got it!"

He tucked Nitpick into his shirt and grabbed Sara's other hand. Together they raced at top speed for all of two seconds before Sara screamed and reared back, pulling Flissa and Galric with her.

"No," she mewled. "I can't. Please don't make me."

Flissa stared ahead of them in complete disbelief.

All across the ground, as far as the eye could see, holes as round and wide as a dinner table opened in the ground. Like fish mouths, they circled open, then closed again, each time revealing an angry red abyss lined with sickly black dots. The holes popped up randomly, dozens at a time, like an endless array of diseased throats.

Flissa wheeled to look behind them, but the holes were there too, opening and closing. As she watched, one opened up beneath a dragon. It screamed as it fell, but the screams ended with a horrible swallow as the pit devoured its meal.

"No," Sara said, her lips white with fear. "No-no-no-no-no . . ."

Flissa herself couldn't make a sound. The dragons were getting close, with one so far ahead of the others Flissa could count its teeth when it opened its mouth to roar.

If they stayed still, they'd be dead. But if they ran into the minefield . . .

Just then, a flash of color caught Flissa's eye. When she looked down, she saw a circle of grass beneath them had changed from bright orange to carnation pink. Flissa's heart pounded.

"JUMP!" she screamed.

Galric and Sara listened. The three of them leaped away, and the circle opened into another giant maw . . . just as the lead dragon pounced hungrily on the spot and fell to his howling demise.

"The pink!" Flissa screamed, running full speed now, and pulling Sara and Galric with her. "The grass turns pink before the holes open! Stay away from the pink and we'll be okay!"

"Define 'okay,'" Galric said as he sidestepped away from a patch of pink grass, twirling Sara with him.

"Alive!" Flissa retorted.

"This way!" Primka cried, suddenly flapping above their heads. She pointed a wing to the nearest mountain. "I found a path up—you can get away from the dragons."

"Great!" Flissa yelled, tackling both Sara and Galric to the ground and rolling them away from another ravenous maw just as the orange grass turned pink. Galric got up immediately and helped her pull Sara to her feet.

"I don't like this place anymore, Flissa!" Sara whimpered. "I don't like it at all."

"Like it?!" Primka snapped. "It's a magical prison!

You think just because it looks pretty it's going to be nice?"

Sara didn't answer, but Flissa knew it was exactly what Sara had thought. Flissa had kind of thought so too, for a minute. Now she knew better.

"Single file!" she called to Galric and Sara. She saw a route to Primka's path, but gaping maws and pink circles lined it on both sides. Single file was the only way they'd make it.

"No!" Sara cried. "Don't let go of my hand!"

She sounded so scared it ripped Flissa's heart. "I have to! We have to move fast!"

"I'm right behind you, Sara," Flissa heard Galric cry. "Just run!"

Flissa sprinted for the bottom of the mountain path, and she heard Sara's and Galric's pounding feet behind her. Her breath tearing at her throat, she lunged up the path, then turned and offered her hand to Sara to help her up too. Galric was next . . . but the second his foot hit the ground for his last step, the grass turned pink beneath him.

"NO!" Flissa roared. She firmly pushed Sara aside and grabbed Galric's hand with her own, bracing herself on a rock with her other one. Her arm nearly popped out of its socket when the ground went out from under Galric, but he quickly braced his dangling feet on the mouth's edge, and propelled himself onto the path.

"Thanks," he panted breathlessly.

"We can't stop now," Sara said. "Look!"

She pointed, and Flissa followed her gaze. The dragons were still coming. Though many had fallen prey to the carnivorous ground, twenty were still running their way. Flissa saw their forked, barbed tongues and sharp fangs from which red foam bubbled and dripped. As Flissa watched in stunned awe, one of the dragons cocked back its head and spit toward her. Flissa jumped away a second before its red foam spittle hit the rock where Flissa had been leaning. It bubbled, hissed, and melted away.

"They spit acid foam!" Flissa called to Galric and Sara. "We have to climb the path—as high as we can!"

They started climbing, Galric and Flissa pulling Sara up between them. They made it as high as a single story before Flissa looked over her shoulder again to see the dragons still giving chase . . . but now they had unfurled their wings and were rising through the air. The dragons were far more agile on their muscular legs than their puny shoulder wings, but they were gaining altitude each second, and Flissa had no idea how far their poison could shoot.

"Sara? Galric?" she began, but Sara clearly heard the warning dread in her voice because she shook her head.

"I don't want to know," Sara said. "Just tell me what I have to do and how to get away."

"Up here!" Primka shouted, and they all looked up. Just a little higher and to the right, Primka fluttered outside a crevice. "It's a cave! We can take cover! Just *get* here!"

They changed their angle and climbed toward Primka's voice. Flissa heard a *SPLAT* and a *sizzle* and looked down. Another dragon had spit its acid venom against the wall beneath them, knocking away big chunks of rock. Any moment now the dragons would be close enough to easily hit them all.

In the blink of an eye, Flissa ran through her options.

Grab her sword? She couldn't possibly wield it while balancing on the steep rocks. Keep scrambling higher? They'd be out in the open for the next spit attack. Look for another weapon in her bag? She had no idea what was there, and nothing was popping into her head like before.

"The broken rocks!" Sara yelled. "Grab them, throw them! Primka, you too—help!"

That snapped Flissa out of it. "Yes! Great idea! You stay here, Sara."

Sara didn't fight her on that. She knew she'd be more of a danger to the group if she put herself at risk.

Flissa scrambled a little lower and grabbed a heavy chunk of loose rock. She hurled it at the nearest dragon with all her might and smacked it right between the eyes. It fell down, tumbling into three other dragons along the way. All four pinwheeled to the ground, but Flissa didn't watch to see what happened after. Sixteen more dragons still flapped their way toward them, spitting venom she dodged to avoid.

"Good shot," Galric said, and Flissa realized he was right there next to her, a heavy rock cocked in his hand. "Let's keep playing."

He hurled the rock hard, and it hit the next-closest dragon, knocking it out. That beast also took out another as it fell, and Galric grinned. "Only two points for me. I better catch up."

Flissa smiled, and together they grabbed rock after rock, always careful never to touch the ones that were red with venom, and hurled them down at the dragons. Then Primka soared past with an impossibly large boulder grasped between her tiny feet. "Incoming!" she shouted, and Flissa and Galric pressed themselves closer to the side of the mountain as Primka dropped the boulder, taking out five more.

"Down and to your left!" Sara shouted. "Two getting close!"

Galric and Flissa threw their rocks at the same time and knocked both dragons out.

Together, the two of them and Primka hurled and dropped rock after rock until all twenty dragons writhed and moaned at the bottom of the mountain. The beasts were down, but they were very much alive, and there was no telling when they'd perk up and charge again.

"Let's get to the cave," Galric said.

Flissa was happy for the direction. Together they scrambled up to get Sara; then all three of them maneuvered their way to the crevice Primka had found, and squeezed their way inside.

"Now what?" Sara asked, but Flissa put her hands to her lips. She had heard the dragons screeching. The ones who had been knocked out were starting to get up, and like the vines of the Brambled Gates, they were not happy. She wordlessly urged Sara as far back into the cave as they could go, and Galric and Primka joined them. Nitpick peeked out of Galric's shirt for just a second, then ducked back down again as the loudest dragon shriek yet echoed outside the cave. Flissa grabbed Sara's hand and saw her sister exchange a glance with Galric.

They all froze, not even breathing. Barely moving, though Flissa felt Sara tense up as the *FWOOF FWOOF FWOOF* of wings drew inexorably closer and closer.

Flissa shut her eyes against the sound and only listened as the wing beats passed their cave entrance, blowing in dust and fetid air that smelled like old meat.

She held back a sneeze.

The sound died away, and Flissa's body relaxed—until she heard a *thump*. She opened her eyes and saw the long scaly feet of the last dragon perch on the rocks just outside the crevice. Its legs and lower body filled the entrance. Then its long toothy beak lowered, and Flissa heard the hideous sound of poison-wet snuffles as it tried to sniff them out.

Could Flissa pull out her sword and lunge for it? It might spit acid venom and destroy her as it died, but at least she'd save Sara and the others. Then Sara could go on and save Mother.

The snuffling got louder, and Flissa moved her hand to her pouch.

Suddenly she jumped as a monstrous roar caromed through the cave—a deafening bellow unlike anything they'd heard before, followed by a river of fire that flowed past the cave opening and baked their skin.

Flissa smelled burned flesh, and for a second, she thought it was her own.

Then the flames outside their cave faded away, and Flissa heard only massive wing beats, then beautiful silence.

She was fine. Sara, Galric, Nitpick, Primka . . . they were all in one piece too. It seemed like they'd survived, but none of them trusted the silence. They waited, breathlessly hoping all would stay calm, until finally they all let out their breath in a giant whoosh and collapsed to the floor.

Chapter 13
Sara

Sara knew she shouldn't relax. Yes, they had shelter, and they had made it past the dragons, but they were in a cave high on a mountain. Sara had just seen an entire mountain—a mountain that looked like it was full of people who lived there—implode into dust.

She wasn't safe. She should have been as terrified as she'd been when she first saw all those horrible mouths in the ground, opening and closing. Instead, she felt more alive than she ever had in her life. They had escaped those mouths. And dragons. *Dragons!* And she hadn't gotten them in trouble like she had in the Brambled Gates. When no one else had known what to do, she'd come up with the plan to throw the newly broken rocks. And it had saved them. *She* had saved them. Sara took a deep breath and savored the moment.

When she felt like an eternity had passed with no signs of danger, Sara got up and tried to check out their surroundings. She almost immediately walked into a wall. The crevice of the cave opening wasn't big enough to let in much of the purple sunlight. Sara reached into her pouch. "I need light!"

She had no idea what she was looking for specifically. She knew she and Flissa hadn't packed anything that would help, but Katya seemed to have thought of things they hadn't, so it was certainly worth a try.

SMACK! Something large and round slapped into Sara's palm. She pulled it out. The thing was whitish in the cave's dim light, but it was just—

"A ball," Sara said aloud.

Primka flitted over and hovered in front of Sara. "It does seem that way," she admitted, "but you reached into a magic pouch and told it what you need. There has to be a reason this ball came to you."

Sara smiled. "It's magic." Then she frowned. "But I'm *not* magic. So how do I make it work?" Primka opened her mouth to answer, but Sara cut her off, excited. "No, I want to figure it out. Katya *knows* I'm not magic, so she wouldn't have put it in my pouch unless I could use it. And the only magic thing I know how to use now is the pouch, and that gives me what I want when I ask for it, so . . ."

Sara grinned. She'd figured it out. She cupped the ball in her palms and said, "Give us light!"

She squealed as the ball glowed blue. Bright enough that they could see, dim enough that it wouldn't shine too brightly and attract unwanted attention. "I did it! It works! We have a magic light!" She was so excited she tossed the ball into the air but completely missed when she tried to catch it. Flissa rolled across the floor and caught it seconds before it would have smashed to the ground.

"It's perfect," Flissa said. Then she scrunched her face. "Are you limping?"

"A little. I kinda twisted my ankle when we were running from the dragons." Sara blushed and felt silly admitting it. It was ridiculous that after all the running and climbing and stone throwing Flissa and Galric had done, *she* was the one who'd gotten injured. "It's not a big deal."

Sara took the light back and held it up to illuminate their little cave. "Hey, look at that," she said. There was an opening in the back, a space between two rocks that had been hidden in shadows. When she leaned into the space and held the blue orb toward it, she realized what she'd found.

"It's a tunnel," she said. "A long one. I think we should check it out."

"I don't think going into the mountains is a good idea," Flissa said. "Did you forget about the collapse?"

"I don't think going back outside is a good idea," Galric said from his spot against the cave wall. "Did you forget about the creature-digesting ground?"

"No, I did not," Flissa said pointedly. "I think the intelligent thing to do is figure out logically which path is the safest, then—"

Primka flittered over to Flissa and landed on her shoulder.

"Flissa," she said gently, "there is no safe path. We're in the Twists. It was created from magic. Its sole purpose is to punish dark mages and make sure they never come back to Kaloon. Anything can happen here, none of it good."

"*Some* of it good," Sara countered softly. "The land and

the dragons were all really pretty . . . until they tried to eat us."

"That's a pretty big 'until,'" Flissa said.

"Indeed," Primka agreed. "And the path I saw to the marketplace was filled with even worse. Fires, and tornadoes, and—"

"And that's why we should explore this tunnel!" Sara said. "It might bring us out somewhere with a better path to the marketplace and Dorinda."

"*Or*," Flissa countered, "it could bring us to a dead end. At least Primka got a look at what's along our path out there. So we can prepare."

"Prepare how?" Galric asked. "Things change out there. Whatever Primka saw, it won't last. It doesn't even matter. No offense, Primka."

"It's all right," Primka said. "You're correct."

"Yes, but we *have* to get to Dorinda in the marketplace," Flissa said. "If we don't . . ."

Flissa didn't have to finish the sentence. They all knew what would happen if they failed. But there was no way Sara wanted to go back the way they'd come. Sara couldn't explain it, but she knew—she knew in her bones that if they went back out there something horrible would happen, and they wouldn't succeed.

But without a logical way to explain that, how could she convince Flissa?

Then it hit her. "Let's flip the coin."

"Yes!" Flissa agreed. She eagerly pulled out her locket.

Sara smiled. She'd made up her mind that if she needed to, she'd lie for the second time. No matter what the coin said, she'd tell Flissa it wanted them to go down the tunnel.

Sara held out her hand for the coin, but Flissa shook her head. "I'll do it," she said. "I don't want it to get lost in the cave."

"Are you sure?" Sara asked, her heart beating faster. "I'll be careful."

"I have it, thank you. King, we go out the way we came; queen, we go down the tunnel." Flissa balanced the coin on her thumb, flicked it expertly into the air, where it spun around and around and around; then she snatched it and held it in her right fist. She smacked her right hand down on the back of her left, closing her eyes as she slowly lifted her right hand away—she didn't want to see the verdict until she was ready.

Sara, however, saw the coin the second Flissa's hand lifted. It was their dad's face. King. They go out the way they came. Sara's heart sank and she closed her eyes, devastated. She wished with all her heart the coin had come up the other way.

"Queen," Flissa said. "We take the tunnel."

Sara's eyes snapped open. "What?"

"Queen." Flissa held out her left hand. Sitting on the back of it was their mom's face, smiling on the back of the coin.

"Really?" Sara asked. "Did you . . . flip it or something?"

Flissa looked confused. "You mean after it landed? Of course not. Why would I ever do that? That takes away the whole point of having the coin." Then Flissa's eyes widened. "What are you saying?" she asked nervously. "You think the coin's wrong?"

"No-no-no!" Sara said quickly. "I see it now. Queen. Totally clear. Sorry, it was the blue light. I saw it weird for a second. The coin's right. The coin's always right. We take the tunnel. Come on, everybody."

As Sara led the way holding the blue-glowing orb, she couldn't stop thinking about the coin. *Did* she see it wrong? Had it been queen all along?

No. It wasn't. It wasn't the light, or her eyes playing tricks on her. The coin had come up king. But by the time Flissa looked at it, it was queen. And the coin hadn't moved. Neither one of them had touched it.

There was only one answer, and Sara didn't know if she loved it, or if it scared the living daylights out of her.

Magic.

The very sound of the word in her head thrilled her, but she wasn't sure what it actually meant. It's not like she flipped the coin on purpose, so it's not like she'd found a power she could harness again. It just happened. She wasn't even sure how she could come up with a way to test it, even though she'd love to.

She was so lost in her own thoughts, she didn't pay attention to the walk. She barely registered the drippy, moss-covered walls that pressed close around them, didn't listen to anyone talking or what they had to say. She just kept thinking about the coin, and how it flipped, and what it meant.

Then she realized it was cold. She wrapped her cloak more tightly around her.

THUD.

She turned around and saw Galric had toppled forward. He lay sprawled out on the ground. Sara knelt down next to him. "Are you okay?"

Her breath came out in white plumes. When did it get so cold?

Galric nodded, but it was more a violent tremble. "C-c-c-can't feel my feet. D-d-d-do you have any more cloaks in that bag?"

"I th-th-think we need more than cloaks," Flissa said through chattering teeth. "Look."

Hands shaking, Flissa pointed down the tunnel, back the way they'd come.

As Sara watched in horror, a wave of whiteness pushed its way through the tunnel. It moved slowly but inexorably, and everything in its path froze solid.

And it was heading their way.

"Flissa!" Primka squealed.

Primka plummeted, her wings at an odd angle to her body. Flissa dove and grabbed her a second before she'd have hit the floor.

Sara had never heard a chattering beak before. Primka's sounded like castanets, and she could barely get the words out between clacks. "My wings f-f-f-froze."

The chill tore into Sara's face. The wall of white was getting closer. She still held the blue orb in one hand, but she reached out the other to Galric. She wanted to pull him to his feet and run, but when he grasped her hand, she felt nothing. Her hand was a cup-shaped wax slab, not her own at all. Even when she concentrated and tried to grip him back, her freezing fingers wouldn't listen.

"I c-c-c-can't move, F-F-F-Flissa!" Sara cried. "I'm too f-f-f-freezing."

“We *have* to m-m-move,” Flissa said. “The w-w-w-wall of cold . . . it’s m-m-m-magic. If we don’t move before it reaches us, we’ll f-f-f-freeze like everything else.”

“We’re alr-r-r-eady freezing!” Galric retorted. And from the depths of his shirt, Nitpick mewled and agreed.

Flissa shook her head. She took a single determined stride, but her legs buckled under her and she dropped. Amazingly, she tucked Primka in the crook of one arm while catching her fall with the other. She wasn’t hurt, but she was next to Sara and Galric on the ground now, and Sara saw her sister’s lips were as purple as her eyes.

Sara looked down the tunnel. The wall of whiteness was only a few feet away. Even if they had their footing, they couldn’t outrun it now.

This was her fault. She’d done something to the coin. It didn’t want them to come this way, but she’d changed it somehow, and now they were going to freeze to death.

She cried, but the tears froze in the corners of her eyes.

The cold was seeping into her brain. She could feel her thoughts moving slower. They weren’t connecting. She squinted to try to see Flissa through their steamy breath.

The wall of whiteness was very close now. They only had moments.

“F-F-F-Flissa,” Sara whispered. She held out her hand to her sister, then looked at it curiously. The orb was still clutched there, even though Sara couldn’t feel it at all. It glowed blue. A pulsing blue. Almost lulling and mesmerizing, but something about it tugged at Sara. Like it was trying to get her attention.

She looked back at Flissa. Flissa was staring at the orb too. And even though the cold froze out all sound, all feeling, all hope . . . when Flissa's eyes flickered back to her, she felt a spark.

It might not work, but they both felt it. They had to try. As the wall of magical, freezing whiteness oozed toward them, they both muscled a numb, lifeless hand on top of the orb.

"Give us heat!" they cried in unison.

The orb glowed bright orange. Brighter and brighter until Sara had to squeeze her eyes shut against the glow.

She felt warm. Gorgeously warm, like she was lying out on the palace lawn in the middle of summer, the sun caressing her from head to toe. She melted into the sensation, felt the pleasant prickle of pins and needles as her fingers and toes came back to life. The heat was so delicious, she forgot everything else. She was alone, and she was warm, and she was glowing, and all she wanted to do was bask in the moment forever.

Then she remembered everything. Her eyes popped open.

She saw orange. No longer so bright she had to squint against it, but everything around her was tinted orange. Even Primka's yellow feathers glinted orange-gold as she flitted around in a small circle.

"Primka!" Sara cried. "You're flying!"

"I'm not frozen anymore!" Primka cried happily. "You saved us!"

Sara looked at Flissa, who was on her feet, turning in slow circles as if she couldn't believe what she was seeing. Sara was so happy, she jumped up and threw her arms around her sister. "We did it!"

"*Katya* did it," Flissa corrected her. "She packed that

magic ball. We're just lucky we figured out how to use it in time."

Sara scrunched her eyebrows. They *were* lucky, she supposed, but it felt like more than that. Putting their hands on that ball at the exact same time, saying the same thing in perfect unison . . . it felt like magic. More than just Katya's magic. It felt like maybe she and Flissa had something to do with it too.

Of course, her brain had been practically frozen solid at the time, so maybe what she'd felt didn't matter all that much. She should probably just listen to Flissa.

Suddenly she frowned. "Where's the orb?"

"We're in it," Galric said behind her.

Sara wheeled around and laughed. He was back on his feet, but Nitpick was perched right on the top of his head. The kitten had reared back on his hind legs, and batted at something just slightly too high to reach—the edge of a spherical, glowing orange wall. It was transparent, and now that Sara looked, she could see through it to the long tunnel stretching behind and ahead of them, completely frozen solid.

"The magic freeze thing came right over us," Galric said, answering her unasked question. "It froze everything. But we were okay 'cause we're in the ball."

Sara looked harder at the icescape just outside the sphere. "So . . . we're stuck here," she said.

Galric grinned. "We're not. It moves with us."

He strode to the edge of the sphere and kept going like he'd walk right through it, but just before he'd hit the edge, the entire sphere turned to give him more room.

"I made a toy like this for a mouse once. So I could

run around and play with him outside and he wouldn't get hurt. He was a cute little guy, gray and fluffy. That's what I named him. Fluffy."

The name was almost as adorable as the way Galric lit up when he told the story. "Awww," Sara cooed, but Nitpick wasn't as amused. He rowred and swatted Galric on the head.

"Ow! Claws!" Galric complained. "And don't worry. I didn't love him as much as I love you."

He pulled Nitpick off his head and cuddled the kitten in his arms.

"Charming story," Primka said drily. "Now shall we find a way out? We still have much to accomplish."

Galric blushed, and Sara bit her cheeks so she wouldn't laugh.

"Let's keep going this way," she suggested. It felt weird to stride toward the orange wall. She couldn't help but wince as she got closer, positive she'd either slam right into it or walk through the transparent glow and into the frigid tunnel. But just like it did for Galric, the ball rolled forward for her, and she led the group farther into the unknown.

Chapter 14
Flissa

Flissa wasn't sure what was worse: that they were walking inside a magical ball, in the middle of a magically frozen tunnel, deep inside a mountain very similar to the one she saw implode when they first arrived in the Twists . . . or that thanks to Galric's story, she currently felt like a mouse.

They'd been walking inside the ball for . . . honestly, she'd long since lost track of time, but far too long. Long enough that she wondered if the tunnel would ever end, or if they'd just reach a solid block of ice and have to walk all the way back to the cave where they'd started.

Flissa shook the thought from her head. The coin had said they should leave that cave and take this tunnel. There had to be a reason.

An odd thumping sound got her attention. It was Sara. She'd been limping since they'd first arrived in the cave, but now it was far more pronounced. Sara leaned heavily to the right, trying to take the weight off her injured left ankle.

Flissa quickly slipped under Sara's left arm to steady her. "Your limp is worse. Does it hurt?"

Sara nodded, and Flissa saw spots of red high on her

sister's cheeks. Clearly, her ankle hurt more than she wanted to say.

"We should stop and rest," Flissa said. "We just have to find a good spot."

"What about right here?" Galric asked. "We're in a ball. We're good."

"Uh-huh," Flissa retorted. "And what happens if there's limits to the magic Katya put in the ball? What if it runs out and pops?"

Flissa saw Galric's eyes take in the frozen walls all around them. He paled. "We find a good spot, then," he said. "Good plan."

They kept walking, and Sara leaned even more heavily on Flissa's shoulders. Galric stepped to Sara's other side and helped her too, and Nitpick climbed out of Galric's shirt to curl comfortingly on Sara's shoulder. Primka was worried too, Flissa could tell. She didn't say anything, but she fluttered just above Sara's head making nervous clucking sounds.

Despite what Flissa had said about the ball running out of magic, if they didn't find another option soon, they'd have to stop where they were and risk it.

"Oh!" Primka cried. "I see something! I do! Another tunnel, up ahead on the right."

Primka had far better eyes than her, but after what seemed like an eternity, Flissa saw it too—a large, triangular gash in the tunnel wall, which opened to another craggy tunnel. When they got close, Flissa peeked inside. Her heart quickened.

"It's not frozen in there! The magic—it only went down the one tunnel. We'll be safe!"

In a split second, every magical horror they'd already witnessed flashed through her mind.

"Safe . . . ish," she corrected herself.

They turned down the new tunnel, and the orange ball rolled with them. Through its transparent glow, everything changed. Instead of a frozen white landscape, the rocky walls seemed to glow with bright purple light.

"Sunlight," Sara said. "It's purple sunlight."

They moved faster, despite Sara's injury, until the tunnel opened into a massive cavern, with walls that stretched up high and curved toward each other but didn't meet, leaving the top open to the sky and the purple sun. Flissa felt woozy, and she flapped her cloak away from her body. The combination of the hot sun and the hotter orange ball made it almost impossible to breathe.

"How do we get out of this?" she asked.

Sara threw back her head. "No more heat!" she cried.

In an instant, the ball around them collapsed into itself, until it was just a clear ball again, sitting in Sara's palm. She held it to the mouth of her pouch. "Inside," she said. It whooshed back in.

"I could get used to this magic thing," Sara said with a grin.

Flissa rolled her eyes. The sooner they accomplished their mission and got *away* from magic, the happier she'd be.

With the orange ball out of the way, Flissa could see the cavern more clearly. The walls were striated with green, purple, and yellow bands of rock, and several smaller passageways branched in every direction from what was clearly a main atrium. None of the other passageways showed any signs of ice. If there were magic traps in them, Flissa imagined they were different from the one they'd left behind.

"I'll pick where we go next," Sara said. She limped farther into the giant room, but almost immediately tripped on a divot and turned her left ankle—the same one she'd already hurt. She sucked in her breath, and instantly Flissa and Galric were by her side, holding her up.

"We're not going *anywhere* next," Flissa said. "Not yet. We said you're resting a little, remember?"

"Yeah," Sara said. She put her foot down and winced. "I mean, I remember *now*."

"It's the only choice," Primka said, flittering in Sara's face. "And to be honest, it's probably good for all of us. We've been out here awhile, and we still have a long journey ahead. It's wise to rest and eat a little something."

Flissa hadn't even thought about food until Primka mentioned it, but now she was ravenous. "Good idea," she said, and for the millionth time, she was grateful that Primka had come along. She and Galric walked Sara to the nearest wall and leaned her up against it. Flissa's heart hurt as she watched Sara slide painfully to the ground, but then she realized something so obvious she could have smacked herself in the head.

"Of course!" she blurted, then reached a hand into her own velvet bag. "I need medicine for a twisted ankle!"

SMACK! She felt something hit her palm. When she pulled it out, she gripped a small cork-stoppered glass jar, filled with some kind of paste.

"Brilliant, Flissa!" Primka crowed. "Of course Katya would pack first aid. She's your nurse!"

Flissa beamed proudly until she pulled the stopper out of the jar. The paste smelled like a combination of menthol and a privy chamber. The odor smacked them in their faces, and they all started coughing.

"Is she trying to heal us, or torture us?" Sara asked.

"It is pungent," Flissa admitted, "but if Katya gave it to us, I'm sure it's only because it works."

Flissa pulled off her sister's boot and rolled up her pants, then took large fingerfuls of the horrible-smelling paste and rubbed it all over her ankle. Flissa used very little pressure, but the pain still brought tears to Sara's eyes. It was awful to see. By the time Flissa finished, even Galric, Primka, and Nitpick were staring at Sara with big sad eyes.

"Don't look so tragic!" Sara laughed. "I'm fine! Let's eat. We'll have a cave picnic!"

Flissa thought "picnic" was an awfully frivolous way to describe what they were doing, but she wasn't going to complain. Together, the two of them reached into their pouches and called out all of Mitzi's delicacies: tiny sandwiches, vegetables carved to look like flowers, and the mini tea cakes and scones in flavors no one else would dare try, like lavender and honey. Plus the butter, jams, and other spreads. And while none of that would do for Nitpick, Katya had of course seen to his well-being—Flissa found some corked glass jars of minced meat just for him. Flissa took off her cloak and set all the food on top of it, and the whole room seemed to rumble with the sound of their growling stomachs.

Sara laughed. "We must be seriously hungry to want to eat with this paste smell around."

"Starving," Galric confirmed. He dove in and started chowing down. The rest of them unabashedly did the same.

Sara raised a tea cake up high. "To Mitzi!" she said. "For making the most incredible food in the entire universe."

They all echoed the toast—Nitpick with a meow—and ate . . . well . . . like royalty. For the briefest of moments, Flissa almost forgot where they were and what they were doing. Much as she hated to admit it, it felt like a picnic. They all chatted as they ate, but not about their mission. Galric told ridiculous stories that couldn't possibly be true—stories about Balustrade and how unsophisticated he acted when he and Galric were alone. Primka talked about how hard it was to get Flissa to learn to speak when the twins were little, because Sara liked talking for both of them. And Flissa and Sara each revealed their favorite hidden spots in the castle. Then Sara decided the feast should be a celebration of their progress thus far, and everyone but Nitpick touched tea cakes in a toast. Nitpick couldn't be left out, of course, so Galric offered him the frosting off one of the cakes. Nitpick took one sniff, then arched his back, hissed as if the tea cake were attacking him, then batted the cake right out of Galric's hands. They all laughed; clearly Mitzi's frosting was no match for Katya's minced meat. They uncorked another jar and let him eat his fill.

Flissa suddenly couldn't help herself. She yawned so loud and long she sounded like a lowing cow. It was mortifying! She turned bright red and smacked both hands over her mouth. The whole thing made Sara laugh so hard she snorted the juice she was drinking out of her nose.

"*Manners*, Sara!" Primka scolded.

"Flissa started it!"

"I did," Flissa admitted with a smile. "And I'm sorry. I'm just so . . . *exhausted* all of a sudden."

"It's catching," Sara said through a yawn, but Flissa barely heard her. She was even *more* tired now. It was as if she could feel the energy draining out of her—the opposite feeling from when she'd eaten Katya's puffy gingersnap. Her eyelids were lead weights.

"I apologize," Flissa said. "I honestly don't think I can keep my eyes open."

"Strange," Primka agreed, stifling a yawn of her own. "I'm also rather spent."

Nitpick looked at them all curiously. He meowed several times and batted Sara with a paw.

"I'll get you more food later," Sara said, her words slurred. "After we nap."

"Mm-hm," Flissa agreed, her words equally slurred. "Nap. Just a short one."

"Perhaps someone should stay on guard, though," Primka suggested as she lit down to the ground and fluffed the pillowy feathers under her wing. "Galric?"

Galric snorted and jumped at the sound of his name. "Huh-wha-huh? I'm up. I'm awake."

Sara and Flissa both laughed, but it sounded like they were underwater. "I bet we can all sleep," Sara said. "Just for a little. It's safe. Katya even said we might nap, right? Look."

As proof, she reached into her pouch and asked for two bedrolls; then Flissa followed her lead and asked for the one in her pouch as well. Flissa tried to arrange the three bedrolls neatly next to one another, but just touching their puffy softness was too tempting. She closed her eyes and lay down. She heard Sara and Galric collapse down next to her, and she thought she heard Nitpick wail—was he pawing at her arm?—then she fell fast asleep.

She did wake up at one point, or at least she thought perhaps she did. Her eyes fluttered open, but they couldn't stay that way. They were too heavy, and her whole body felt thick and drained. She propped up the littlest bit to see if anyone else was awake, but it was hard to tell. Everything looked blurry. And wavy, like she was underwater.

She let her head thump back down on her pillow. The only person in view was Galric, just a couple feet away. He looked blurry, but he also looked . . . misty. Flissa squinted, and as Galric breathed out, she saw a dark green mist flow out of his mouth and cover his body. A mist like the one she saw over her mother after she was cursed. It was strange, and Flissa knew she should be alarmed, or at least look more closely, but her body wouldn't listen. That was fine. Flissa was obviously dreaming. And she liked the dream. The mist was beautiful, really, coming out of Galric in long tendrils with each loud snore. Like ocean waves. Flissa watched it ebb and flow, in and out of Galric's body, waves and waves of misty green . . . until her eyelids thumped down again, whisking her off to yet another dream.

The next thing Flissa heard was gruff laughter, and it did *not* sound like something out of a dream. Her eyes snapped open, but the only thing she saw was a giant thick-soled black boot with silver rivets right in front of her face. She sat up with a gasp, only to find a wooden spear with a razor-sharp metal tip pointed at her face. Black Boot was holding it. In addition to the boots, he wore a rough-hewn tunic and short pants tattered enough to reveal the enormous muscles on his arms and legs. His black hair was scraggly and hung down to his shoulders, and he smiled at Flissa with several silver teeth.

"'Mornin'," he said.

Flissa could have disarmed him. She knew the exact moves she would use. She would lean back on her arms and leg-swipe the spear out of his grip, then bound upright and grab the spear herself. She would have it pointed at his throat before he even knew what was happening.

But Black Boot was not alone. Flissa darted her eyes around and saw an equally burly, equally scruffy, equally . . . *everything* man, except this one wore a black leather eye patch.

Twins. Identical twins. They had to be. Eye Patch even held a spear identical to Black Boot's, but his was pointed at Galric's heart. If Flissa made a move, Eye Patch could stab Galric immediately, and there would be nothing she could do about it.

Eye Patch moved his spear and gently scraped the tip of it against Galric's cheek. "Wakey-wakey."

Galric was still half-asleep. He tried to roll over and swat what he probably thought was an insect, or just part of a dream. If Eye Patch moved the spear away, that would be fine, but if he didn't . . .

Flissa's heart thudded. She wanted to say something to wake him, to warn him, but what if that was the thing that made Eye Patch so upset he attacked? She bit her lip and let out a mewl smaller than any of Nitpick's.

Eye Patch did move the spear, and Galric didn't get cut as he stretched and smacked his lips. But then he opened his eyes, and Eye Patch grinned down at him. Unlike his twin, his teeth were gold. "Hiya."

Galric screamed and scooted back against the wall, as far away from the spear as he could get. His shriek woke Sara and Primka, but the minute they opened their eyes, two other people stepped forward. These weren't twins. One was younger than the men but tall—a head taller than Galric—with long tangles of dark hair and a ring through her nose. The other guard looked like a feral girl—maybe no older than Flissa. She dressed in a patchwork of leather scraps and skins with fingerless gloves, and her piercing blue eyes glinted ferociously. Her dirt-streaked white-blond hair was shaved in intricate patterns except for a single high ponytail at the back of her head. One look and Flissa knew to take both of them very seriously—especially since they both held short thick daggers with serrated blades with the easy confidence of people who knew how to use them.

In one swift motion, Nose Ring knelt down by Sara, while Ponytail crouched next to Primka. They both pointed their daggers at their victims' throats.

"What's going on?" Sara cried, curling away. "Fl—"

"I'm right here," Flissa said quickly, before Sara blurted out her real name. "Everything's going to be okay."

Crackling laughter echoed through the atrium. "You really think so? That's sweet. Sweet . . . but very, very wrong."

Chapter 15
Sara

Sara pushed her body back closer to the stone wall—anything to get away from the blade that Nose Ring flicked toward her. The throaty voice that had echoed through the atrium now filled it again. "You picked the wrong place to nap, my sweet morsels."

Sara heard nothing, but she felt something moving closer. Something large, with musky breath that sucked the air out of the room.

Then she appeared: a lioness, sleek and sinewy and silent on her paws. Her flaming yellow eyes danced over Sara and her friends as she paced in front of them, licking her fangs.

Sara couldn't breathe. Her pulse thudded in her ears, and she had to fight not to pass out. She focused on the sharp edge of the dagger in her face and forced herself to stay alert.

"Now let's see what we have," the lioness said, pacing in front of the group. Her eyes rested on each of them in turn, then narrowed. "Four of you. Five, if you count the puny excuse for a feline."

There was something terrible in the way the lioness spat the words, and Sara heard the terror in Galric's voice as he cried out. "Nitpick! Where is he? What did you do to him?!"

Galric leaned forward to try to see for himself, but Eye Patch waved him back with his spear, nearly taking out Galric's eye.

"You'll want to stay calmer around me and my pride," the lioness purred. "Bad things happen to those who act rashly. The cat is fine."

The lioness waved a massive paw. A small cage slid out of the shadows, blue sparks dancing around it. Nitpick was crammed inside. He had a collar around his neck, and a short leash that tied him to the top of his thick-barred prison, so he couldn't lie down even if he wanted to. His tiny mouth was muzzled so he couldn't meow.

"Those blue sparks . . ." Flissa said, gaping at the lioness. "You just cast magic! Animals can't do that!"

For a second Sara thought Flissa had lost her mind. Weren't they traveling with two magical animals? But then she realized neither Primka nor Nitpick had ever *cast* any magic, and they certainly didn't have a magical signature. Sara had never thought about it before, but Flissa must have known it from her books.

The lioness turned slowly to Flissa. She smiled. "Then I suppose I'm no ordinary animal. All the more reason for you to fear me."

"We're afraid, okay?" Galric said, scurrying farther away from the spear pointed at his heart. "Just let Nitpick out of there. He's only a kitten."

In a single motion, the lioness pounced to Galric. She

pushed his guard out of the way and swatted Galric down, placing her paws on his chest as she leered into his face. "I was a kitten once too, and I did *not* answer to humans or jump around and meow trying to wake them up and protect them from great cats like myself, Raya the Lioness."

Raya sat back, but her eyes still bored into Galric's.

"The kitten is where he deserves to be," she said. "Be glad he's alive at all. As for the rest of you . . ." Raya padded away from Galric now, and Eye Patch stepped immediately back into place with his spear. "I'd like answers. There are five of you. Am I to assume you've been very lucky, or have you found a way to avoid the Rule of Three?"

Sara shivered, thinking about the carnivorous plant, the mouths in the ground, and the moving wall of ice.

"We haven't been very lucky," she said, looking down at her lap rather than face Raya's fiery eyes.

"What's the Rule of Three?" Flissa asked.

Raya smiled slowly, revealing her deadly incisors. "If you don't know, you *are* lucky. Lucky to be alive. Conspiring isn't allowed in the Twists. The Rule of Three says only three creatures can be together at a time. If more congregate, the Twists sense it and attack."

Sara felt her jaw drop open. Everything they'd experienced in the Twists so far had nothing to do with the coin or even their choices. The actual *land* had been trying to kill them.

"What you're saying doesn't make sense," Flissa said, her voice logical and uncowed. "There are five of you too. Shouldn't the Rule of Three make the Twists attack you all the time?"

"Yeah," Galric agreed, "and there's way more than

three of us in here now. Shouldn't the whole room collapse or something?"

Sara saw his eyes dart around nervously, as if by saying it, he might make it actually happen.

"In theory, yes," Raya said. "But we work for a supremely powerful mage. His magic counteracts the Rule of Three. It removes it from us, removes it from anyone with us as long as they're in our presence, and removes it from anyplace we wish to claim. Like this, our lair. So tell me . . ."

Sara tensed as the lion strode toward her and Flissa.

"You're clearly twins. You're reasonably well-groomed and didn't know the Rule of Three, which means you were only recently exiled . . . and yet you're nearly grown. How did that happen? How did you get to be so old before the Keepers found you? Were you born into the Underground? Maybe friends in high places?"

The lioness locked eyes with Sara, as if knowing she was the one who might break. Sara shivered inside, but she could feel Flissa's intense gaze begging her to stay strong, and Sara understood. She could only imagine what Raya might do if she knew her prisoners were actually Kaloon's undercover twin princesses.

They needed a good story.

Luckily, Sara loved good stories.

She gulped down her fear. She even let out a confident laugh.

"If we had friends in high places, we'd still be in Kaloon," Sara said. "We just had *regular* friends. At least, we thought we did. Right up until they turned us in. Then the Keepers came. Grabbed us and our brother. We didn't even have time to run and hide."

"I see," Raya said. "And they grabbed your pets too? Not so wise on your part, getting a black kitten when you're already twins. You were asking for trouble."

"I got the kitten," Galric offered. "And yeah, probably not the best idea."

Raya strode closer to Primka. "And this is your songbird?"

She took a deep sniff of Primka's head.

"Rude!" Primka snapped. "I don't care who or *what* you are, I won't have some *cat* sticking her nose in my feathers!"

Raya's chuckle was low and terrifying. "A *magical* bird," she cooed. "You might prove useful, then. Perhaps I won't eat you."

"*Eat* me?!" Primka hollered. She tried to fly at Raya's face, but a close swipe from Ponytail's dagger made her settle back down.

The guard's move was so swift and sudden, it jarred Sara as much as it did Primka. All four of Raya's guards had remained remarkably still during the conversation, their weapons aimed at their captives as they waited for any movement or command. It was the kind of trained obedience Sara was used to seeing among her father's guards, and for a moment, she wondered how Raya had won their loyalty.

Raya flicked her ears at Primka, annoyed. "I said I *won't* eat you," she snapped. "What I *will* do is take you to Kravein. He rewards us nicely for newcomers like you."

"Who's Kravein?" Flissa asked.

Raya smiled and stretched, baring all four sets of claws. "An old friend. And our employer. *And* the strongest and most powerful mage in the Twists. It was his direct ancestor Maldevon who was framed for the Dark Magic Uprising."

Flissa frowned and shook her head. "Framed? No. That's not true. Maldevon *did* start the Dark Magic Uprising. He gained King Lamar's trust; then he and his followers turned *against* King Lamar and slaughtered most of the royal family, as well as innocent people in the palace. He would have done worse, but Grosselor and his band of friends—all strong, ethical mages—risked their lives for what was right. They rose up and fought off Maldevon and his people, then started the Keepers of the Light for Kaloon's continued protection. It's the only reason Kaloon still exists and wasn't completely overrun by dark magic. Every Kaloonian knows that."

Sara had heard Flissa's lecture before. It was the basic history of Kaloon that every student was supposed to be able to recite by memory, exactly like she just had. But even though Flissa was looking right at Raya as she spoke, it was as if she didn't notice the effect her words were having. With each sentence, Raya's shoulders tensed, until her entire body was poised to pounce. She lunged, stopping just short of Flissa.

"Fool!" Raya snarled.

Flissa paled. She shrank back as Raya leaned even closer, fangs bared.

"You're a parrot," the lioness said, enunciating the word and making spittle fly in Flissa's face. "Everyone in Kaloon says the exact same thing, but they're all wrong. Grosselor's lying. And the only reason he gets away with it is that everyone else who was there mysteriously died. All of Grosselor's own mages *and* all those innocents of which you speak."

Astoundingly, Flissa met Raya's eyes and looked at her stubbornly. "He's the only one alive because his magic's the strongest."

Sara wanted to grab her sister, but the glint of Nose Ring's dagger stopped her. Instead she said softly, "Please stop talking, Flissa. Just let it go."

Both Flissa and Raya ignored her. "*Grosselor* says his magic is the strongest," Raya said. "*I* say maybe so . . . but only because he makes sure no one stronger stays alive."

"No one except the Shadows," murmured Ponytail, the girl watching Primka.

Raya wheeled on her and snapped her tail. "The Shadows are a *lie*!" she roared.

It was a big reaction, and as much as Sara wanted Flissa to stop talking for her own good, she also kind of hoped her sister would ask what the Shadows were and why they got Raya so upset.

But the lioness didn't give her the chance. She whipped her head back to Flissa and growled into her face. "Grosselor is a liar. Didn't you ever wonder how he showed up at *just* the right time the night of the Dark Magic Uprising? Soon enough to spare the king and one heir, late enough for the king to lose the rest of his family and be a broken man?"

"It wasn't coincidence," Flissa said. "Grosselor woke in the night with a magical warning in his head. He rallied his family and followers who lived peacefully with him on a compound and . . ."

Flissa's voice trailed off, and Sara thought she knew why. Grosselor's story was one they'd been told since birth.

They'd recited it out loud for Primka in history lessons for years. The whole kingdom recounted the story on Turn to the Light Day, the anniversary of his heroism. Kaloonian kids came to the palace to reenact the event in plays. It was basic historical fact.

But hearing Flissa say it now . . .

Sara didn't know if it was the story itself, or the look on the scornful lion's face, but it all sounded suddenly hollow and fake.

Raya eased back on her haunches.

"There *was* no magical warning," she said. "Grosselor wanted to take over Kaloon, but he couldn't because the kingdom was filled with mages who would fight him off. When King Lamar became close with Maldevon and brought him to live in the castle, Grosselor saw his chance. Maldevon didn't do anything that night. He didn't *have* followers. He was asleep in bed. *Grosselor* was the one with the followers. They used magic to get into the castle, and the first thing they did was take out Maldevon."

"But—" Flissa objected.

"You're going to say Maldevon got captured and sent to the Twists. Don't. It's a lie. They took him out." Raya bared her teeth. "Then Grosselor and the rest of his friends showed up at just the right time because they'd set the whole thing up. They 'saved' King Lamar and Prince Regland, and King Lamar was so grateful and such a wreck from losing his family, he didn't think twice about signing over Kaloon to the Keepers of the Light."

"With the Magic Eradication Act," Flissa murmured.

Raya nodded her large feline head. "Yes. The act that lets Grosselor banish or destroy anyone who threatens him—anyone who even *might* threaten him, including regular Kaloonians who happen to be born with a possible sign of magic—so he can rule the kingdom with impunity."

Flissa looked pale. Sara knew her sister had always trusted the Keepers, but if what Raya said was true, then everything Flissa had ever believed had been a lie. Even their lives as Princess Flissara—if Raya was right, the charade wasn't for Kaloon's security at all; it was just bending to Grosselor and helping him keep control.

Sara believed the lion. She wished she could ask Flissa if she felt the same way.

Flissa swallowed hard. "Why are you telling us all this?" she asked Raya.

"To give you some perspective." Raya calmly licked her front paw. "When I take you to Kravein, he will test you in truly terrible ways to see if you have magical abilities. No matter how bad it gets, remember: It's better than being in Kaloon."

Raya rose back onto all fours. "Now let's go."

She waved a paw, and Sara looked down at herself, alarmed. She was covered in blue sparks. Before she could react, she was tugged to her feet, pulled by some kind of invisible magical rope attached to her chest. Her arms were welded to her sides.

"My wings!" Primka wailed as blue sparks danced over her tiny body. "I can't move my wings! You won't get away with this, you . . . you . . ."

Raya growled and more sparks bounced over Primka's beak. When they disappeared, Primka could only moan in wordless frustration. Her beak had been magically sealed shut.

The Ponytail guard—the youngest one—scooped up Primka and grabbed Nitpick's cage with her other hand.

"Did Kravein give you this power?" Flissa asked, and Sara was amazed that her sister was somehow more fascinated than frightened by what was happening. "From everything I've read, animals—even magical ones—can't cast spells. You said Kravein was powerful. Did he—"

"Enough!" snapped Raya. "Story time's over. The next one of you who talks will be my evening snack."

The blue sparkles crackled over Sara again, and she felt her body grow even more rigid. Now her neck wouldn't move, so she couldn't look at anyone else. She could only stand, straight up, shoulders back, arms plastered down, all the while feeling like a giant suction cup was attached to her chest, pulling her and keeping her on her feet.

Thankfully, her eyes could still move. She shifted them all the way to one side and could just make out Flissa and Galric. They both looked like dolls brought to life, hauled to their feet against their will, stiff and unnatural. Their guards still stood over them, their blades tauntingly close to Galric's and Flissa's throats.

Sara ached to call out, but she wouldn't dare. She'd only use her voice if she needed it. She didn't want it magically taken away.

"Move!" Raya cried, then bounded down one of the tunnels branching out of the room.

More sparks. Then Sara's body spun around jerkily and followed the lion, though Raya was already so far ahead she couldn't see her. Sara's legs spasmed down the damp, dark cave tunnel, as if maneuvered by a clumsy puppeteer. Now no matter how hard she tried, she couldn't see Flissa, couldn't see Galric, couldn't see Nitpick or Primka. She could only imagine they were part of the sounds behind her, an echoing cacophony of shuffling, dripping, stomping, breathing, and crunching.

Even her heart was beyond her control. It thudded in her chest, so hard she couldn't breathe without gasping, and tears pooled in her eyes.

For the first time since they started their adventure, Sara was afraid they'd never make it home.

Chapter 16
Flissa

It was the strangest feeling, Flissa thought as she moved down the tunnel. She was under magical control, that was certain. She stood uncomfortably upright, like a parody of good posture. She couldn't move her arms or neck, and her legs were walking without her telling them where to go. Yet at the same time, she wasn't totally helpless. It was as if the magic told her body where to go, but she was still helping it obey. She was fairly certain that if she refused to move, the magic wouldn't be enough to keep her going and she'd collapse on the floor.

Doubtless that's why Raya kept her squad of armed guards and why Black Boot walked directly behind her and to one side. If Flissa tried to fight the magic, he'd be right there to take over.

The smart thing to do, Flissa decided, was to use this time when her body was not entirely her own to come up with some kind of plan. Yes, things looked dire, but now they'd spent enough time with Raya and her gang that she could evaluate their weaknesses and come up with some ways to get free. Then, when she and Sara could talk again, Sara would help her figure out which idea was best, and they could get back to finding the marketplace and Dorinda, who would lead them to Gilward.

She *wanted* to do that, but her head was too full of everything Raya had said about Maldevon, and Grosselor, and the Keepers. Was it even possible that the lion was right? Was Grosselor behind the Dark Magic Uprising? Was he behind this second uprising and what happened to her mother?

No. Impossible. Yes, it's true that only Grosselor was still around from that time, but plenty of Keepers were almost that old. Like Rouen, and Quendrick, and Bartlos, and Tzaz. Flissa had heard their stories. They were just little children when the Dark Magic Uprising happened, but they were alive. If the Keepers were based on a lie, they would know about it . . . wouldn't they?

Of course they would. And it was insanity to think the most important law in Kaloon, the Magic Eradication Act—the entire reason why she and Sara had become one person, and those like Primka and Katya had to live in secret—was based on anything except the best interests of Kaloon and all who lived there.

And who was Flissa going to believe? Her tutor and a lifetime of history lessons, or a big magical cat whose best friend was a dark mage in the Twists? An impossible cat with the powers of a mage, something Flissa had never heard of before . . .

She changed her mind about using this time to think. Better *not* to think. Better to focus on Sara and make sure she was okay.

Sara and her guard, Nose Ring, walked a few feet

ahead of Flissa. She wasn't limping anymore; Katya's cream had done its job. But the ground was unsteady, and even though her motions weren't entirely her own—or *especially* because of that—Flissa could see that Sara had a hard time keeping her balance. She kept tripping and catching herself, and struggled to stay on her feet. Each time it happened, Nose Ring grabbed Sara's arm roughly and shoved her ahead, which only knocked her further off-kilter.

Then Sara tripped over a root, thumped onto her knees, and cried out in pain. Flissa gasped, but Nose Ring had no sympathy. She grabbed one of Sara's braided buns and yanked her to her feet. Sara whimpered.

"I said *enough* of that!" Nose Ring growled. She yanked Sara's head back further and held her dagger to Sara's throat. "You keep fighting like that and you won't make it out of here alive. You hear me?"

Sara whimpered again, and Nose Ring moved the blade even closer to her throat.

Flissa couldn't take it. *No one* could hurt Sara like that. *No one*. Flissa burned with fury, and in her mind she sent all the flames toward Nose Ring. She imagined herself moving her arms, grabbing her scimisword, and slicing the guard off at the knees as easily as she'd sliced the carnivorous plant.

Then Nose Ring yelped in terror. "Hey—no, stop it! *Stop it!*"

"I'm not doing anything!" Sara insisted.

But someone was, because Nose Ring was still brandishing her dagger, but it was pointed at her own forehead.

Nose Ring's *own hands* were thrusting it toward her. She fought against herself to keep it away and sank to her knees to avoid it, but the blade kept coming closer. *"Stop it!"* Nose Ring shrieked. *"Stop your magic!"*

"I'm not magic!" Sara screamed.

And then she started to cry.

Flissa's rage vanished and Nose Ring's dagger dropped to the floor.

Everything around Flissa was swimmy after that. She had some sense of Raya darting back down the corridor and chiding Nose Ring for overreacting. Then the lion rubbed up against Sara, thrilled that she was bringing not just twins but at least one *mage* to Kravein. She commanded a switch in guards, so Black Boot took Sara, Ponytail took Flissa, and Nose Ring was relegated to Nitpick and Primka.

But all Flissa saw was Nose Ring's own body turning against her.

It was the blackest of magic. It was what Galric had accused the Keepers of the Light of doing with their bloody spikes in the dungeon. It was what the girl with the sickle mark on her hand had done to her friend in the hills. Not just harming someone, but taking over their body, robbing them of their free will. It was the stuff of Flissa's worst nightmares and the reason she feared all magic.

And it was what Flissa had just done herself.

She couldn't explain it any more than she could explain how the word "scimisword" came to her when she needed it to save Sara's life, but she had done it.

Was she magic?

Flissa tried to focus on her own body, tried to focus all her fear and anger on the spell that bound her so it would break.

Nothing.

Then she was *not* a mage.

Except she was when she wanted vengeance. Like against the plant, and the Brambled Gates, and Nose Ring.

Was she a *dark* mage?

Flissa went hollow inside. She didn't even notice when she emerged out the end of the corridor and into the purple sunlight, or when her body climbed into a metal box on wheels that attached to Raya's horse-drawn carriage. She didn't balk when her captors locked the door. She was actually grateful. At least now she and Sara could talk.

Raya reared back on her hind legs and rested her paws on the box so she could look in the only window—a small barred opening at the back. "Next stop, the marketplace—and Kravein. And because I'm a kind and benevolent captor . . ."

Flissa saw blue sparks, then felt a sweet release as the spell dissipated and her body was her own again.

Almost her own. Her rear end was stuck firmly and magically to the bench on which she sat, but the rest of her was blissfully free. No matter how mixed up she was in her head, she couldn't help but luxuriate in the feeling. She rolled her neck all around, then stretched her arms high above her head.

"Mmmph! *Mmmph!*" Primka struggled to speak.

"Sorry." Raya smiled. "No reprieve for you. I don't like birds."

Flissa heard a whip snap and the carriage started

to move. Raya dropped back down to all fours and ran. Apparently the carriage was just for her human cohorts and their prisoners. Raya was faster on her own.

They all stayed silent, listening to the hoofbeats and the squeaks and strains of the metal box on wheels, until they felt they could talk without the guards hearing from the carriage.

Galric grinned. "Did you hear what she said? We're going to the marketplace! That's exactly where we need to be, right? It's where we're supposed to find Dorinda."

Neither Flissa nor Sara responded. They only had eyes for one another. Sara leaned forward, arms on her thighs, as close to Flissa as she could get.

"It was you, wasn't it?" she asked.

Flissa was so relieved she didn't have to explain. Sara just knew. She mirrored Sara's position, so their faces were just inches away.

"I don't know how it happened," Flissa said. "She was hurting you. I wanted it to stop. You have to believe I wasn't *trying* to do something so horrible, and I never would have—"

She was going to say she never would have let Nose Ring kill herself with the dagger . . . but could she say it honestly? If it was the only way to save Sara's life, could she truly guarantee she wouldn't be that vicious?

Sara's eyes widened and she grabbed Flissa's hands. "Flissa, do you think I'm upset? I'm not! She was hurting me. She had a knife at my throat, and you stopped her."

"Wait, what?" Galric said. "What did I miss? What did you do? I couldn't see anything. I was behind you—I just heard a lot of screaming and shouting."

"But I used—" Flissa looked at Primka and Nitpick, who were both staring at her. Galric was also hanging on her every word. She couldn't say it. She leaned even closer to Sara. "And it wasn't the first time. In the Brambled Gates too. I have no idea what a scimisword is; I have never heard of such a weapon in my life. But I called for it because—"

Sara looked at her intently. "I did it too."

The words smacked Flissa. "What?"

"The coin. In the first cave. I knew in my bones that if we stayed, we'd never get out in time to save Mom. I couldn't explain it, I just knew. Then you flipped the coin and I *saw* it—it came up king. And I wished like crazy I could change it . . . then by the time you looked at it, it was queen."

"You flipped it?"

"I didn't touch it."

That wasn't the same as saying she didn't flip it. Flissa couldn't believe it. It went against everything the coin stood for. It went against their trust. It went against *them*.

"So the coin wanted us to stay in the cave," Flissa said accusingly. "And if we *had*—"

"If we had, we'd be dead. I wasn't sure before, but after what you told me, I'm positive. Whatever happened, it worked for you when you needed to save my life, and it worked for me when I needed to save yours."

"How can you know that?" Flissa asked. "The cave was safe. Leaving it—"

"Was the only choice," Sara finished. "We had to get out. And now we're on our way to the marketplace, just like Galric said. Exactly where we want to go."

"As prisoners, on our way to an evil mage," Flissa objected. She sank her head in her hands. "Maybe we deserve to be in the Twists."

Primka *mmmmphed* loudly, but Flissa ignored her.

"No," Sara said. "*No one* belongs in the Twists. I don't know if Raya's story is true, but I do know there's good magic out there. Like Katya's, and Primka's . . . and ours. We shouldn't be punished for it. We shouldn't have to stay in hiding. We shouldn't have to live our lives so terrified of the Keepers that we pretend we're one person just to keep them happy."

It was like Sara had reached inside Flissa and twisted her stomach.

"I like sharing a life with you," she said. "I thought you did too."

Sara sighed. She looked tired. She squeezed Flissa's hands. "I like *you.* I *love* you. But I don't want to *be* you, and I don't want you to have to be me. It's not fair. To either of us."

Tears sprang to Flissa's eyes and she hated it. What Sara wanted was so clear and basic and normal. It shouldn't rip her heart out. But it did. And she wished she could stop talking about it because it only made her feel weak and hopeless, but she couldn't help it. She lowered her head.

"I don't know who I am if I'm not part of you."

"Me neither," Sara said, and Flissa was so surprised to hear her sister's voice break that she lifted her head. Sara's eyes glistened with tears. She let out a wet laugh. "Just on this trip I'd be dead a million times over if it wasn't for you. But we'll do it. We're the princesses of Kaloon. We have power. We'll save Mom, we'll go back, we'll tell Mom and

Dad everything we know . . . and somehow we'll get Kaloon back from the Keepers. Then we can just be ourselves. It won't be easy, but it'll be good."

Flissa still didn't know what to believe about the Keepers, but she did know things in Kaloon had to change. There had to be room for good magic. And a sign of potential magic, like twinhood or left-handedness, should never be enough to get someone exiled to this terrible place.

Things would be different, and that meant she and Sara would have to be different too.

She looked hopefully up at Sara. "Can I still flip your coin to make decisions?"

Sara laughed through a sob. "Sure. Until maybe you won't need to. Can I still hold your hand if I'm running and I don't want to fall?"

Flissa nodded; then her voice broke as she added softly, "Until maybe you won't need to."

The sisters looked at each other, holding hands, and even though they were in a tiny box on their way to an evil mage, Flissa was sure they'd succeed.

They had far too much to live for.

"It's sundown," Galric said, cutting into Flissa's thoughts.

"Sundown?" she and Sara echoed, then twisted their positions so they could peek out the window too.

Galric was right. The purple sun hung low in the sky.

"That's not possible," Sara said. "How long were we in the cave?"

"Not sure. We got there, then there was the tunnel, and the ice, and then we slept. . . ."

Her voice trailed off and the hairs on the back of her neck stood up. She had a sudden flash of seeing something green and wavy. . . .

She shook it off. It must have been part of a dream. "However long it was, it's dusk now," Flissa said, "so we have approximately sixteen hours to accomplish what we need to do, then get back to Kaloon."

She said it matter-of-factly, but Flissa knew sixteen hours wasn't much, and she could tell it hit Sara that way too. They silently took it in; then Flissa realized they weren't the only ones who were silent. Their jail cell had stopped creaking, and the horses had stopped clomping. Instead, Sara was buffeted by the sound of a million different voices, shouting and talking and all running into one another.

"Hoods up," Flissa said quickly. So far they'd been lucky; Raya and her gang hadn't recognized them. They might not be so lucky in the marketplace.

She and Sara pulled on their hoods just as Ponytail opened the back of the box. Raya stood next to her, not the least bit out of breath from her run. "Out," the lion said.

Blue sparks flew and Flissa's body went rigid again—arms flat to her sides, head and chest up—but her rear end came free of the seat and she marched herself out of the box, right behind Galric. She couldn't turn, but she heard a *thump* when Sara fell to the ground behind her, then a squeal when someone pulled her back up.

Flissa heard the roar of a million voices, though all she could see was a rough-hewn street, with parked carriages shoved together at every angle. Hitching posts lined the street, and horses jostled against one another for spots at drinking troughs. Clumps of people—men, women, families pulling along children—thronged across the street to the roar behind her, which had to be the marketplace itself.

Apparently the Rule of Three didn't hold in this part of the Twists.

Flissa heard Raya's voice. "Take them to Kravein. I'll meet you there."

After that she heard scuffling sounds; then Flissa felt her body turn.

Sara, Galric, Nitpick, Primka, and their guards were all gone. What she saw was pure bedlam. It was some kind of town square, she supposed, but there was no way to tell its size. Mostly she just saw a mad crush of people and animals. Voices roared, and the smell was overpowering—a mix of exotic foods, spices, incense, and perfumes, plus a rank undertone of sewage, barnyard animals, and filth.

"Keep resisting," Ponytail said, her voice hard and too close for Flissa's comfort. "I dare you."

Flissa didn't even realize she'd been resisting until that moment, but now she resisted even more. She did *not* want to enter the marketplace. There were too many people, too many bodies, too many ways for things to go horribly wrong.

She'd been so foolish. She and Sara had spent the whole ride to the marketplace talking about the future, when they could have been planning for the moment they arrived and how they'd escape. What would they do now? She didn't even know where Sara was.

That made Flissa stop resisting. Sara was going to the same place Raya had sent Flissa, so if she wanted to see her sister again, she had to release her body to Raya's magic.

She started walking.

It wasn't easy. The magic kept her head high, and though her hood helped shield her face a little, it was still dizzying to see all the bodies thronging and shoving so close. Several times people slammed into her, and she tripped back into Ponytail so often that she felt like Sara.

Flissa took deep breaths and tried to get her bearings. From what she could see, the marketplace stood on a patch of flat ground maybe three times the size of the palace courtyard. The purple sun had all but completely set—darkness loomed over buildings at the ends of the square—but here the sky was full of thousands of tiny flying, flickering lights. So many that the marketplace was bathed in the equivalent of the midday sun.

"Oof!"

Someone had slammed into her, ramming into her stomach. She tilted her eyes down and saw two grimy boys, completely identical, and no more than five years old. Flissa had just enough time to wonder what such small children were doing alone in a place like this, when one of the boys snatched the magic velvet bag off her waist; then they both ran off and disappeared into the crowd.

"Hey!" Flissa yelled. "Come back here!"

She tried to lunge after them, but a blinding headache jerked her back and to her knees. She wailed out loud as stars and fireworks exploded behind her eyes.

And she smelled lavender. The overpowering stench of lavender.

The pain went away, but Flissa's head still throbbed.

She opened her eyes, and there was Ponytail, crouched over her, a cold, satisfied smile on her face.

"Remember me . . . *Princess*?"

Deliberately, she peeled off the fingerless leather glove on her right hand . . . to reveal a large, sickle-shaped purple blotch.

Flissa stopped breathing. Her heart thudded until it shook her whole body.

It was her. The girl. *Here.*

Ponytail's grin widened.

Flissa had to fight. She *had* to. She tried to rear back on her hands, ready to kick out and sweep Ponytail's legs out from under her, but Ponytail merely quirked a brow when Raya's spell made Flissa flop uselessly to the ground.

Ponytail knelt down and pinned the lower half of Flissa's body with her knee. Her cold blue eyes boring into Flissa's, she casually drew her knife and placed its serrated edge against Flissa's cheek. Without breaking the skin, Ponytail traced a line from Flissa's cheek up to her eye.

"Still want to fight?" Ponytail asked.

"No," Flissa said breathlessly. "I won't. I promise."

"Good."

Ponytail withdrew her knife and got up, leaving Raya's magic to take over and pull Flissa to her feet, chest up, arms pinned down. A marionette all over again.

"So here's the question," Ponytail said as she walked through the crowd, Flissa moving helplessly by her side. "How do I get the most out of your secret? Do I tell Raya? Or Kravein? Or do I go right to one of the Keepers and tell her that not only is the princess of Kaloon right here in the Twists, but she's actually a *twin*?"

Flissa desperately wanted to turn her head to see if anyone had heard, but her neck refused to move. No one in the throng ahead of them seemed to hear, though. Everyone was too busy gathering around the marketplace's stalls, jockeying for position and haggling over prices.

"Please don't tell anyone," Flissa begged. "I'll give you whatever you want."

"Really?" Ponytail laughed scornfully. "You'll give me back my life? My freedom? My family? Everything else you stole from me?"

Flissa's heart sank. Promises wouldn't help.

"I wasn't trying to take anything from you at all," she tried instead. "I was eight. I was scared. I saw you hurting your friend, and—"

"*Hurting* her?!" Ponytail exploded. "I was a little kid too, remember? I was mad. I got out of control. Spinning her around like that was an *accident*, and she was *fine*! When I tell your secret to the Keepers and they drag you through Kaloon in chains, you look for Anna and she'll tell you herself. She was *fine*. We might have fought, but she was my best friend and she wouldn't have wanted this for me."

Flissa stopped in her tracks, so stunned she didn't even realize she was fighting Raya's magic until her knees threatened to buckle. She took the tiniest possible steps forward. Ponytail continued on several paces before she realized Flissa was dragging her feet.

"You're gonna make this hard again, huh?" Ponytail said. "Great. More fun for me."

"You don't know," Flissa said somberly, and something in her face made Ponytail pause.

"Know what?" she asked.

When Flissa didn't answer, she moved closer, getting right in her face. "Know *what*?"

"I can't ask Anna," Flissa said softly. "Her family was run out of Kaloon. They were tormented because everyone thought they'd kept your secret. Their home was ransacked, old friends threatened them . . . they had to leave everything, and run from the kingdom in shame."

Ponytail looked pale and stunned. Then she shook it off. "You're lying."

"I'm not," Flissa said. "It was awful. My father got the report—I made him tell me everything. They tried to sneak away in the middle of the night with the few belongings that mattered to them, but their neighbors saw. They became a mob—they grabbed the family's things, said they didn't deserve to leave with anything but the clothes on their backs. And even then it wasn't enough. People were spitting at them—throwing things. Anna and her sister were—"

"Enough!" Ponytail snapped. "That's not my fault. What happened to Anna and her family, that's on Kaloon. It's on the Keepers, and the stupid royal family, who tells everyone that all magic is evil. You know who it's on? It's on *you*."

Ponytail shoved Flissa, hard, knocking her back to the ground. Then Ponytail reared back to kick her and Flissa flinched, but the blow never came. Instead, Ponytail kicked at a stump, whacking it again and again with all her might, each *thump* and *thwack* ringing out . . . until she fell to her knees, all her energy gone. She collapsed on top of the stump, buried her face in her hands, and let out a ragged sob.

Raya's magic had retaken Flissa's body and she'd been dragged upright again. Frozen in place, she watched the tears run down Ponytail's cheeks. For the first time, she noticed the scars all over the other girl's skin. Deep scratches from claws or thorns, a thick uneven gouge on her leg that looked like it came from a serrated knife, and a long line of puckered and burned skin that stretched across her collarbone. Flissa tried to fit this image with the innocent, doll-like child Flissa had seen romping through the grass with her friend.

It was almost impossible.

"I'm sorry," Flissa said.

Ponytail sniffled, big and wet. "I didn't want that to happen to her. Or her family. They were always so nice to me." She tried to rub away her tears with her forearm but only smeared them across her unwashed face. "She was my best friend."

"I know," Flissa said. "I could tell."

Flissa wished she could offer more comfort to the girl, maybe even put an arm around her, but she wasn't sure she could fight Raya's magic long enough to make it work.

She *did* have something to offer, though, Flissa realized. She could open up and share something that might make the girl feel better . . . but the girl could also use the information against her. Flissa didn't *think* Ponytail would do that, but she couldn't be sure.

Flissa's frozen fingers itched for her locket. More than anything she wanted to open it up and flip the coin to help her decide . . . but she had to make this choice for herself.

"I did the same thing," Flissa offered. "You all thought my sister attacked your friend with the nose ring, but that was me. And I didn't try to do it. I didn't even want to do it. I was just so mad, I didn't have control."

Ponytail looked up at her, her face blotchy from tears but her eyes curious. Flissa took a deep breath and went on.

"I was so scared when I saw what you did," Flissa admitted. "It made me hate magic more than ever. But now I know what it feels like. For the first time . . . I understand what happened to you that day."

Ponytail snorted ruefully. "So I guess we both belong in the Twists."

"Maybe," Flissa admitted. "Or maybe no one does. Maybe if magic was allowed in Kaloon, mages wouldn't have to fight so hard to keep it in. And then it wouldn't be so hard to control when it came out."

"Sure," Ponytail agreed. "But that's not how things work."

"It can be," Flissa said. "My sister and I want to change things in Kaloon. We want to get rid of the Twists, and we want to take the kingdom back from the Keepers. I don't know if we'll succeed, but we'll never have a chance if you turn us in."

Ponytail narrowed her eyes. Flissa saw hope there but also doubt, and she wished there were something else she could do to earn the girl's trust.

Only one idea came to mind. She looked around, then lowered her voice and did something she'd never done before.

She introduced herself.

"My name is Flissa."

Ponytail blinked. "Half of Flissara, I get it." She gave a half smile. "I'm Loriah. And I'll keep your secret."

Flissa felt a triumphant grin split her face. Loriah

rolled her eyes. "Don't get too excited. Whatever you're doing, it's probably a suicide mission, so I'm not sticking my neck out. I'll keep my mouth shut, that's it. I can't do anything about Raya's spell—you're standing there like a board, so you know it's still on you. It'll make you walk right to Kravein, and I have no clue how you'll get away from him . . . but I won't get in your way."

"Thank you!" Flissa cried. She was so grateful she dove down for a hug, but it was like swimming upstream against a powerful current, and a single shove from Loriah sent her right back into her upright, head-back, cemented-arms stance.

Loriah got to her feet and leaned in close. "I don't do hugs," she said. "And I don't do favors. So if you get out of this, you'd better do what you promised."

The words were tough, but Flissa could see Loriah's half smile.

She couldn't help but smile back.

Chapter 17
Sara

Sara had tried looking for Dorinda as Black Boot led her through the marketplace, but it was impossible. Not only was she unable to turn her head, but people were constantly right in front of her, blocking her view, or jostling into her. Someone even yanked off her velvet pouch, though she had no idea when it happened, and Black Boot was continually pulling her by the arm to keep her on her feet.

Even still, for all the shoving and the yelling and the being-held-captive-ing, there was something . . . well . . . magical about the marketplace. It teemed with vendors and stalls—some dilapidated tents, some mini palaces that shot off fireworks—and each one offered something more impossible than the next. A six-fingered man made spun sugar shaped like unicorns out of thin air. A woman transformed her long black curls and sparkling blue gown into a cap of green straight hair and a bright pink tunic and tights. A crowd of people cheered for two mages in a boxing ring, each of whom controlled a battling dragon made of sparking red-and-orange light.

Sara also saw flashes of yellow-robed mages in the

crowd. Keepers of the Light, watching over everything. Sara remembered what Katya had said, that Keepers also roamed the Twists *without* their robes, which meant they could be anywhere. She imagined Flissa's voice in her ear, and she tried her best to pull her head farther back into her hood.

For a second, Sara wondered which would be worse, getting turned over to Kravein, or being spotted by the Keepers. Raya said Kravein's magical tests were terrible, but Galric had told her the Keepers' tests were too. And while Kravein might torture Sara, Flissa, Galric, Primka, and Nitpick horribly, the Keepers would probably extend their vengeance and punish her parents, and Katya . . . maybe even Mitzi and everyone else they loved in the palace.

Kravein was probably the better deal . . . though to be honest, Sara hoped she and her friends would find a way to escape them all.

Sara jumped as something lit on her arm. Raya's magic snapped her back into position almost immediately, but Sara cast her eyes down as she walked and saw a tiny glowing *girl* in a green tunic and tights, with silvery wings and eyes and bright red hair. The fairy shook out her hair, smiled, and waved to Sara, then flew back off into the crowd.

"A fairy!" Sara squealed. "I can't believe it—it's a fairy!"

Next to her, Black Boot grunted. "So what? They're everywhere."

Sara's heart jumped. These were the first words Black Boot had spoken to her. If she could keep him talking, maybe she could convince him to help her instead of taking her to Kravein. Maybe he'd even help her find Dorinda!

"So . . ." Sara said, searching desperately for a topic he might find fascinating. "There's a ton of people around. What happened to the Rule of Three?"

"Doesn't hold in the marketplace."

He didn't elaborate. Sara looked around for inspiration.

Not far off, a group of children were playing some kind of game, running around waving brightly colored ribbons. A couple of adults looked on indulgently. It almost looked like a party, which was weird after all the terror Sara had experienced here so far. Could some exiles be *happy* in the Twists? Or were they happy in spite of them?

A small child squealed, delighted, as he toddled across her path and into his mother's arms, and Sara gasped as she realized he might not be an exile at all. The Twists had been around for generations—long enough that some people were probably *born* there, and never knew Kaloon at all. What could that possibly be like?

"A lot of kids around," she said, trying again to engage her guard. "Seems like kind of a weird place for kids, right? I mean, with people magically dragging other people off to evil dark mages and all."

Sara winced. She was usually much better at this kind of thing. Clearly the Road to Doom wasn't her best venue for brilliant party banter.

Black Boot shrugged. "Same deal. No Rule of Three. Lots of people can get together. Kids too."

Aaaand he was done again, while Sara's magically controlled body still led her jerkily toward Kravein.

"I know it's night," she tried again, "but it's so bright

here." She rolled her eyes up so she could see the sky, which was full of tiny lights—*thousands* of them—so bright it hurt to look at them. Each light shone for several moments, then flickered off again, but there were so many that the light in the marketplace remained steady. "Are the lights magic?"

"Magical creatures," harrumphed Black Boot, his eyes still staring dead ahead. "Brightening bugs. Mages let them out at night to light up the square."

More silence after that. Sara waited a moment, then tried to ask if he knew any good glassblowers in the marketplace—possibly one with raven hair and one glass eye—but he cut her off the second she made a sound. "No more talking," he said. "Gives me a headache."

So much for Black Boot becoming an ally. Sara would clearly have to rely on herself to find a way out. She mused that it was probably good she didn't have to think about controlling her body. It freed her up to concentrate solely on a brilliant plan to escape. She tuned out everything else and fled into the deepest recesses of her mind to scheme.

"We're here," Black Boot said several minutes later. "Kravein's tent."

Sara came back from the deepest recesses of her mind... with absolutely no ideas whatsoever.

Black Boot nodded ahead of them, and she followed his gaze.

She blinked, disoriented.

It was like she'd stepped back into the palace.

The "tent" was a sparkling golden pavilion encrusted in jewels, so enormous that the entire throne room could have fit underneath. The ground beneath it was marble, but it looked like the starry sky, with constellations slowly moving around one another in a languid dance. It was filled with people and animals—too many to take in with a single glance. They laughed and talked in groups, and Sara saw many of them completely change their hair or clothes mid-conversation, with just a wisp of colored smoke or some other magical signature Sara couldn't see or hear or smell to signal it.

Sara jumped and lost her footing when she heard a loud growl, lower and fiercer than Raya's. She fell into Black Boot, who propped her back up. "Kravein's pet dragons," he said by way of explanation. "He brought two of them tonight."

She followed his gaze to a cage. Two dragons, just like the ones that had chased them earlier, were muzzled and chained inside. They thrashed against the bars and roared. Sara hated to see them locked up, but would rather someone free them far away from her.

"Looks like he's feeding them tonight," Black Boot said.

He pointed to another cage hanging from a post. It looked like a glass case, teeming with tiny, glowing winged boys and girls. Sara recognized them immediately. "Fairies!" she gasped.

"Uh-huh," Black Boot said. "Told you they were everywhere. Good dragon food."

Sara's stomach turned as she watched the fairies fly around furiously, looking for an escape. Then she gasped. *Her* fairy—the beautiful glowing girl with silvery wings and bright red hair—was in the cage too. Unlike the others, she stayed perfectly still, pressed up against the glass and staring at the dragons. Tiny rainbow tears pooled at the corners of her silvery eyes.

Sara's eyes welled up too. Suddenly she wasn't scared of Kravein—she was furious with him. She glared around the tent, but he wasn't hard to find. The mage sat on a gilded throne lined with plush red pillows. It floated in the air, and just like in her parents' throne room, people gathered on either side, men and women eager to gain favor and get closer to their leader.

Then one of them turned her way, and Sara's breath stopped.

Katya had been right. Keepers in the Twists didn't always give themselves away by wearing yellow robes. Sometimes they gave themselves away by having a face like a fist, pockmarked and swollen and as craggy as an orange with a loose, bumpy peel.

It was Rouen. And he was staring right at her.

Sara quickly turned away and shrank further into her hood, but it was too late. Rouen had seen her. She knew he had.

Then Raya strode into the tent and moved in front of Kravein's throne. She gracefully bowed her head. "Presents from the field."

Raya's tail flicked. Sara saw blue sparks dance over her body; then it moved of its own volition to kneel in front of Kravein. Galric and Flissa moved into line to kneel next to her, and Nose Ring set down Nitpick and Primka to finish the row.

Raya gave them all a lethal feline grin. "Don't do anything foolish when I remove the spell. There's far more magical power under this tent than you can possibly imagine. It would be a shame to make it all the way here only to be rent to pieces."

Blue sparks flew, and Sara's shoulders slumped blissfully as the magical chain holding her upright gave way. She saw the same thing happen to Galric and Flissa, and the box, leash, and collar that had been confining Nitpick disappeared. He meowed loudly, and jumped into Galric's arms.

"Mmmm-*MMMMPH!"* Primka wailed through a closed beak.

Raya gave a growling chuckle. "Ah, yes, my bite-sized little friend. I believe you're fine just the way you are. Besides, I'm hoping Kravein will let me keep you. Songbird's my favorite snack."

The lion licked her chops. Primka continued to scream through her closed beak, and rocked back and forth as she tried in vain to move her wings.

Though the magic had released Sara, her skin prickled with nerves. Without getting anyone's attention, she tried to lean forward and catch Flissa's eye, to warn her about Rouen. It was hard, but that was okay—it meant Flissa's hood hung far over her face, keeping it in shadow. Rouen had definitely seen Sara, so he knew Princess Flissara was in the Twists, but at least he wouldn't know they were twins.

On his throne, Kravein looked them over appraisingly. "Thank you, my dear huntress. You never cease to amaze," he said. "I look forward to testing them all. In the meantime, perhaps a special treat as a reward?"

He flicked a hand and one of his followers raced to the fairy cage. He opened the door for just an instant—enough time for a single bright blue fairy boy to frantically fly out.

Raya's haunches flexed, preparing to pounce. Sara felt dizzy with horror, but she wouldn't give in to despair. While everyone else in the tent looked on, transfixed, as Raya chased her meal, Sara reached out and squeezed Flissa's hand. When Flissa looked her way, Sara darted her eyes toward Rouen, to warn her.

It was a bad idea.

Flissa turned . . . and gasped out loud. Rouen's eyes immediately flickered to them. The *pair* of them. And despite the cover of their hoods, his eyes narrowed and Sara knew he had seen them both.

It was all over. Any second now, Rouen would step forward and take them away. They were already in the Twists, but Sara was sure he wouldn't just leave them here to punish them. She and Flissa were princesses. If the Keepers were planning a second Dark Magic Uprising, she and her sister had just saved them the trouble. The Keepers would make them an example and use them to take down the entire royal family.

Sara thought about the pit of Forever Flames beneath the castle, and the box where the Keepers had held Galric as a boy.

Is that what would happen to her and Flissa? To all of them?

Thunderous applause and cheers echoed through the tent. Out of the corner of her eye, she saw Raya bow, triumphant, before slinking to Kravein's side. Inside the fairy cage, the girl with the red hair had collapsed down to the floor, where she sobbed, her head in her hands.

Sara's throat closed as she realized this might be the

last thing she'd see before the Keepers locked her away forever. Her sister and friends, trapped in the Twists, surrounded by powerful and cruel mages, at least one traitorous Keeper of the Light, and a crush of innocent fairies doomed to become dragon food.

Their whole mission had been in vain. They wouldn't save their mother, they wouldn't save their father, and they wouldn't save themselves. They had accomplished nothing.

Sara thought that; then her heart thumped heavily.

No.

It couldn't be for nothing. They'd gone through too much. She had to do *something* to make things better, even if it was small.

She looked at the cage of fairies, the redheaded girl sobbing.

That fairy was *not* going to be eaten by a dragon. Not if Sara could help it. She needed to act quickly, before anyone noticed and stopped her. She summoned all her will, then ran and lunged for the fairy-cage door.

In her mind, she saw herself grabbing and opening it and freeing every fairy inside.

In reality, she tripped. Her legs tangled up like always, and she fell into the cage post, knocking it to the ground. She heard a crash; then she slammed to the ground herself, her head banging against the hard marble floor.

Everything went swimmy. Then she had the strangest sensation . . . she thought she smelled lavender. A whole field of lavender. The last thing she saw before she blacked out was a rush of fairies zooming out of the smashed-open cage. Sara smiled and shut her eyes.

Time passed. At least, Sara thought it did. She wasn't sure. She thought she maybe heard noises, voices, but mostly everything was black and thick with silence.

"Princess. *Princess*."

The gravelly voice was oddly familiar, and it hissed in her ear. Then she heard other sounds too—chaotic sounds. People screaming and things breaking, but none of it made any sense.

Then something hideous attacked her nostrils, and she bolted upright.

"Smelling salts," Rouen explained, tucking the tiny vial into his cloak.

Rouen. Rouen was right in front of her, in her face. She scrambled to get away, but he took her hand.

"The fairies," Rouen explained. "You saved them. And in return they bought you time. They released their fairy flame on the whole tent. Your mage friend and I were the only ones who reacted quickly enough to shield our eyes—and yours."

"My mage . . . friend?" Sara asked, totally confused. Did he mean Flissa? "And what's fairy flame?"

"It's a poison fairies have in their bodies. It's blinding. Makes catching them tough, but clearly not impossible. The effects are only temporary, though, which means you have no time. Kravein, Raya . . . they'll all be back to themselves very soon, so you need to concentrate and listen to me."

Sara focused on Rouen's craggy face. Was he trying to help her?

"Katya changed the plan. You'll meet Dorinda *after* you get Gilward, and she'll get you back to Kaloon. She'll be right outside the marketplace, where you got out of Raya's carriage, but she needs to leave by dawn. She'll stall as long as she can if you're late, but we can't have the Keepers suspicious of her, so you need to hurry. Here."

He pressed something into her palm. Sara tried to look at it, but Rouen shook his head. "Not now," he said. "Just hold it. It's an amulet, and it will point you to Gilward, but it must be in Galric's hands to work. There's no time to explain more than that. Now *go*!"

Rouen reeled back and started screaming and holding his eyes. Sara was confused; then she realized he was acting like everyone else so when the poison faded, they wouldn't wonder why he hadn't been affected.

Sara scrambled to her feet. Careful to keep her footing, she ran across the marble floor until she found Flissa, Galric, Primka, and Nitpick. Still unable to fly, Primka was tucked in Galric's pocket and Nitpick was back inside his shirt, but they all stared into the chaos, and it looked like they were desperately searching for her. Flissa was pale as a ghost.

"I'm here," she said.

Flissa jumped at her voice, then threw her arms around Sara for a desperately tight hug.

Then Flissa called, "Found her!" and Raya's ponytailed guard ran over from another side of the tent, where she'd been looking in at the chaos. Sara shied away as the guard came closer.

"It's okay," Flissa said. "She's with us. Her name is Loriah."

Sara was ready to object, but then she remembered Rouen's words. "Our mage friend," Sara echoed.

"She doesn't know Dorinda," Flissa continued, "but maybe she can help us find—"

"The plan changed," Sara said, cutting her off. "I'll explain it later, but now we just need to get out of the marketplace and find Gilward. Once we have him, *then* we find Dorinda here, but we have to be back by dawn."

"I can get you out of the marketplace," Loriah said. "But we need to go now, before the fairy flame wears off. Follow me, and don't slow down for anything. No mistakes. Right?"

They all nodded; then Sara turned to Flissa. "Me running is by definition a giant mistake. Take my hand?"

Flissa shook her head. "We'll go faster if I don't. And your last 'mistake' just saved our lives, remember? You can do this."

"Yeah." Sara smiled, taking in Flissa's confidence. "Yeah, okay. Let's go. Lead the way, Loriah."

Loriah took off running, and together Flissa, Galric, and Sara ran full speed, weaving their way through the marketplace.

Chapter 18
Flissa

The mad crush of life in the marketplace had seemed awful before, but now Flissa was grateful for it. It gave them the perfect cover as Loriah dodged and darted around and between booths, always finding that one aisle with no one around to block their path. She never looked back to make sure they were following, and she didn't have to. Flissa and Sara ran together, matching each other stride for stride, and kept Loriah in sight at all times. Galric followed them closely, Nitpick and Primka tucked in his clothing.

The walk to Kravein's had taken forever; the run back felt like it took no time at all. Flissa was shocked how quickly they emerged at the other side of the marketplace, where Raya's carriage and prison box sat waiting.

Loriah turned to face them, and they all huddled around her. "I have to get back before Raya knows I'm gone. Wherever you're going, you need speed. If it were me, I'd take horses. But remember the Rule of Three—the second you're out of the marketplace area, it holds. And a horse counts as one of the three."

"So I'll ride with Sara, and Galric can hold Primka," Flissa said.

"What about Nitpick?" Galric asked. "You want him to, what, run after us? He's a cat, he can't keep up with a horse."

The kitten meowed indignantly, hopped out of his arms, then looked up at him and meowed again.

"I think he's telling you he can," Sara said.

"He shouldn't follow too close anyway," Loriah said. "If you're within speaking distance, that's close enough for the Rule of Three."

"Got it," Flissa said.

"And don't think you're safe even if you obey the rule. The Twists won't go after you specifically, but they're still treacherous. The temperature can change suddenly, and storms come out of nowhere. Fires, tornadoes . . ."

"Imploding mountains?" Galric asked.

"Exactly." Loriah looked around as if she'd heard something, then turned back to them. "You got it from here?"

Flissa nodded. "Thanks for sticking your neck out."

"I didn't," she said, giving Flissa a flinty glare. "I saved your butts *without* risking mine. That's how I like it. That's why I've gotta get back."

"I understand," Flissa said. "I just . . . I really hope we see you again."

"Oh, you will," Loriah said with a hard smile. "When you break open this prison like you promised. Or if you get home and forget all about me, and I find a way to break out and refresh your memory."

She raised a knowing eyebrow, then turned back toward the marketplace.

"Wait!" Sara called before she'd gone more than a step. Flissa saw her flinch a little under Loriah's irritated glare, but she went on anyway, "What are 'the Shadows'? In Raya's lair, you said something about 'the Shadows' being stronger than Grosselor."

Loriah nodded, already edging back toward the marketplace throng. "That's what people say. The Shadows are mages just as old as him—some even older. After they were banished to the Twists, they used powerful magic to go into hiding . . . in the Shadows. Now stop talking so I can get back before Raya knows I'm gone."

Flissa watched Loriah until she disappeared in the crowd. She promised herself she *would* come back and help her. But first they had to move.

"Horses," Flissa said. "That's what Loriah said." She pointed to the nearest hitching post, where five horses waited for their riders. "What do you think, Galric? You're always at the stables. Which ones look fastest?"

Galric shook his head. "You tamed Blusters."

"Balustrade!"

"Whatever. You're way better with horses than me. You choose."

Flissa felt sweaty and not just because she'd been running. She didn't want to choose. She *couldn't* choose. What if she picked the wrong horses and Kravein or Raya caught up to them?

"The coin," she said, but Sara shook her head.

"You don't need it," she said. "Trust yourself. You *know* this."

Flissa wasn't sure she did, but time was short and a whole series of coin flips to choose between each possible combination of horses would take forever. She nodded and looked the horses up and down: their stance, their musculature, the way they tolerated being tied to the post.

"The gray and the black," Flissa said. "Sara, you and I will take the black one; Galric, take the gray with Primka."

The black horse blew through his lips.

"Good choice," it said, in a clipped, upper-crust accent. "We *are* the fastest. But perhaps you'd consider releasing *all* of us."

Flissa reared back in shock. She exchanged stunned looks with Galric and Sara, then walked up to look the black horse in the eye. "You're *magic*."

"Of course we are," he said. "We're in the Twists. Many animals here are. Not all, of course—"

"Enough with the yakking, more of the freeing," said the gray horse. "We're not getting paid for what we do. We got horse-napped a long time ago, and we could use some help."

"R-right," Flissa stammered. "Of course. Galric, Sara, could you help me work the knots?"

As they untied the horses from the hitching post, Flissa kept an eye on the marketplace. She knew it was only a matter of time before their captors rushed out and grabbed them. She was also very aware that she was freeing horses that some magical people doubtless believed belonged to them, and they wouldn't be happy if they came out and saw Flissa, Sara, and Galric in action.

The second they were free, all the horses except the black one shouted quick thank-yous and raced off.

Tried to race off. The black one lunged and grabbed the gray one's reins in his mouth before he could bolt.

"Terrible manners!" the black horse scolded. "These people did us a favor. Now we need to do one for them."

"I got a family!" the gray horse complained. "Do you know how long it's been since—"

"After," the black horse insisted.

Flissa, Galric, and Sara fidgeted nervously, staring between the horses and the marketplace.

"I'm so sorry," Flissa said, "but we're *really* in a rush and—"

"Hop on!" the black horse said, and Flissa obeyed. She swung easily onto his back, then reached out to help Sara up as well. Galric, with Primka still in his pocket, swung onto the gray horse.

"Where to?" the black horse asked.

"He'll tell you," Sara said. She leaned over and handed Galric the item Rouen had pressed into her palm. "It's an amulet," she told him. "You're the only one who can use it, and it'll tell you how to find Gilward."

"How did you get that?" Flissa asked.

"I'll tell you when we have time," Sara said. "I promise. Just tell us where to go, Galric."

Galric held up the large amulet on a chain. The center stone was green and in the shape of a snakelike dragon with its wings spread wide. "It's just a snake," he said. "It's not telling me anything."

Flissa swore she heard familiar voices yelling from the marketplace. "We should just go," she said.

"No," Sara insisted. "We don't have time to go the wrong way. Galric, please, try to make it work."

"I'm not *not* trying! It's just a necklace! See?"

He placed it in his palm and held it out to show her . . .

when the snake gem glowed bright green, except for its eyes, which burned red.

"Whoa!" Galric exclaimed. He dropped it, but Flissa leaned over and caught it.

"Sara was right!" she said. "It's responding to you. Now do that again but don't drop it."

Galric nodded, and Flissa handed the amulet back to him. He returned it to his palm, and again the gem lit up bright green with glowing red eyes. But then the glow faded in every area except the snake-dragon's right wing. Flissa's heart thudded excitedly. She knew what this meant.

"It's pointing!" she said. "It's pointing you in the direction we need to go. The wings are left and right, the head is forward, and the tail is backward! It's like a compass pointing to Gilward!"

"Go!' Sara urged. "We'll follow you, but we won't stay close."

Galric looked nervous, but he nodded. Then he called down to Nitpick. "You'd better follow us, you hear me? Keep your distance and be safe, but don't lose us."

Nitpick meowed, then ran away.

"I haven't even started yet!" Galric called after him. "You don't know where I'm going!"

"He knows what he's doing," Flissa insisted. "Hurry!"

"YA!" Galric hollered, kicking into the gray horse's flank.

"Really with the kicking?" the horse replied. "All you had to do was say, 'Yo, Gus, go fast to the right, and—' "

"Stop stalling!" said the black horse. "These people are in a rush!"

The gray horse—Gus—rolled his eyes. "Fine." Then he cantered off fast as lightning.

Flissa forced herself to count to ten slowly. "Think you can follow him but stay far enough away?"

"Indeed. I'm very familiar with the Rule of Three," he replied. "Let's ride!"

He broke into a canter just as the door to the nearest building slammed open. Flissa heard shouts of "Hey! My horse!"

The black horse gently suggested they duck. They did, just as the smell of burned onions hit their noses and a giant tree branch swung sideways, sweeping right where their heads would have been.

"Was that your—" Flissa was about to say "owner," but that seemed like the wrong term for a horse who was clearly his own person, so to speak. "Was that the mage who horse-napped you?"

"It was!"

"Do you think he'll come after us?" Sara asked.

"Impossible! He hasn't got a horse!"

The horse laughed, and Sara laughed right along with him. Flissa turned to check on her. "You okay? Hold on tight with your legs and keep your arms around my waist."

Sara grinned. "I'm good. This is incredible!" Then she called to the horse. "You're incredible!"

"Actually," said the black horse, "I'm Klarney, and it's my pleasure to help you. I'll keep us a safe distance from Gus and your friends, but I won't let their trail out of my sight."

"Thank you so much," Flissa said.

Klarney stayed at a full canter, and Flissa easily molded her body to his jolting rhythms. It should have been strange riding a magical horse, she thought, but it really was no different from riding Balustrade. She could feel Sara bouncing around a little behind her, but she was in no danger of getting thrown, Flissa could tell.

They rode for a long time over packed dirt paths among scattered bare trees that reminded Flissa of the outskirts of Kaloon, where they'd found Katya's house. She saw wooden homes here and there, but very few people and animals. She leaned over Klarney's neck so he could hear her speak. "Where is everyone? Where does everyone in the Twists live?"

"'Everyone' lives separately," Klarney said. "Rule of Three and all. But even the groups of three never live in one place very long, because you never know when— Are you the kind of mages that can magic up an umbrella?"

"An umbrella?" Flissa asked. "No. Why?"

That's when thunder roared, and Klarney reared back to avoid a bolt of lightning right in front of them.

"Sara!" Flissa shouted, but Sara had miraculously stayed on the horse's back.

"I'm okay," she said.

"Sorry about that!" Klarney yelled over the sudden storm. "You'll want to hold on. These things happen."

The sky opened up, pelting Flissa and Sara with hailstones that bit into their skin like wasps.

"How can it possibly be hailing?" Sara cried. "It's *hot* out!"

“Maybe we should find shelter,” Flissa suggested, just as a massive tree in front of them was struck by lightning and fell in their path.

“Shelter’s a bad idea,” Klarney said. “Just have to get through it.”

He vaulted over the giant tree and kept cantering, while Flissa and Sara yelped and winced as the hail came harder and faster.

Then they turned a corner and the hail was gone. So were the trees. They were in a flat meadow, and the green moonlight lit up only low grass and flowers as far as the eye could see.

“It’s beautiful,” Sara said.

“Mm-hm,” Klarney agreed. “But smell.”

Flissa did. She expected to smell freshly mown grass and flowers. Instead the air reeked of something sharp and vinegary. “What is it?” she asked.

“Tar pits,” Klarney responded. “I’ll have to slow down if I don’t want to dip in a hoof and get stuck for the rest of eternity. Do you mind terribly?”

Flissa exchanged glances with Sara. What could they possibly say to that? “Nope,” Sara said. “All good.”

Klarney meandered circuitously through the meadow, carefully testing the ground with his hooves before putting his full weight down. Flissa knew he had to do it, so she didn’t want to ask if Klarney could still see Gus’s trail up ahead, but she worried. She sucked on the end of her braid and kept wiping her sweaty palms on her pants until the landscape changed again.

Now they were in a lush orchard filled with blue-leaved fruit trees. There was no path, so Klarney simply picked his way around the trees until he stopped short.

"What's wrong?" Flissa asked. "Did we lose Gus?"

Klarney blew through his lips. "Not at all. Gus stopped too. He's having a snack, no doubt." Klarney nodded at a glowing, bulbous purple fruit. "Blarnages are truly delicious. Mind if I indulge?"

"Of course not," Sara said. "Eat up."

"Thank you," he said. He reached up for one of the fruits, chomping it down in a few bites. Before reaching for another, he turned to Flissa. "You're very good on a horse, you know. Very easy to carry."

Flissa beamed. "Thank you. One of my best friends is a horse."

"Indeed? Excellent." Klarney nodded approvingly, then went back to his snack.

"I wish I could give him a sugar cube," Flissa told Sara, "but someone stole my pouch in the marketplace."

"Mine too," Sara said.

"But you also got the amulet," Flissa said. "How? Did you find Dorinda?"

Sara shook her head. "Rouen gave it to me."

"Rouen?!" Flissa exclaimed. "Sara, what are you thinking? This whole thing could be a trap!"

"It's not," Sara said. "It can't be. It doesn't make sense. If Rouen wanted to hurt us, all he had to do was arrest us. He's a Keeper. He saw us. He saw we're twins. Whatever he wanted to do with us, no one would've stopped him."

Flissa had to admit that made sense, but still, it was strange. "I just don't understand. Does this mean the Keepers *want* us to find Gilward? Are they trying to stop the bad Keepers? The ones behind a new Dark Magic

Uprising?" Flissa sucked on her braid, trying to put the pieces together, then shook her head. "No, that doesn't make sense. They're Keepers. If they wanted Gilward, why not just find him themselves? Or join us, if they needed Galric to hold the amulet?"

"That's the thing," Sara said. "After Rouen helped me and gave me the amulet, he pretended he'd been blinded by fairy flame, just like Kravein and the others. I don't think the Keepers want to help us at all. I think *Rouen* does. In secret."

Flissa furrowed her brow. "So . . . you think Rouen's . . . with the Underground?"

Sara shrugged. "Maybe. Katya is, and he mentioned her. He said *Katya* changed the plan. And he knew about Dorinda—he said we should meet her *after* we get Gilward instead of before."

"Right, but . . . do you really think he's on our side? I mean, you've never liked Rouen," Flissa said. "You've never trusted him."

"I know," Sara admitted. "But I kinda do now. I kinda feel like we need to."

"Best be going," Klarney said. "Gus is on the move!"

Flissa and Sara held on while Klarney led them farther into the Twists. They clomped through woods with red leaves that chimed like crystals, past farmland with melons as big as wagons, and even trudged through silvery swampland that smelled oddly like fresh-baked cookies.

"Some things here are so beautiful," Flissa mused as Klarney tromped through the shiny puddles. "You really think there's a way to bring the good parts of this to Kaloon, and not the awful parts too?"

“I don’t know,” Sara said. “But I think we have to try.”

Flissa noticed something up ahead: a small, wood-slat cabin with a wide porch. The cabin sat in the middle of the swamp water, and as Flissa looked closer, she realized what she thought was a porch wasn’t that at all.

“It’s a balcony,” Flissa said out loud. “It’s the second floor. The first floor’s underwater.”

“Flash floods,” Klarney said. “Happens all the time in the Twists. If there were other houses here, looks like they didn’t make it. I’m guessing you’ll find out, though. All you have to do is ask.”

“Ask who?” Sara asked.

“Whoever lives here,” Klarney said, coming to a stop in the knee-high water. “Gus has stopped moving. Looks like this is your destination.”

Chapter 19
Sara

"So . . . how do we do this?" Flissa asked.

Sara looked at the cottage, the green moon shining down on the silvery swamp water. "We just walk, I guess. It looks like there's a little bridge from the shallower water to the balcony."

"No, I mean the Rule of Three," Flissa said. "If Gilward's in there, he's one. Galric needs to be two. . . ."

"I'll go with him," Sara said quickly. "I'd like to."

Flissa frowned a little. Sara blushed, though she couldn't say why.

"Okay," Flissa said. "But how do we tell him the plan?"

"That's easy," Klarney said. He reared back on his hind legs and splashed his front hooves in an ornate pattern on the swampy water.

"Whoa!" Sara cried, gripping desperately onto Klarney with her legs. "What are you doing?"

"There are ways to work around the Rule of Three," Klarney said. "Gus and I happen to have exceptional eyesight, so we've gotten quite adept at nonverbal communication."

Klarney squinted his eyes and leaned forward for what seemed like an eternity.

"Ah," he finally said. "Message understood. Galric will meet you at the start of the bridge. The bird will stay with Gus."

"Thanks, Klarney," Sara said.

The horse walked her to the shallowest spot he could find, then with Flissa's help, Sara slid off his back and splashed down in the silvery water. It came up to her knees, and she expected it to feel cold and clammy against her skin, but it didn't.

"When you see Gilward, make sure you're wearing your hood," Flissa said. "He was just in Kaloon. He might recognize you."

Sara nodded, then started wading through the swamp. It was like walking through smoke. It didn't feel wet, just warm, and the movement of her body made the water dance in swirling patterns.

Sara had a long way to wade until she got to the end of the bridge, but was it far enough? When she reached Galric, would they be too close to Klarney and Flissa for the Rule of Three? Would they be too close to Primka and Gus? What if Nitpick accidentally moved to the wrong spot and *he* broke the rule?

Sara tried to see below the waterline for any danger, but the silvery swamp was completely opaque. She couldn't even see her own feet. It was far too easy to imagine an unseen underwater creature wrapping a snakelike tentacle around her ankle and yanking her below the surface, then dragging her deeper . . . deeper . . .

Sara shook the thoughts away. Instead of thinking, she

counted her steps and concentrated on her balance. She focused her eyes on the end of the bridge, which turned out to be one in a series of floating wooden discs that led to the house's balcony. She was so deeply inside her head that she didn't even realize she wasn't alone until she was only a couple feet away from that first disc.

"Hey."

Sara looked up. Galric stood there, calf-deep in the silvery water, glowing in the green moonlight. His hair hung in his face, and when he pushed it away, he met her eyes, and smiled, and Sara's heart leaped. She hadn't even realized how alone and nervous she'd felt tromping through the swamp until she was back with a friend. She threw herself in his arms and hugged him. He squeezed back; then they both quickly pulled away.

"Sorry," Sara said. "I guess I was a little scared."

"Me too," Galric admitted. He nodded to the cabin. "So I guess this is it. At least, that's what the amulet says."

"I guess so," Sara said. She watched him shake out his hands, then run them through his hair. "Are you okay?"

"Just a little nervous, I guess," Galric said. "I mean, what do you say to the guy who left you when you were two years old? I mean, I know what I have to say. I have to get him to come back and take the curse off your mom, but . . ."

"Whatever you want to say is good," Sara assured him. "I'm right here with you."

"I kept thinking about it on the ride here, you know? The amulet. My father had to think about that in advance. Like, he *knew* he was going to do something and get taken away from me. He thought about that part, and he was still okay with it . . . you know?"

Every part of Sara wanted to tell him he didn't have to do this if he didn't want to, but she couldn't. All she could do was reach out and squeeze his hand.

"Whatever happens, it'll be okay," she promised him. "I know it."

Galric nodded. Then he ran his hands through his hair again and looked at the bridge.

"Guess we should go," he said. "You first. I can help you on."

Sara nodded. She took his hand, and he helped boost her onto the first floating disc. It was as big around as the top of a well and floated on the silvery water like a cork. She crouched low when she first got on, expecting it to wobble horribly underneath her, but it was actually steady, like a rooted stepping-stone. She stood tall.

"It's good," she assured Galric. "Easy to walk on."

She stretched her legs long and stepped onto the next disc, which was just as well rooted, and heard Galric clamber onto the first behind her. Ten steps and they were at the balcony rail.

It was strange. This was clearly the second story of the cottage. Sara could see windows and what would have been the first floor below the balcony, disappearing into the water. Yet the front door was up here, with a large window next to it. Sara also noticed that while the cottage itself was covered in old, peeling paint, the balcony and door were bare wood. Sara could imagine what happened—a whole neighborhood of houses like this, wiped out in a massive flood, only this one left standing. Then Gilward, probably displaced by some other horrible Twists storm someplace else, found it and magicked up a new way in, just so he'd have someplace to live.

Still deep in the daydream, she climbed off the last disc and onto the balcony. The curtain over the big window was closed, but it was thin and diaphanous, and Sara could see the glow from an inside lamp. She leaned close to the windowpane.

"I see him," she said.

At least, she imagined it was him. A shrunken old man huddled over a weathered wooden table in a nearly empty room that looked like it was his kitchen. With a dull blade, the old man tried to slice the mold off a hunk of cheese, but he lacked the strength. The knife kept slipping and slamming into the table.

"He looks so old," Sara said. "Is he that old?"

Galric joined her at the window, and Sara watched his face. It was unreadable, but when he spoke, his voice was soft and low. "He wouldn't be that old, but that's what they say the curse did, right? All the stories. They say it bounced back and aged him."

Sara nodded; she remembered that too.

Gilward tried and failed again to slice the cheese, so he simply picked up the entire hunk and took a small bite.

"He seems so sad," Sara said.

"He should be sad," Galric said. "He messed up his life."

Sara heard the edge to Galric's voice and knew she should be feeling it just as much. Gilward had tried to kill her mom—twice. He'd probably meant to kill her and Flissa too. She should be furious at the man.

But he just looked so pitiful. And so helpless.

"I don't understand," she said. "Why can't he cut a piece of cheese?"

"The spell," Galric answered. "He's old and weak."

"Yeah, but he was strong enough to sneak out of the Twists, curse my mom, sneak back *into* the Twists . . . and now he's so weak he can't use a knife?"

"Maybe he had help," Galric suggested. "Or maybe his body is weak but his magic is strong."

"Then why didn't he use his magic to prepare his food?" Sara asked.

"I don't know," Galric said, pushing away from the window. "I don't need to know. If we're gonna do this, let's do it."

He knocked on the door. Sara remembered Flissa's warning and quickly put up her hood.

No one answered.

Galric knocked again.

Nothing.

He looked at Sara and shrugged, then tried the doorknob.

It turned easily.

The door opened, and Galric and Sara walked inside. Without the curtains in the way, Sara could better see the cottage. The whole upper floor was just one room, sparsely furnished but clean. A tidy bed on a thin wooden frame sat in one corner, a pump basin and some dried hanging herbs signified the kitchen, and a faded tapestry blocked off what had to be the privy. Gilward remained seated at the wooden table, the only major piece of furniture in the room. He hadn't heard the knocking, but the door opening got his attention. He looked up, and his eyes locked on Galric.

The hunk of cheese fell from his hand and thunked

down on the table. Gilward's eyes widened. His mouth worked, but no sound came out.

"I think he recognizes you," Sara whispered.

"I recognize him too." Galric's voice was raspy, and his skin had gone waxy-pale. "He looks like me."

Sara frowned. She didn't think Gilward looked like Galric at all. The man was a million times older, and stiff and stooped, while Galric was tall and loose and gangly. Yet as she looked more closely, she started to see the resemblance. Galric and Gilward both had the same angular face, the same ever so slightly hooked nose, and exactly the same deep, dark eyes.

Galric took a step closer to the old man. He held the amulet in his palm so the dragon head pointed directly to Gilward, and glowed with blinding light.

"I . . . I think this is yours," Galric stammered.

Gilward slowly rose to his feet, gripping the table for support. His eyes filled with tears. "My son?" Then he laughed, and the tears rolled down his face. "My son!"

He staggered across the room and squeezed Galric's upper arms again and again, as if feeling to make sure he was really there. Then he wrapped himself around Galric in a tearful hug that Galric allowed but didn't return. "My boy . . . you're here . . . it's really you." He pulled back from the hug and smiled tearfully. "I always knew you'd learn the truth one day and come find me, and you did . . . and you're here."

Another hug, but this time Galric frowned and stiffened in the embrace.

"My boy, my boy, my boy . . ." Gilward chanted it like a spell.

Galric cleared his throat and gently but firmly pulled out of his father's embrace. "Yeah," he said. "It's me."

Gilward looked around and for the first time seemed to notice Sara. He beamed, and fresh tears rolled down his face. "You're from the palace, aren't you?" he asked. "You've come to pardon me. Does that mean you found the mage who actually cursed the queen? Is that why you've brought me my son?"

For a second, Sara was confused. Had he recognized her as the princess? Why else would he think someone younger than his son had come from the palace to pardon him?

Then she remembered her face was covered by the hood. He probably had no idea how old she was. And since Keepers didn't always wear their yellow robes in the Twists, he probably assumed that's what she was—a Keeper who accompanied Galric on his journey to the cabin.

But *why* would he think that? If he was working with the Keepers to plan a second Dark Magic Uprising, shouldn't all his questions be about that? Sara was very confused, and when she didn't answer Gilward right away, he got confused too.

"That *is* why you're here . . . isn't it?" he asked.

"We're not here to pardon you," Galric said. "*You're* the mage who cursed the queen. And now you've cursed her again. So we need you to come with us to undo what you did."

Gilward shook his head. He staggered back and sat heavily in his kitchen chair, then looked up at Galric, utterly baffled. "I cursed her . . . *again*? How?"

Looking at this weak, withered man, Sara believed him. At least, she wanted to believe him. But she kept hearing Flissa's voice in her head. Flissa would say this is exactly what a crafty mage would do—put on a show and act feeble so they'd take pity on him, when actually he was plotting their demise.

It was possible, and maybe Sara was being completely gullible, but she didn't think so. She believed Gilward had no idea what she and Galric were talking about. But she had to be sure.

She took off her hood.

Gilward furrowed his brow, so obviously perplexed that Sara felt sure she'd been right—he hadn't expected the person under the hood to be eleven years old. She sat across from him at the table, and spoke slowly and clearly so he'd have to understand. "Gilward, someone cursed Queen Latonya yesterday morning. A mage ambushed her in the woods. Now she's dying, and the only way to heal her is if that mage who cursed her removes the curse and saves her."

"But . . . why me?" Gilward asked, and again, the question in his eyes seemed real.

Still . . . they had proof it wasn't.

"It has to be you," Sara said. "I saw the green mist. *Your* magical signature. Just like before."

Gilward stared at her.

Then, impossibly, he started to laugh. A deep, rolling laugh that made him lean back in his chair as it went on and on and on.

Sara glanced at Galric, but he looked as alarmed as her.

Finally Gilward stopped. He looked at them, red-faced and teary. "That's it, then!" he said through a grin. "This *is* my pardon. Because the green mist is *not* my magical signature. It never was!"

Sara frowned. "But it is. Twelve years ago, people saw you cast a spell with green mist. Everyone in the throne room saw it."

"Did they?" Gilward asked. "Or did they see me cast *a* spell, then get blinded by a bright light and look away, then see the green mist only when they could finally open their eyes?"

Sara shook her head. "I don't understand the difference."

"Ah, but I do, because I've had twelve years to do nothing but think about it, so I can tell you in intimate detail. And, Galric, please sit. I've made terrible mistakes, and I want you to learn from them."

He patted the chair next to him. Galric hesitated but obeyed. Sara, meanwhile, couldn't stop staring at Gilward. The man was so fired up by this turn in conversation, he looked like he'd dropped ten years from his age and he practically thrummed with energy. It was strange.

Gilward patted Galric's knee. "Good, good. Now here's what you have to know. I believe I am a good man. But I was not always a good man. I had a little magic in me, but I knew the rules and I kept it hidden. I had a respectable position as court jester in the palace, and no one knew."

Then he turned to Galric. "No one except your mother."

"My mother?"

Galric looked like he'd just had ice poured down his back, and Sara realized she'd never heard him mention his mother, not once, and she suddenly wondered if this was the first time he'd ever heard anything about her.

Gilward nodded and smiled dreamily. “A young woman from one of the outer villages. I met her during a local celebration—the king and queen and their entourage had come to join the celebration. It was a very big deal for the town. I fell in love at first sight, and I thought she did too.”

Then his smile hardened into a grimace. “Turned out she was in love with the idea of someone from the palace. She thought I was royalty, some cousin or other of the king. The next morning, when she found out I was only the jester . . . she wasn’t happy. She kicked me out, and I never saw her again.”

He fixed his eyes back on Galric. “Nine months later, I leave the throne room and go back to my quarters and you’re there, in a basket on my bed. With a note, of course, telling me not to look for her, that by the time I read it she’d be long gone, off to another kingdom, and that she wouldn’t ruin her life by being tied down to a lowly court jester and his offspring.”

Sara scanned Galric’s face to see how he was handling this. He didn’t look hurt, or sad . . . just stunned. Sara wondered if he could even take it all in. Gilward seemed to be wondering too. He leaned closer toward Galric, as if waiting for a response, but Sara could tell Galric wasn’t ready to say a thing.

“What happened next?” she asked, pulling Gilward’s attention back to her. “After you found the baby?”

“I looked for her, of course,” Gilward said. “Asked all over the palace if anyone had seen her. Some had, but no one knew where she’d gone. I called in every favor I could, reached out to people in her village, but she’d told the truth—she was long gone from Kaloon. All because I was nothing but a court jester."

The story was settling in for Galric, Sara could tell. She could almost see that baby in his face, sad and abandoned.

Then he set his jaw, cleared his throat, and ran his hand through his hair. "None of this matters," Galric said. "It doesn't have anything to do with the curse."

"But it does!" Gilward insisted. "You deserved a mother, and I deserved a wife. I still loved her. I knew I'd be good to her. And all I had to do was elevate my position. Become more than a court jester. And I knew I could do it because I was a mage. I started practicing my magic, training it, getting it stronger. But at the same time, no matter how strong I got, I knew it was hopeless. I could be the strongest mage in Kaloon, but it would only get me sent to the Twists. So I got angry. I was furious that I'd never be able to reach my true potential, and I blamed the king and queen for that. I believed they were the ones holding me back. I wanted justice—not just for myself, but for *you,* Galric. For the life you should have had."

Gilward's face was red and his nostrils flared. Sara suddenly wished she hadn't taken off her hood. The mage hadn't recognized her yet, but so far, despite the tragic beginning, his story went along with everything she had always heard: He was a man with a grudge against the royal family, and out for revenge.

"I *wanted* justice," Gilward reiterated, "but I didn't know what to do. And then I started getting these notes. Unsigned. Slipped into my shoes, my pockets, on my lunch plate. Notes that said I needed to make a statement. For myself, and for all hidden mages."

That didn't make sense. Sara jumped in. "Wait. If you hid your powers, how would anyone know to leave you the notes? How did they know you were actually a mage?"

Gilward pointed to her, his eyes twinkling. "Excellent question! One I didn't bother thinking about at the time, but believe me, I have over the years. I told you I'd been practicing. I thought I was careful about it, but clearly I wasn't careful enough. Whoever left those notes saw me do magic. And the very fact that they could leave the notes in my things meant that it was someone who worked in the palace, so they knew my situation, and how angry I was. They preyed on my weakness and told me what I wanted to hear. The notes said I could use my powers to show that mages weren't meant for hiding but for greatness. They said I could prove I was even more powerful than the royal family or the Keepers of the Light, and I could do it by casting a curse on the queen and her unborn child at the party to celebrate her ninth month of pregnancy, right under the Keepers' noses."

"And that was supposed to make you, what, a hero?" Galric asked. "Killing the queen and her babies?" He quickly caught himself and shook his head. "I mean—*baby*?"

Gilward didn't seem to notice the slip. "Hero, yes," he said. "Killing, *never.* No one was even supposed to see me cast the curse. My magical signature is subtle and easy to miss. My plan was to put the queen to sleep. That's what the notes recommended, and that's what I wanted to do. Not a long sleep. A week maybe. Just enough time for all Kaloon to worry before I heroically swept in, showed off my true magic, and removed the curse just in time for the baby to arrive. I'd be celebrated throughout the land. And then, Galric, your mother would know I was far more than a court jester, and she'd come back to me."

Sara took a second to try to match that with the story she'd always known. It didn't line up.

"But . . . the story says you pushed to the front of a huge crowd to cast your curse," she said. "And then you thrust out your hands and started screaming words that no one else understood."

"Yeah," Galric agreed. "That's not subtle."

"No, it's not," Gilward said. "But I didn't do that. Whoever cast the real spell was watching me. As I was casting it, that mage controlled my body and made me take everyone's attention. The shouting should have been enough to prove it! Who needs to shout to cast a curse? No mage does! None that I know."

It was true that Gilward was the only mage Sara had ever heard of who shouted strange words to cast a curse, but that didn't mean it couldn't happen. And getting his body taken over by someone else sounded like an awfully convenient excuse.

And yet Sara herself had had her body taken over by a lioness's magic, so she knew it was possible. Still . . .

"Okay, what about the hero thing?" she said. "You just told us you thought you'd be a hero when you removed the curse, but a curse can only be removed by the mage who cast it. If you *had* cursed the queen with a long sleep, like you said you wanted to, then waited a week and saved her, you wouldn't have been a hero at all. You'd have proved you were the villain."

"Untrue," Gilward said. Then he raised a withered finger. "*Generally*, yes, it's much harder for a mage to take off someone else's curse, but a mage with the right strength can do it. And I would have made everyone believe I was a mage with that kind of strength. I was sure of it."

Then his face clouded over and his voice dulled. "I was filled with hubris, you see. Anger and hubris. And whoever sent me the notes knew it. That mage knew what I'd planned—what *he'd* planned—and timed his curses right along with mine. He moved my body; he filled the room with bright light, no doubt to hide my own magical signature, which wasn't as strong or as lasting; and he cast his own curse on the queen at the exact same time as I cast mine. Of course, when magic meets magic, the result is unpredictable. It's why everything is so chaotic in the Twists: The whole realm is made of the mixed magic of the time's strongest mages. In my case, the magic recoiled. I was hit with a blast of mixed magic, and became what you see now. I entered that room a young man; I left it stooped, withered, white-haired, and feeble, and I was sent to the Twists before I could even try to prove my innocence."

Gilward looked at them now, waiting for their reactions. Sara glanced at Galric. He looked angry, sad, and uncertain all at once. She wanted to reach out and take his hand, but he had pushed his chair back and his hands were in his lap, kneading one another as he worked through his thoughts.

"I don't know," Galric said. He wouldn't meet his father's eyes.

"I'm not saying I'm blameless, son," Gilward told him. "I let my pride get the best of me. Maybe for that I even deserve this body, this exile. But I need you to know that I did not do the crime for which I was sent here. I did not try to kill anyone. Never."

Then Sara realized something so terrible it sucked her breath away.

"But if you didn't put this new curse on the queen, you can't take it back off," she said, her voice small and broken. "You were only going to pretend you were that strong. You can't help us at all."

"You're right," Galric said, putting the pieces together along with Sara. Then he slid back his chair and turned to Gilward. "And that means we have no reason to bring you back."

Gilward paled. "What?! The reason is I'm innocent! I told you! And as for the curse, my magic is much stronger than it was then. I've had twelve years to do nothing but practice. If the queen is cursed, I can remove it!"

Sara shook her head. "We saw you. You couldn't even cut a hunk of cheese. If your magic's so strong, why didn't you use it for that?"

Gilward rose and leaned heavily on the table. Spittle clung to the sides of his withered mouth as he cried out desperately, "Look at me! I'm old and feeble. Every time I do magic it weakens me, and I need time to recover, so no, I won't do it to slice a hunk of cheese. But that doesn't change the power in me. If you want a curse taken off the queen, bring me to her and I can do it—and you'll be liberating an innocent man in the process."

Galric looked at Sara, lost and uncertain. Sara wasn't sure what to do either . . . until the perfect idea exploded into her mind.

"I've got it!" she shouted. "We have a friend who was cursed. Her wings are stuck to her sides and her beak is stuck closed. If you can remove the curse, we'll know you can help the queen. And if you do it in front of Galric, he'll see your magical signature, so he'll know if you're telling the truth about the past too."

Gilward smiled. He nodded so hard that his whole body bobbed up and down. "Yes," he said. "Bring her to me. I'll do it." Then he turned hopefully to Galric. "And you'll watch?"

"I will," Galric said. "But . . . the Rule of Three . . ."

"I won't be here," Sara said. "I'll wait with Fl—"

She stopped herself, remembering that Gilward still didn't know who she really was.

"With my sister. You get Primka and bring her back here. If we see her fly out, we'll know it worked!"

"Primka?" Gilward asked. "A bird named Primka? When I worked in the palace, there was a bird named Primka. . . ."

Sara thought it was best to avoid this conversation. "Good luck!" she called. Then she raced out of the cottage, flying over the bridge discs like she was made of air.

If Gilward was telling the truth, she and Flissa were finally well on their way to saving their mom.

Chapter 20
Flissa

"I would give anything to see what's going on in that room right now," Flissa said.

She and Sara were sitting on Klarney's back, staring at the faraway cottage. Since she'd returned, Sara had told Flissa Gilward's entire story. The whole time Sara told it, Flissa shook her head, not buying a word of it. The pieces all fit together too neatly for Gilward and gave him an excuse for everything.

At the same time, if someone *had* framed him, and they'd been smart about it, every piece of evidence *would* point to Gilward, and anything he said to deny it would sound like a far-fetched story, too complicated to be true.

Plus, Sara had come up with her brilliant idea that would uncover the truth, so they didn't have to take Gilward at his word at all.

"If we still had Katya's pouches, we could ask for a pair of binoculars," Sara said.

"Or you could just ask me," Klarney said. "I have very good eyesight. I can see in the side windows."

"What?!" Flissa cried. "You didn't tell me you could see inside the cottage! Sara was in there forever and you didn't tell me anything."

"You didn't ask," Klarney said. "Besides, we were having a lovely conversation about the proper care and feeding of horses, which I for one enjoyed tremendously."

Flissa smiled. "I liked it too. But since you can see . . . do you think you could tell us what's happening?"

"My pleasure," Klarney said. "Galric and the bird just entered the cottage a moment ago. Now Galric is holding the bird out to Gilward, who has his hands out to accept her. He has a big smile on his face, like he's eager to do the job."

"Or because he knows her," Sara said. "He remembered her from his time at the palace."

"Oh dear," Klarney said. "Primka is thrashing around like crazy. She does not want Gilward to touch her."

"'Course not," Flissa said. "Even if Galric told her everything, I doubt she believes it. She probably thinks Gilward's going to kill her."

"Poor Primka," Sara said.

"Luckily she's small, so she's very easy to corral, even for the old man," Klarney went on, "especially with her wings and beak stuck. He has her now . . . he's holding her cupped in his hands. . . ."

Flissa had a sickening worry that they were wrong, and Gilward *would* hurt Primka. She imagined the old man crushing the tiny bird in his hands, while they did nothing to help. Worse, they'd be the ones who sent her to her death.

Flissa's upper lip broke out in beads of sweat, and she

gripped Klarney's mane tighter. "Do you think we made the right choice?" she asked.

"He won't hurt her," Sara said. "Not in front of Galric. The worst that'll happen is he won't be able to remove the curse."

Flissa hoped she was right. "What's happening, Klarney? What do you see?"

"Gilward's concentrating. . . . He's closing his eyes. . . . Oh my!"

" 'Oh my'?" Flissa echoed urgently. " 'Oh my' good or 'oh my' bad?"

" 'Oh my' his head dropped back so far it looks like it's about to fall off," Klarney said.

"Oh my," Flissa and Sara said in unison. They both leaned forward as if to get a better view, but they couldn't see anything at all, just the glow of the faraway window.

"Gilward's hands are shaking now," Klarney said. "Shaking quite violently, I have to say . . . oh, and now they stopped. He's standing quite upright, no stoop at all. And very stiff, like there's a steel pole running through his whole body."

"Ow," Sara said.

Then Klarney whinnied, delighted. "It worked!" he cried. "Her wings are moving! And her beak too!"

"What about the magical signature?" Flissa asked urgently. "When he magicked away the curse, what was his magical signature?"

Flissa could hear the satisfied smile in Klarney's voice. "A light lemon-yellow mist. Difficult to see, and very easy to overlook."

"He was telling the truth!" Sara cried. "He was telling

the truth, and now he can come take the curse off Mom!"

She hugged Flissa from behind, and Flissa smiled. She wanted to be as elated as Sara, and she was, certainly about saving their mother. But if Gilward was telling the truth, the whole story of his curse and what happened the day they were born was just one more thing she'd always believed that turned out to be a lie.

And if Gilward didn't curse their mother twice . . . who did?

"Sara," Flissa asked. "Do you think Mother and Father know that Gilward was innocent?"

"Are you kidding?" Sara asked. "No. No way. They have no idea. But we'll tell them. We'll tell them everything. We just have to get back home and make sure Mom is cured. Flissa, we're gonna save her!"

Then Primka soared out the door. Small as she was, Flissa and Sara could see her shadow against the light from Gilward's window. They saw her loop exuberantly upside down, before she flew off beyond where they could see.

"Where is she going?" Sara asked, but Flissa knew right away.

"Rule of Three," Flissa responded. "She knows we have to get back to the marketplace and meet Dorinda by dawn, and if Galric's bringing Gilward, she needs to stay away."

"What about Nitpick?" Sara asked. "We haven't seen him since—"

Klarney cut her off with a whinny and nodded up toward the large moon, now low on the horizon. Standing out against the green orb, Flissa and Sara saw the silhouette of an apple-sized bird, carrying a kitten in her feet.

Flissa smiled. Primka had Nitpick. Everyone was safe.

Klarney's ears perked up and he leaned forward.

Flissa stiffened, nervous.

"Is Gus signaling you?" she asked. "Is everything okay?"

"Yes, and it's fine," he said. "He says your friends are with him, and they're asking if the plan is still to get to the marketplace by dawn."

"It is," Flissa said. "And I'm sorry, Klarney, I hate to make you go back there. . . ."

"It's fine," Klarney said. "This close to dawn it's highly unlikely the mages who horse-napped us are still there. Most importantly, we said we'd be at your service, and a horse's word is his bond."

As Klarney reared back and signaled Gus, Flissa looked back up at the sky. The moon was still full, and most of the sky was still black, but the edges were turning lemon yellow, and on the opposite horizon Flissa could see the tiniest hint of purple from the rising magical sun.

"Do you think we can make it on time?" Flissa asked.

"Only if we ride preposterously fast," Klarney said. "Lucky for you, preposterously fast is the speed Gus and I like best. Hold on tight!"

With that, Klarney tore off. Flissa felt Sara's arms wrap firmly around her waist, and for a second she wondered how Gilward was handling the ride. Sara had said he was very frail and that magic took quite a bit out of him. She could only hope that Galric kept him steady on Gus's back and nothing went terribly wrong.

Unlike their trip *to* Gilward's cottage, this time Klarney knew exactly where he was going, and he never let up speed for even a second. Flissa couldn't have spoken to Sara even if she'd wanted to—they were buffeted by far too much wind. Honestly, it was better that way. After everything Flissa had learned, she was thrilled to empty her mind and simply ride.

Flissa wasn't even shocked by the Twists' regular pitfalls anymore. When they ran through a desert filled with thorny tumbleweeds twice Klarney's size, she just kept her head low and trusted his dodging skills. When they tromped through mounds of bright red snow that wasn't cold but made her itch, she clenched her fists to stop herself from scratching and was thankful the snow was powdery enough for Klarney to plow through without slowing down. And when they zoomed through a forest of giant fire-spitting cobras that were rooted into the ground like trees . . . well, that was terrifying, but Klarney got through them as fast as he could, while she and Sara ducked under their cloaks and waited for it to pass.

By the time they arrived at the marketplace, the sun was more than peeking over the horizon, and the square was a shell of its nighttime self. Vendors were sparse, and customers sparser.

Flissa immediately glanced across the way for Kravein's tent. It wasn't there. Raya's carriage with the prison box behind it was also gone. In its place was a small single-horse-drawn carriage towing a large open wooden cart with slats on the sides and a closed back.

The cart was moving slowly. Strangely slowly. Almost as if it was hoping someone would catch up with it.

Flissa leaned forward to hiss in Klarney's ear. "Hurry! Get us to the front of that wagon!"

Klarney didn't question her. He pushed himself faster

and didn't slow until he was side by side with the carriage driver—a woman who held her reins in two hands, each with an extra finger beyond her pinkie. When the driver turned to shoot them a mind-your-own-business glare, Flissa first noticed her left eye—a glass orb with a silhouette of a bird where her pupil should be. Then Flissa realized the woman's close-knit cap of jet-black hair had sleek black bird feathers woven into the strands.

"Raven hair," Flissa said, amazed.

"Dorinda," Sara said excitedly. "You're Dorinda, aren't you?"

All pretense melted away. Dorinda smiled and exhaled with relief. "Yes!"

She looked around at the few scattered people on the street and the square. "No one who will care, but that could change any second. Where are the rest of you? I was told there'd be more."

As if on cue, Gus barreled up behind them. Galric and Gilward were both on his back, Gilward in front so Galric could hold on to him for the ride.

"You made it!" Sara cried.

Galric nodded. "Where's—"

He didn't even finish before they all heard a meow, and looked up to see Primka swoop down. She released Nitpick into Galric's hands, and he cuddled the kitten close.

"That flight felt absolutely *wonderful*!" Primka exclaimed as she landed on Flissa's shoulder and fluffed her feathers. "After all that time unable to move my wings—"

"Can't talk," Dorinda said. "Must hurry. I need you in the back."

Everyone dismounted and quickly said their goodbyes to the horses. Flissa was a little teary when she realized this might be the last time she saw Klarney. She scratched just above the softest part of his nose, where Balustrade loved it best.

"Ride well and ride free," she said.

"You too," he said. "It was a pleasure and a privilege. Onward, Gus!"

Flissa watched them as they cantered out of sight; then Dorinda grabbed her by the arm. "Focus," she said. "Not much time." She took them all to the back of her wagon, which was full of wooden boxes. "My glassware," Dorinda explained. "I have a special arrangement with the Keepers of the Light. People like my glassware, so I get to bring it to Kaloon and hand it off to a seller for money. Nothing like what it's worth—the Keepers make a fortune when it's sold—but it's something, and it means I get a corridor through the Brambled Gates. But it's only open at certain times, so we need to move *fast*."

Dorinda opened two of the boxes to reveal that they were empty. "One for you two and the bird," she told Flissa and Sara; then she turned to Galric and Gilward. "And one for you two and the cat. It's a tight squeeze, but it'll have to do."

"I look forward to it," Gilward said, looking at Galric. "Give us some time to catch up."

Then a lion roared. "You!"

Flissa bit back a scream. It was among the last voices she wanted to hear. She wheeled around.

Raya stood right in front of them, Eye Patch and Black Boot on one side of her, Nose Ring and Loriah on the other.

Flissa desperately scanned Loriah's face for any sign of their earlier understanding but saw none. Like the others, Loriah only scowled and brandished her weapon.

"You belong with *me*," Raya growled. She waved a paw, and Flissa braced herself for blue sparks and the full body stiffening she knew was about to come.

Instead, Raya and all four of her gang members collapsed to the ground.

"What happened?" Dorinda asked, alarmed. "Are they dead?"

But Primka was already fluttering over their bodies. "Asleep. It must have been a sleeping spell."

"Did one of you do that?" Gilward asked.

Everyone shook their heads, but Flissa was suddenly overpowered by the smell of lavender, and in her mind she ran over and hugged Loriah. She'd come through for them again. Flissa could only hope that Raya hadn't smelled the lavender before she passed out, and that Loriah using the spell on herself as well would convince Raya it came from someone else.

"Doesn't matter who did it," Dorinda snapped. "Corridor closing. In."

Galric, Gilward, and Nitpick folded themselves into one of the boxes while Flissa and Sara curled into the other with Primka. They lay like puzzle pieces, each folding into a comma and fitting perfectly into one another, with tiny Primka nestled in a spot by Sara's feet. The lid came down; then Sara heard Dorinda rearranging boxes of glassware on top of them.

They were packed tight. They couldn't get out even if they wanted to.

Flissa tried to stay calm, but she couldn't. She couldn't bear being stuck, with no room to move. Her breath came in sharp, quick gasps.

"Flissa," Sara said soothingly. "Look out the slats. Don't think about the box, okay? Focus on outside."

Flissa had been too panicky to even notice the slats, but Sara was right. Their box had long, thin panels of light between each board. If Flissa kept her eyes focused out there, it was easier to try to forget how cramped she was inside. She kept hyperventilating a moment longer, but then her breath slowed. "Thanks, Sara."

"Anytime."

Flissa saw thick foliage through the slats. "I think we're back in the Brambled Gates."

"But this time we're not being attacked," Sara said. "I like it better."

"Me too."

"Remember?" Primka said. "You weren't going to tell me about what happened to you in the Gates. I'll have nightmares. Even if you did make it through okay."

Flissa smiled and Sara laughed.

"We made it through the hard part," Sara said. "Now we just go home and cure Mom."

"Yes," Flissa said. "And then what?"

"Figure out who really cursed her, I guess," Sara said. "And find out if someone's actually planning a second Dark Magic Uprising on our Ascension Day."

"Yes," Flissa said, "but we can't do it alone. We'll need to tell Mother and Father everything we know. And find out everything they know too. Especially about the Keepers of the Light."

"And if it turns out they're really bad?" Sara asked.

Flissa took a deep breath and let it out. "Then we get a lot of good people on our side and try to change things. Good non-magic people *and* good mages."

"And maybe one day we close the Twists for good?"

"Maybe . . . and maybe we bring the best of it over to Kaloon."

"Where we take our place in the royal line side by side," Sara declared. "Princess Flissa and Princess Sara. Twins and proud of it."

Flissa heard a loud sniffle and an even louder sob.

"I'm so proud of you both!" Primka wailed.

Flissa and Sara both laughed out loud.

Suddenly the carriage jolted to a stop. Sara gasped. "Are we here?"

Flissa looked through the slats, but it didn't seem like they were anywhere near the palace. Everything looked desolate and dry, like the flatlands. Then she saw a flash of canary yellow.

They heard Dorinda climb out of the carriage. "Praised be the Keepers of the Light," she said. "Is there a problem?"

Flissa's breath caught, and she felt Sara urgently tap her leg. Dorinda had used the formal greeting for a reason. It was a warning.

Flissa heard a woman's voice, pleasant and polite. "Just a checkpoint. Three people escaped into the Twists yesterday. Most likely they're already dead, but we're inspecting every vehicle that comes through the checkpoint, just in case."

Sara tapped Flissa's leg harder, which really wasn't

helping. Flissa wondered if Gilward and Galric heard what was happening too, and if they were panicking or keeping calm. Flissa herself was closer to the panic side of things. Judging from the fevered tapping, so was Sara. Primka remained quiet, but Flissa was quite sure that if she could do it silently, she'd be pulling out her feathers.

They heard only silence, but Flissa smelled peanuts—the magical signature of the Keeper who had chased them on their way into the Twists. Flissa held her breath. What was happening?

"Please be careful with those boxes you're levitating," Dorinda implored the Keepers. "And please watch where you set them down. My merchandise is all very fragile."

Flissa mentally thanked Dorinda for once again letting them know what was going on. The Keepers were using their magic to unload her carriage, one box at a time, and no doubt to open each box as well.

"Of course," said the female Keeper briskly.

Dorinda's warning was nice, but it didn't help Flissa figure out what to do at all. It was only a matter of time before the Keepers worked their way down to the bottom two boxes, and then there was no way out. They'd be discovered.

Flissa's head throbbed. It wasn't fair. They'd come too far for it to end here. They'd braved the Twists, they'd escaped Raya and Kravein, and found Gilward and brought him back . . . there was no way it could all end now.

The peanut smell became overpowering, and it grew lighter inside her box as the lid started to levitate away.

Flissa did the only thing she knew how to do. Sara's knees were right by Flissa's arms. She grabbed her sister, squeezed her eyes shut, and hugged her as tightly as she could. Sara did the same.

Then the lid drifted away, but everything sounded echoey and distant. Like Flissa was underwater and voices had to carry from far away. She kept clinging to Sara, but she opened her eyes and looked up.

The two Keepers stared down into the box, stared right at them, but showed no sign of recognition. None at all. And though Flissa recognized them from their altercation by the Gates, they appeared different now. There was a pink tinge to their faces that hadn't been there before. Pink tinged their yellow tunics too. It was strange. But what was stranger was that the Keepers frowned at one another.

"This one's empty," the man said. "Let's keep looking."

How was that possible?

Flissa didn't let go of Sara. She didn't release her breath. She lay there, waiting, staring up the pink tinge that now colored the very sky, as she listened to the Keepers levitate the rest of the box lids, all the ones that had been stacked on the bottom, including Gilward and Galric's. But the Keepers said nothing. In fact, when they finished, they put all the box lids back on, restacked them carefully, and thanked Dorinda for her cooperation before sending her on her way.

Still, Flissa didn't move. She stayed stone still, squeezing Sara tight, until Dorinda's carriage was back on the move and she had made it through a slow count to one hundred. Only then did she release Sara, and the strange pink tinge disappeared from view.

"Did you do that?" they asked each other at the

same time. Then they answered together. "I don't know. I don't think so."

"Someone did something," Primka noted. "Because the Keepers were looking right at us and said they saw an empty box."

"Same with Gilward's box," Flissa said. "It must have been, or we wouldn't be here now. Do you think he did a spell?"

"He must have," Sara said.

Flissa agreed, and she didn't say more after that. She was too busy hoping with all her might that they didn't get stopped at another Keeper checkpoint. She wasn't sure if Gilward would have the strength to protect them a second time.

After a while, the carriage slowed to a stop again. What Flissa saw through the slats still didn't look anything like the palace grounds, but she supposed they couldn't stop anywhere too close to the castle, or someone would notice.

Flissa heard scrapes and grunts as Dorinda moved around boxes. She heard her open Galric, Nitpick, and Gilward's first, then sunlight—regular yellow sunlight—shone into their box as Galric and Dorinda lifted the lid to their box.

"Nice work with the hiding-us-all spell," Galric said as he extended a hand to help out Sara, then Flissa. "You saved us."

"What do you mean?" Flissa asked as she hopped off the back of the carriage. "Wasn't that Gilward?"

The carriage had stopped in a barren, dusty expanse, dotted with tangled knots of brush, one of which gave them some cover as they unloaded. It wasn't the most attractive part of Kaloon, but Gilward smiled like he was in paradise.

"A pink force field big enough to make us all invisible?" he asked. "I wouldn't know where to begin." Then he spread his arms wide and threw back his head to feel the sun on his face. "Kaloon is so, so beautiful." When he looked back at Flissa and Sara, tears brimmed his eyes. "Thank you, Flissa. Thank you, Sara. You are most royal highnesses indeed, and I will be honored to save your mother."

"I filled him in on everything on the ride here," Galric said as he helped Dorinda reload her boxes. "Hope you don't mind."

"I'm glad you did," Sara said. "And I promise you," she continued to Gilward, "we'll make sure your name is cleared throughout Kaloon."

"That's beautiful," Dorinda said, "but you'll have time for beautiful later. Katya's house isn't far from here. She said Primka and Nitpick will know the way."

"I do," Primka said, and Nitpick meowed in agreement.

"Good," Dorinda said. "From there you can get to the palace. If anything goes wrong, I'll swear I've never seen you before in my life, but . . ." She quickly hugged both Flissa and Sara. "Good luck, Your Highnesses."

She quickly got back in her carriage and drove away, leaving Flissa, Sara, Galric, Gilward, Primka, and Nitpick in the tangled brush.

"Katya's house?" Flissa echoed. "But that's nowhere near the palace."

Sara grinned. "It is, though," she said. "Katya's chair! Primka, Nitpick, lead the way!"

Chapter 21
Sara

Flissa thought it made more sense for them to split up so they weren't as obvious, running in a giant group across the barren landscape. She wasn't wrong, and Sara started out running with her and following Primka, but when she looked over her shoulder and saw how slowly Galric was moving with Gilward leaning heavily on him, she had second thoughts. Galric was working so hard to help and encourage his father, it hurt her heart to leave him on his own.

"Keep going," she told Flissa. "I'll catch up with you there."

"Sara!"

"It's fine—I'll be fine. We'll all get there faster this way."

Flissa hesitated, then turned and kept running, following Primka's path in the sky, while Sara doubled back to Galric, Gilward, and Nitpick, who led the way.

"Here," she said, ducking under Gilward's other arm. "You can lean on me too."

"Thank you, Princess," Gilward said. "You're very kind. She's very kind, Galric."

Galric blushed. "I know she's very kind, Dad."

Sara stifled a giggle. "Thank you, Gilward. Galric's very kind too. And you don't have to call me Princess. Sara's fine."

"Sara, then. I'll always be grateful to you, Sara, for bringing my son to me."

"*You* brought your son to you, actually," Sara said. "With the amulet."

"Yeah," Galric said. Then he frowned. "I don't really understand, though. If you didn't plan to get thrown in the Twists . . . if you thought your curse would make you some kind of hero . . . why'd you make the amulet? I mean, why did you think I'd need to come find you?"

"I'd planned to give it to you when you were grown," Gilward said between panting breaths. "So wherever you went in life, wherever you might go to follow your dreams, you'd know you could always find me."

"That's beautiful," Sara said.

"I made it the week I found him on my bed," Gilward told her. "I worked so hard to try to find his mother . . . I never wanted him to have to work that hard to find me." Gilward hugged his arm tighter around Galric's shoulder, and Galric smiled, blinking away tears, and hugged him back.

"I was wearing it the day . . . you know," Gilward said. "But the Keepers took it from me. How did you get it back?"

"A Keeper gave it to me," Sara said. "Rouen. He was there in the Twists."

"Rouen? Ugh." Gilward scrunched up his face distastefully, and Sara laughed. She kept forgetting that he knew almost all the same people she did.

"I know." Sara laughed. "It was weird. He *helped* us. Flissa and I still don't really get it."

Galric shrugged. "He helped you 'cause he's married to Katya."

Gilward and Sara both wheeled on him. "What?!"

Galric paled. "Oops. You, um, probably weren't supposed to know that. Shoot . . ."

"Married?!" Sara repeated. "But Keepers aren't allowed to get married. They can't have families."

"Well, yeah," Galric agreed. "That's why you're not supposed to know. It's a secret. It only happened like a year ago."

"A *year* ago?!" Sara cried.

Galric looked over both shoulders. "Wanna keep it down a little? We're kind of on the run, remember?"

"No, no, that makes no sense," Sara said. "If he's married to Katya, why didn't he just come out and talk to us from the start? Why didn't he give us the amulet right away?"

Galric recoiled like he was being attacked by projectiles. "I dunno, you'd have to ask Katya. Maybe there's things he didn't know at first. I know they don't see each other all the time—that's part of the whole 'secret' thing—and if she was dealing with your mom, and he was dealing with some big Keeper uprising . . . maybe he didn't know. And maybe he didn't give you the amulet right away 'cause he didn't have it. Grosselor had it for twelve years, right? It might not have been easy to find."

Sara supposed he was right, but still . . .

"Katya and Rouen?!" Gilward blurted in disbelief.

"I know, right?!" Sara wailed. Then she turned to Galric. "Have you ever seen them kiss?"

Galric scrunched up his face like he'd just eaten an onion. "Ew. Stop. Just stop. We're here."

They walked into Katya's house and found Flissa already standing behind Katya's chair, drumming her fingers anxiously on its back. Primka waited on her shoulder.

"Finally!" Flissa said. "Who goes first?"

"Did you know Katya's married to Rouen?" Sara blurted.

"What?!" Flissa exploded.

"Of course!" Primka replied.

"What?!" Sara and Flissa both wheeled on Primka.

"For how long?" Flissa asked.

"Like a *year*!" Sara responded. Then she turned to Primka. "How did you never tell us this?"

"Frankly, it's none of your business," Primka said.

Flissa looked at Primka and grimaced like she was nauseous. "Did you ever see them kiss?"

"That's what I asked!" Sara cried.

"Girls?" Primka said. "A little focus? Saving your mother? Listen up, please. A mage needs to be in the chair to make it work, so Gilward and Galric should go together—with me, because they don't know the royal quarters. But if the king is there, I don't see him reacting well to the three of us appearing in his room first, so—"

"I'll go first," Sara said. "How do I make it work?"

"Sit in the chair, and think about where you want to go. Think hard."

Sara plopped into the chair, scrunched her eyes shut, and visualized every detail of her parents' room.

Then her stomach flipped upside down, and she had the strange sensation of being stretched apart without any pain. She opened her eyes, but everything was dark. Her ears filled with a rush of sound, like a giant was blowing into them, then *ZIP*—all her sensations returned to normal and she was just sitting in the chair . . . but in her parents' bedroom.

Katya blocked her view of the bed. She was on the side closest to Sara, leaning over the mattress. On the far side of the bed Sara could see her dad. He sat in a chair and leaned over heavily.

He was sobbing.

Sara had never seen her father crying like that. It ripped her in two. She desperately wished Flissa was already here so she could grab her hand.

She stood and approached the bed.

Her mom was a skeleton. All but three wisps of hair had fallen out. Her skin was thin and yellow-white as parchment. Sara could have counted the bones in her hands, her arms, her face. Her breaths rasped, and an eternity seemed to pass between when one ended and the next began.

Her dad looked up and saw her, but he had no words. He rose . . . but then his eyes became hard steel, his face reddened, and the tips of his mustache reached out like barbs.

Sara wheeled around. Flissa was right behind her, and Galric, Nitpick, Primka, and Gilward had just appeared in the chair. She hadn't even heard them come in.

"You . . ." the king seethed, eyes boring into Gilward. "You did this to her. You did this to her, and you're going to take it back *now*."

"He will," Sara said. "He'll take off the curse. He can do it. But you need to know, he wasn't the one who cursed her."

"We have proof," Flissa added quickly. "It wasn't him now, and it wasn't him before."

Their father's mustache twitched. He wouldn't take his eyes off Gilward for a second. "I *saw* him do it. I saw the green mist. Then *and* now."

"That's not his magical signature," Sara said. "Galric saw it. Primka too," she added quickly, knowing Galric's word would hardly be enough for their dad.

"Primka?" Katya asked. She had turned away from the bed and studied the group in the room.

"It's the truth," Primka said soberly. "And you know I wouldn't believe it unless I saw the proof with my own eyes. The man is innocent, but the girls are right—he can still help. He took a curse off me, even though he wasn't the one to cast it. I believe he can do the same for Queen Latonya."

Katya looked to the king. "Your Highness."

The king didn't look at her. He still stared daggers at Gilward.

"Edwin," Katya said gently. "She has very little time. We need to let him try."

The king nodded. His face remained menacing, but his voice was calm. "My daughters believe in you," he said to Gilward. "And I believe in them. Cure her."

He nodded to the bed, giving him leave to approach. Leaning heavily on Galric, Gilward made his way to the queen's side. Katya stepped away to make room for him. Sara barely breathed as she watched Gilward reach out and gently place his hands on either side of her mom's head. He closed his eyes and took long, deep breaths.

Very quickly, Gilward's breaths came harder and faster, and his nostrils flared as he fought to suck in each one. His arms trembled . . . then his chest . . . then his whole body seized, his mouth opened wide, and thick green mist started streaming out of his ears and mouth.

Then his eyes snapped open, but inside were only swirls of green.

He screamed.

"It's the curse! It's hurting him!" Galric cried. "We have to stop him!"

"No!" the king snapped. "He has to save Latonya."

"I don't think he can," Flissa said shakily. "I think it's too strong."

Galric grabbed Gilward around his middle and pulled.

"Wait . . ." the king said, but his voice was small and broken. He looked plaintively at Flissa and Sara. "He has to keep trying. He has to heal her."

Sara wanted that too, more than anything, but she saw what was happening, though it nearly broke her to say it out loud.

"It won't work," she said. "It's killing him, Daddy."

Galric was still trying to wrestle Gilward away from the queen, but Gilward's hands were welded to her face.

"I can't do it!" Galric cried. "I can't get him off!"

Then the green mist from Gilward's ears started flowing into Galric's.

"Enough!" Katya shouted. She swatted Galric aside and yanked on Gilward herself. She strained; then there was a sick, sucking sound as Gilward's hands ripped away from Queen Latonya's face. Gilward reeled and tottered, then crumpled to the ground in a heap.

Galric crouched down next to him, peering into his face. "Dad? Are you all right?"

It took a moment, but Gilward caught his breath and his eyes fluttered open. They were back to normal now but filled with tears. "I'm so sorry," he rasped. "I couldn't do it. The curse is too strong." He looked at Flissa and Sara and shook his head helplessly. "I'm so sorry."

The room suddenly felt very small to Sara, but everyone else seemed far away. The only person she saw clearly was her mom. She walked over to the bed and took one last look through her tears. "That's it, then," she said. "We couldn't do it."

Flissa grabbed her arm. "That's not true, Sara. It's not over. It can't be over."

"Flissa . . ." Katya said gently, but Flissa didn't listen.

"We have to think about it logically," she said, pacing the room. "One person can still remove that curse: the mage who cast it. We need to figure out who that is, and we don't have time to make a wrong choice."

Sara saw that Flissa's upper lip had broken out in sweat. She was nervous, but it wasn't slowing her down.

"Who framed you, Gilward?" Flissa asked. "Who gave you those notes?"

Lying on the floor, his head in Galric's lap, Gilward shook his head. "I don't know. . . . I never knew. . . . I'm so sorry. . . ."

"It's okay," Galric said, squeezing his father's shoulder. "You tried."

"Another angle, then," Flissa said. "There has to be *something*."

Sara realized there was. "The magical signature!" she said. "It's unique to the mage that did this, right? So when else has anyone seen that same green mist?"

The king had perched on the bed next to their mom and was holding her hand. He answered, but he kept looking at her face. "The day you were born," he said. "No other time until this curse."

Flissa stopped pacing. Her eyes widened. "Oh my heavens," she said. "I've seen it. I've seen that mist. I saw it in the cave, when I ate all the food and fell asleep. I thought I was dreaming, but . . . Galric, it was coming out of you!"

"Out of *me*?" Galric asked.

"Yes." Flissa staggered backward and sat heavily on a big tufted chair. "I remember . . . and I remember how sleepy the food made us . . . I thought at the time we were just tired, but . . ."

Sara suddenly understood, but she didn't believe it. She didn't *want* to believe it. Flissa was right, though, they hadn't just been sleepy when they napped in that cave—they'd passed out, totally unable to function. And there was something else too. . . .

"Nitpick!" Sara gasped. "We offered him the frosting. He hissed and batted it away, remember? He knew. He wouldn't eat any of it. And Raya said he was the only one awake when they came in."

Primka put a wing to her beak. "Oh my," she moaned. "You're right! How did I not see it?"

Galric looked around at them, totally confused. "See what?" he asked. "What are you talking about?"

"Our food, Galric," Flissa said. "Our food was cursed."

"And Mitzi made the food," Sara said, stunned to even hear the words in her mouth. "Dad, was Mitzi in the throne room that day? The day we were born?"

"Yes," the king said, "but Mitzi's just a cook. Why would she possibly—?"

"We don't have time for why," Katya said briskly. "Flissa, you're positive about this? The mist from the food was the same as the mist from the curse?"

"Absolutely positive," Flissa said.

"Then there's hope," the king said. He sprang to his feet and strode to the door, his mouth set in a stern line. "I'm having my Guards bring Mitzi up here."

"To the Residence?" Primka chirped.

"I can't exactly bring Latonya to her," he snapped. Then he took a deep breath through his nose and let it out. "But if you're right, she's dangerous. I don't want any of you in here with her. You need to go into Flissa and Sara's room. Now."

No one moved.

"All due respect, Edwin," Katya said. "You can't handle a powerful mage by yourself. You need me for this."

Her father opened his mouth to object, and Sara remembered that he had no idea how powerful Katya's magic really was. He must have seen it in her eyes, though, because he set his jaw and nodded.

"I don't want to go either," Sara said. "Flissa and I deserve to see this through. We all do."

Her dad's mustache pronged out, pointing at her furiously, though his voice stayed calm. "I appreciate what you're saying, Sara. But it's too dangerous. I will not risk any more lives."

"We'll hide," Flissa said. "Behind the tapestry. She won't hurt us if she doesn't know we're here."

"No," the king said firmly, but still no one got up to leave.

"You don't have time to argue this, Edwin," Katya said. "Everyone but me will hide. I'll stay right here," she added, sitting in the thick tufted chair Flissa had recently vacated, "but believe me, she won't see me. And I won't make a move except to protect you. No one can force a mage to remove a curse; she has to decide to do it on her own."

The king looked from Katya, to Flissa, to Sara, all of whom met his gaze with stony strength.

"I understand," he said. "Just stay hidden."

He strode out to talk to his Guards—Sara imagined Abrel was still stationed by the door to the Residence—and Sara, Flissa, and Galric helped Gilward hide with them, Nitpick, and Primka behind a billowy tapestry, which hung like a floor-to-ceiling curtain. They heard the sound of Primka chirping, though the bird stayed silent. Sara smiled.

"Katya," she said, acknowledging their nurse's magical signature. And when she peeked out from the tapestry, she saw Katya had disappeared. She hadn't left—she hadn't been sitting in the traveling chair. Sara knew Katya's magic had made her invisible.

Sara slipped back behind the tapestry. She huddled closest to its edge, with Flissa right next to her, and Galric and Gilward farther back. Nitpick stood at alert on Galric's shoulder, and Primka was perched on the kitten's head. They all listened intently, but there was nothing to hear except the king coming back into the room and pacing back and forth while he waited.

"I get that it's Mitzi," Sara whispered to Flissa as she puzzled it out, "but what was her plan? Was it just to kill Mom? I mean, how could she know for sure we'd go to the Twists?"

"She probably didn't know for sure," Flissa said, and from the tone of her voice, Sara could tell she'd been thinking it through too. "She probably just hoped. She knew the green mist would point to Gilward. She had to know most people would never think he'd sneak back into the Twists once he got out, so Father would look here. But remember Blakely and Ivamore told me the rumor about Gilward going to the Twists with a Keeper?"

Sara hadn't remembered, but now she did. She nodded.

"Blakely said Ivamore heard it from a 'scruffy kitchen boy,'" Flissa said. "Mitzi works in the kitchen. If the rumor started there, I'm sure it came from her."

"And she knew you'd see Blakely and Ivamore, so she knew you'd hear it," Sara said. "And she hoped we'd go."

Flissa nodded. "And when we asked for snacks late at night, she knew we'd taken the bait. So she cursed the food. And she hoped it would kill us."

"But it didn't," Sara said. "We ate it all. It didn't kill us."

"We didn't eat it all," Flissa said. "We didn't even bring it all. And we shared it with Galric, and Primka. And, Sara—she doesn't know we're twins. She may have packed enough cursed food for one princess to die several times over, but by the time we parceled everything out, even though we ate our fill . . . it wasn't enough to kill us."

"So we're alive because we were with our friends," Sara said. "And because we're twins."

Flissa smiled. "Exactly."

Sara grabbed Flissa's hand and squeezed, then tensed up as they heard a knock on the door, and the creak of the doorknob.

Abrel's voice rang out.

"Mitzi, Your Majesty."

Chapter 22
Flissa

As the door creaked open, Flissa wondered what was going through Mitzi's mind. She must have been stunned to get asked to the Residence. Did she think the queen was dead from her curse? And if so, why would she imagine the king would call her of all people to let her know?

Flissa didn't hear footsteps. Mitzi and her father must have still been in the room's entryway, where Mitzi couldn't see the queen on the bed.

"Your Majesty," Mitzi said.

The sound of her voice made Flissa's mouth go sour.

"I was so surprised to be called up to the Residence," Mitzi said, her voice dripping with sweetness. "Is it the princess? Is she ill? I know how much she loves my cooking. If there's anything I can do . . ."

"There is something you can do," he said, and Flissa was stunned by his restraint. He almost sounded polite. She and Sara exchanged looks, then both peeked out from behind the tapestry. Their father held Mitzi by her upper arm and guided her to the bed, where Mitzi caught her first glimpse of Queen Latonya.

Flissa saw it flash over Mitzi's face—a quick smile of smug satisfaction. Then she gasped.

"Oh no!" she said. "I don't understand . . . what happened to the queen?"

"I believe you very much understand, Mitzi," the king said. "You cursed Queen Latonya, and I need you to remove the curse immediately."

Mitzi looked at the king in utter, innocent disbelief. "Me? I swear, I don't know what in the universe you're talking about." Then she bit her lip as if she might cry. "Poor, poor Princess Flissara. The dear must be heartbroken. Does she know?"

Flissa should have seen it coming. She could feel Sara seething next to her, and she knew her twin well enough to realize Sara wasn't just angry about what Mitzi had done, but about her own blind spot with the cook, and how much Sara had always loved her. Still, Flissa was totally shocked when Sara burst out from behind the tapestry.

"The princess *does* know, actually," Sara said. "And she's pretty angry about it."

"Sar—Fli—Flissara!" the king stammered.

Still peeking out from behind the tapestry, Flissa saw Mitzi's eyes widen in disbelief. For just a second, her nostrils flared and her mouth became a hard line, before she contorted herself back into sugar and honey.

"Flissara, I'm so glad you're okay!" Mitzi gushed. "I feel like I haven't seen you in *days*! You poor little thing. Come, let Mitzi give you a hug."

For a second, Flissa thought her sister's head might explode. "A *hug*?! Seriously?! You cursed my mom! You tried to kill me—twice!"

Sara was ranting, and all the while, Mitzi only shook her head like an innocent little bunny. They *knew* what Mitzi had done. They had *proof*, but she was giving Sara nothing. Flissa could tell it was making Sara lose it.

"You're worried about your mom, I understand," Mitzi said gently. "That's why you're acting so strange." She turned to the king to confirm it. "That's why she's acting so strange."

"AAAARGH!"

Sara had reached the end of her rope. She lunged for Mitzi but tripped on the edge of the carpet and fell. Flissa heard the too-loud *THUMP* as her head banged against the bedpost.

Flissa didn't think. She ran out from behind the tapestry. "Sara!"

She was so worried, she was on her knees and inspecting the fast-rising egg-shaped contusion on Sara's forehead before she'd realized what she'd done.

"Twins?!" Mitzi said.

The sugar and honey was gone. Mitzi's voice was now all venom and disdain. She wheeled on their father. "They're twins. You're harboring twins. In direct violation of the Magic Eradication Act."

"What I'm doing is none of your business, Mitzi," the king said. "Now I want you to—"

"None of my business?!" Mitzi railed. "Do you even know how I ended up at the palace?"

The king didn't respond. Mitzi moved toward him, slowly, like a tiger stalking its prey.

"I had a little sister," Mitzi said. "A *baby* sister. Adopted. She was left-handed. We hid that from the Keepers of the

Light, because we knew they'd send her to the Twists, even though she wasn't magic at all. I was, my parents were, but she wasn't. Still, she had the *sign* of magic, so she was the one in danger. We tried everything to stop her from using her left hand. We even tied it behind her back for weeks at a time, which was awful, but we did what we had to do. Nothing worked. She'd remember to act right-handed for a little while, but then she'd forget and do what came naturally. When she was six, and that happened at school, her teacher turned her in to the Keepers of the Light. And then she was gone."

Mitzi's voice caught. She looked away for a moment, and Flissa saw her father reach out as if to comfort her.

"I'm so sorry, Mitzi," he said gently.

Mitzi slapped his hand away and glared into his face.

"I'm not done," she snapped, her jaw tight. "They sent my sister away, so my parents went to the palace and threw themselves at the mercy of the king and queen, *your* parents. Do you know what Their Royal Majesties said? They said giving her up was a public service to the safety of Kaloon. And we should be thankful she was adopted and not blood, or the Keepers would have had every right to throw us *all* into the Twists."

Sara reached out and grabbed Flissa's hand. Flissa squeezed. It was a horrible story. And though Flissa was ashamed of the way her grandparents had acted, she also understood. Before her journey to the Twists, Flissa probably would have agreed that terrible choices had to be made for the safety of Kaloon, and sacrificing one six-year-old for the good of the kingdom might actually be the right choice.

Yet now, with everything she'd learned . . . the whole thing was just tragic.

Their father thought so too. Flissa could tell. His mustache drooped, and his face had gone ashen.

"I truly am deeply sorry for your loss, Mitzi," he said. "And I understand you were acting out in revenge. But my parents have long since passed. Don't make my wife pay for their mistakes. Remove the curse. I'll do everything I can to make things better for you."

Mitzi shook her head. "You can't. You can't bring back my sister. Even if you could, even if she's still alive, you can't take away her years of suffering. And you can't bring back my parents, who died trying to sneak into the Twists and save her. You can't take away my years, all alone, honing my skills and waiting for revenge. All you can do is make them worthwhile."

Mitzi was smiling now, an angry smile that added strange angles to her round face. The king betrayed no emotion, but his body tensed, on alert.

"I don't know what you mean," he said calmly. "But I do understand that nothing can make up for your loss, and—"

Mitzi strode even closer to the king now. Strangely close. She must have thought he'd take a step back, but Flissa could have told her that her father would never cede his ground.

"I don't want you to make up for my loss," Mitzi said. "I want you to suffer for it. That's what I wanted twelve years ago, and I worked so hard to put all the pieces together. But I forgot mixed magic is unpredictable. When my curse met Gilward's, it bounced back on both of us, but I was stronger and it didn't destroy me the way it did him. Still, it took my powers years to recover fully, and all the while I wondered, 'Why didn't it work? How did the princess survive?' But now I know. *Twins.*"

She turned and sneered at Flissa and Sara, spitting the word like a poison dart. Then, impossibly, Mitzi relaxed and smiled. And to Flissa's horror, the cook plopped down on her parents' bed, right next to Queen Latonya. Mitzi piled pillows against the headboard and settled back, smiling beatifically.

The king's whole body trembled with barely contained rage. His nostrils flared. "Mitzi . . ."

"Oh, stop trying to scare me, you big phony," she trilled. "Until Latonya dies—which should be any minute now—you need me, so I know I'm in no danger. But I do have to rethink my plan. You see, Eddie, I put a lot of thought into this."

Mitzi turned on the bed to face him. She sat cross-legged now, hugging a pillow like a giddy schoolgirl. Flissa listened to her, but all she could see was her mother's wrecked body bouncing helplessly on the mattress with every move Mitzi made. It made her sick.

"So all those years I was getting stronger," Mitzi told the king, "I thought about it, and I realized the perfect time to strike again was right before Princess Flissara's Ascension Day—just like what Maldevon did to King Lamar. Curse the queen, send the princess on a suicide mission to the Twists, leave you a wrecked shell with no heir. But unlike Maldevon, I'd finish the job. After Ascension Day came and went with a dead queen and princess but no ascension, I'd finish you off too. No chance for you to have more kids and continue your royal line, and best of all, a signal to all the mages in the land that we're stronger than the Keepers, we're certainly stronger than the royal family, and we deserve to come out of hiding and take back what's ours."

Next to Mitzi, the queen gasped painfully for a ragged breath that tore out Flissa's heart. Mitzi watched Queen Latonya for a moment, pouting with exaggerated sympathy, then turned back to the king.

"That's just about it," Mitzi said. "I'd get ready if I were you. Once she croaks, I'll need to get rid of you three right away, so you don't try anything stupid. Not quite the way I planned it, but it'll do. And it'll be nice when I run out and grab your guard to show him the bodies of *twin* princesses. When word gets out about that, the people will lose their minds."

Mitzi giggled jubilantly.

"Mitzi," Sara said, and Flissa was surprised to hear her use the same measured tone as their father's, "it won't happen that way. If you go get Abrel and show him the entire royal family, dead . . . he's gonna know you had something to do with it."

"He won't, though," Flissa said. "Because we'll all have green mist coming out of us."

Mitzi beamed and pointed at Flissa, "That's right! And *who* does everyone think the green mist belongs to? Gilward! He'll get the blame—again—and I'll be a poor, sweet, innocent victim, lucky to escape all the violence."

"No!" came a strangled cry from behind the tapestry. "Not again!"

Flissa heard a loud scrape as a stone-carved bust of King Edwin slid off its pedestal and rocketed across the room toward Mitzi's head, leaving a faint puff of yellow mist in its wake. A second before it smacked into her face, Mitzi pointed a finger at the bust, and in a blur of green mist it disintegrated into dust.

Mitzi pointed her other hand at the tapestry.

There was a strangled scream; then Gilward fell forward, coated in swirling green mist.

"No!" Galric shouted. He sprang out from behind the tapestry and knelt at his father's side. Mitzi smiled smugly.

"Good to see you again, Gilward," she said. "And thanks for all your help over the years. I do so appreciate it."

In the blink of an eye, Katya materialized in her chair and lunged like a raging bull toward Mitzi, but Mitzi blithely waved a hand around the room.

Even before she felt the effects herself, Flissa saw Katya freeze in a puff of green mist, her body tilted perilously forward, caught mid-lunge. Then she heard Sara's voice plaintively calling her name, but she couldn't turn to look at her. She couldn't move at all. Her whole body had frozen solid, even more powerfully than it had under Raya's spell. She was soldered to the floor, every muscle immobile rock. Only her mouth and eyes could move, and she gazed around the green-hazed room to see them all frozen in place: their father, standing next to the bed, his eyes darting around in confusion and rage; Katya, still lunging for her prey; Primka and Nitpick, peering out from behind the tapestry; Galric, kneeling next to his father; and Sara, on the floor next to Flissa.

Only Gilward was untouched by the freezing spell. His body grappled with something much more dire. He coughed dark green mist as he clutched Galric's frozen hand and looked into his son's eyes. As Flissa watched in horror, Gilward's body shrank and withered. He sank from a feeble old man to a dry husk.

"Dad . . ." Galric said. "No . . ."

Gilward smiled. He touched Galric's face, and tears pooled in both their eyes. "Don't be sad, Galric," he said weakly. "We got to be together again . . . I'm happy."

He coughed again, harder this time. Racking, sandpaper coughs that shook his body, thrashing it up and down . . . until he went slack. Thick green mist oozed out of his mouth, ears, and blank, staring eyes.

"No!" Galric cried. *"No!"*

"That's the last person you'll hurt, Mitzi," Katya said in clench-jawed fury. Her face was bright red, and Flissa was sure she was using all her strength to try to break the cook's curse. "You're saving Queen Latonya."

Mitzi rolled off the bed and touched Katya lightly on the nose, enjoying the nurse's complete impotence in the face of her power. "I'm not," she said. "And honestly, while this has been all kinds of fun, I'm done. And that means all of you are too. First things first"—Mitzi turned to the king and winked—"you get to watch your daughters die."

The king shouted so loudly that for a second Flissa was surprised Abrel didn't run in. Then she remembered the walls were soundproof to make sure the king had his privacy. Probably for the best, Flissa supposed. If he had run in, Abrel would only end up locked in Mitzi's spell, just like the rest of them.

Mitzi swaggered toward her and Sara, smiling with deep satisfaction. "It really is more satisfying knowing you're twins," she said.

Mitzi cocked back her arms, and in that split second, Flissa saw it all: the green mist enveloping her and Sara, withering them like their mother and Gilward, sucking away their lives. She should have been terrified, she knew, but she wasn't. She was angry. She was *furious*, and not just at Mitzi, but at Grosselor, and the Keepers, and everything that had twisted Kaloon into a place where everyone was so scared that they did what they were told, and didn't think about the cost.

Flissa glanced at Sara. If she was going to die, she wanted her sister's face to be the last thing she saw.

Sara was looking at her too.

The second their eyes met, Flissa saw it: pink. The pink they'd seen when the Keepers looked in Dorinda's boxes. The pink shield that hid them all from sight.

The pink shield that *she and Sara* had created.

Flissa saw the recognition in Sara's eyes and knew that she remembered it too.

Flissa's heart thumped faster. "Fight it!" she cried to Sara. "Fight her curse!"

Even as she said it, Flissa herself strained with everything in her against the curse that had frozen her solid. She felt the temperature rise, felt her whole body break out in sweat and start to tremble. And from the corner of her eye she saw Mitzi thrust her hands forward. In her last second, Flissa strained even harder, forcing herself to fight, to pull, to move . . .

. . . until the spell snapped away, and Flissa rocketed into Sara's arms. They hugged each other as tightly as they could.

A pink bubble exploded from their embrace and circled

their bodies. Clinging to Sara with all her might, Flissa looked through it, out at the room. Everything had that same pink tinge she'd seen before, except for one spot, where a green mist pooled against the dome. As if in slow motion, Flissa saw the mist gather and swirl, getting darker and thicker, until it bounced and slammed back into Mitzi with so much force it threw her across the room.

The pink shield disappeared. Flissa was still holding Sara, but now she pulled away to look at her sister. Sara's face was flushed, her eyes wide and frightened . . . but she was smiling.

"We did that?" Sara asked. "We made that happen?"

Flissa nodded. "Second time," she said, her voice shaky. "No way to deny it, I guess. We definitely have magic."

"Yeah, we do." Sara grinned wider. Flissa couldn't return it. She felt woozy and wanted to lie down. Then she heard an ancient moan.

"Mitzi," Sara said. They glanced over and saw the cook crumpled against a far wall, not far from where Galric crouched, still frozen next to Gilward.

"It's like she said," Galric noted dully. "Mixed magic is unpredictable. Whatever you did, her curse bounced off it and back onto her. Just like she did to my dad. Look."

Flissa and Sara moved toward Mitzi and watched, amazed, as her beautiful blond curls receded into stringy white strands. Her skin wrinkled and sprouted thick webs of veins. Her cheeks sank. When she blinked her eyes open, they were rheumy and yellow.

"What have you done to me?" she croaked.

"It's what you did to yourself," Sara said.

"And now you're going to do something else," Flissa said. "You're going to undo your curse and heal our mother. Then take your curses off everyone else in this room."

Crackling laughter wheezed out of Mitzi's throat. "Why would I do that?"

She thrust out her hands to cast a fresh curse, but only the tiniest wisps of green smoke appeared at her fingertips. Sara blew them away like dandelion fluff.

"You're weak now," Flissa said. "Withered and weak. So you have a choice. You'll remove the curses and live out your days comfortably, under guard in a home on the outskirts of Kaloon, or you'll spend your miserable life in the worst prison you can imagine."

"Ooh!" Sara piped up. "Like the Forever Flames under the castle. That'll be super comfortable for you. 'Torment of eternal fire,' right, Flissa?"

Flissa couldn't help but smile a little. "Exactly."

Mitzi's wet, yellowed eyes glowered at them. "What if I don't do it? What if I let your mother die and keep you all frozen so you can suffer?"

"Then we will suffer," the king said, and Flissa was amazed by the strength and control in his voice. "But I promise, you will suffer just as badly."

Mitzi looked his way, then cringed back from what she saw in his eyes. She nodded slightly; then Flissa and Sara helped her to her feet and led her to the bed. As they shuffled to Queen Latonya's side, Flissa heard Galric whisper to Katya, "Can she even do it? She's so weak, she couldn't even cast a spell."

"She can," Katya replied. "Undoing your own curse

is the easiest kind of magic. A mage could do it on her deathbed."

Flissa and Sara moved Mitzi as close to the bed as possible so she could lean and let the side of the mattress support her lower body. Mitzi sighed, then placed her hands on their mother's withered temples. She stood there for a moment, matching her own breathing pattern to the queen's.

At first, Flissa saw only the tiniest trickle of green mist. It seeped from her mother's nose, dissipating into the air. But as Mitzi held the queen's head, the trickle turned into a deluge. Green mist poured from her body in torrents, as if the curse were racing itself to get away from her. As everyone watched, the queen's hair grew back, thick and beautiful. Her body and face filled out. Color returned to her cheeks. And then finally, she bolted upright and coughed . . . and the last wisp of mist floated away.

Queen Latonya sat up for just a moment, shock and confusion fighting for dominance on her face. Then her eyes rolled back and she fell against her pillows.

"What did you do?!" roared the king. "Latonya!"

"It's fine, Edwin," Katya said gently, and Flissa saw their nurse's whole face had relaxed and happy tears pooled in her eyes. "She's fine. Her body's a little overwhelmed, that's all. She'll wake up in a bit."

"Now everyone else," Sara told Mitzi.

The cook rolled her yellowed eyes, but she moved her arm in a wide swoop.

The freezing curse was obviously far less powerful than the curse on the queen. Immediately, puffs of green mist rose from the king, Katya, Galric, Nitpick, and Primka and they could all move again.

"Him now," Galric said, his hand on Gilward's shoulder. "Take back what you did to him."

Katya knelt down next to Galric and put her arm around him. "She can't. He's already gone. It's too late."

Galric didn't want to believe it. He shook his head, and the tears rolled down his cheeks. Then Katya pulled him into her arms and held him close.

Flissa could tell Sara wanted to go to him, but there was something she had to do first. Flissa had always loved feeling like she and Sara were two halves of a whole, each one making up for the other's imperfections . . . but maybe it was time for each of them to stand on her own. She took a deep breath.

"You should take your curse off us too," she told Mitzi.

Sara looked at her, surprised. "Really?"

Flissa nodded. Sara smiled gratefully and took her hand.

"Flissa's right," Sara agreed. "We're ready."

Mitzi scrunched her brows. "For what?" she scoffed. "My curse was meant to *kill* you, and if you'd been one baby, it would have. Instead you shared it and you lived. Whatever else it did to you, I didn't ask for it to happen, and I can't take it away. If you don't like who you are, that's on you."

It was the exact opposite of what Katya had told them, but it was also kind of the same. She and Sara *were* opposites in a lot of ways, and they *did* fill in each other's spaces like a puzzle . . . but for the first time, Flissa understood they were also perfectly complete just the way they were.

Flissa grinned. She squeezed Sara's hand, then let it go.

"Thank you, Mitzi," Flissa said brightly. "You've been extremely helpful."

In bed, their mother moaned a little and rolled over in her sleep. The king rushed to her side.

"She'll be up soon," Katya said. "I think we should clear the room. Don't want to disturb her." She squeezed Galric's shoulder and nodded toward Gilward as she added gently. "Go with Primka, Galric. I promise I won't leave him behind."

Galric took a deep breath and nodded, then sat in the armchair. Nitpick hopped onto his lap and Primka lit on his shoulder. The songbird shut her eyes, and Flissa saw them flip away to Katya's house. Katya gave them a second to get out of the chair on the other side, then scooped Mitzi under one arm and Gilward under the other, before plopping down with them. An instant later, they were gone.

Their mother moaned again, and Flissa and Sara both rushed to her side. When the queen's eyes fluttered open, the king, Flissa, and Sara were all hovering over her, staring down into her face.

The queen yelped. Then she laughed and sat up.

"You scared me! What are you all doing, leaning over me like that? Is everything okay?"

Flissa hadn't realized how certain she was that she'd never hear her mother's voice again until it rang like joyful bells in her ears. She felt tears well up in her eyes, and she knew her mother saw them because she looked worried and sad.

"Flissa? Are you all right?"

Flissa couldn't even get out the words. She nodded, then threw herself onto her mother's lap, wrapping her arms around her neck. Sara tackled their mom from the side, tumbling her over onto the bed.

The queen laughed. "What's going on? Did I sleep through to my birthday?"

"We just love you, that's all," Flissa said.

"So, so much," Sara added.

"More than you can possibly imagine," the king said, and he scooped their mother into his arms and spun her around. The queen squealed with surprise and delight.

"I love you all too," she said. "But honestly, you're acting very strange. I'm not complaining, mind you, but . . . what happened?"

Flissa and Sara looked at one another. That was a question with a very long answer, and one that could wait. Not for long—soon they'd tell both their parents everything, and they'd all work out together what was right for Kaloon.

But maybe they could ease into it.

"We just want to spend time together," said Sara.

Then Flissa lit up with an idea. "You could read us a book!"

Their mother laughed. "Read you a book? You haven't asked for that in years."

"That's why it's such a good idea," Sara said.

"And I have exactly the right one," Flissa said. She darted out to her and Sara's room, and came back a moment later with a giant leather-bound tome. She handed it to their mother, who wrinkled her eyebrows as she looked at the cover.

"A textbook?"

Flissa nodded. "Just seems like something we should brush up on."

The queen looked to the king, who shrugged and laughed. "Latonya, I'm just happy to hear your voice. If the girls want it, I say read it."

"Okay, then," she said. She climbed back into bed and sat up tall, propped on pillows. Flissa and Sara leaned in on either side and laid their heads on her shoulders as she started to read: *"A History of Magic in Kaloon . . ."*

Acknowledgments

First and foremost, I'd like to give the most gigantic shout-out ever to Disney Hyperion editors Kieran Viola and Mary Mudd for trusting me to bring this concept to life. This book has been such a gift, and it was always a joy to get your notes because they drove me to look deeper and push further. You are both magical.

Also brilliant and indispensable to me on this book was Dawn Ius. Dawn, you are the wizard of beta readers. I am so thankful for the way you always put me at the top of your to-do list, and equally thankful for your brilliant insights. Since Dawn and Kieran are both fabulous authors in their own right, I'm plugging them here. Check out www.dawnius.com and www.kieranscott.net. You'll be glad you did.

Huge thanks to the wonderful team at Disney Hyperion: Designer Jamie Alloy, Managing Editor Sara Liebling, Publicist Amy Goppert, Danielle DiMartino and Holly Nagel in Marketing, and Copy Chief Guy Cunningham. I so appreciate all your hard work and support.

To Jane Startz, my manager, I don't know what I did right to earn the privilege of working with you, but I'm grateful every day. Thank you for everything you do.

To Nancy Kanter and Brad Butler at Disney Channel, thank you for being such fans of *Twinchantment*, and championing it from the start.

On a personal note, I'd like to thank Mom-Mom Sylvia, who at 102 is sharp as a knife and still one of my favorite people to hang out with. I completely recognize how lucky I am to have you, and I take not even a second for granted. Mom-Mom Eva, Pop-Pop Irv, and Pop-Pop Nate, you are always with me in my heart.

Finally, I want to thank my husband, Randy, without whom nothing I do would be possible; our daughter, Maddie, who is easily the most incredible human being I've ever met (not that I'm biased or anything); and our dog, Jack-Jack, who likes to sit on my lap when I write, occasionally taps on the computer, and is doubtless responsible for all the best parts of this book.

Okay, I was wrong about the "finally" part. There's one more group to thank, and that's *you*, everyone who reads this book. Stories only come to life when they're shared, and I'm beyond honored that you let me share this one with you. Thanks for reading, and absolutely feel free to reach out and say hello at elise@eliseallen.com, or on Twitter @EliseLAllen—I'd love to hear from you!